MONTCLAIR

Portraits

Balcony

Blind Faith

Endangered

Entangled

Gentle Touch

Heaven's Song

Impasse

Masquerade

Montclair

Stillpoint

Walker's Point

MONTCLAIR

SARA MITCHELL

BETHANY HOUSE PUBLISHERS
MINNEAPOLIS, MINNESOTA 55438

Montclair
Copyright © 1997
Sara Mitchell

Cover illustration by William Graf

Published by Bethany House Publishers
A Ministry of Bethany Fellowship, Inc.
11300 Hampshire Avenue South
Minneapolis, Minnesota 55438

Printed in the United States of America.

Library of Congress Cataloging-in-Publication Data

Mitchell, Sara.
    Montclair / by Sara Mitchell.
       p. cm.—(Portraits)
     ISBN 1–55661–963–4 (pbk.)
     1. Horse sports—United States—Fiction. 2. Equestrian centers—United States—Fiction. I. Title. II. Series: Portraits (Minneapolis, Minn.)
PS3563.I823M66   1997   97–4712
                                             CIP

SARA MITCHELL is a popular and highly-acclaimed author of numerous novels, including the gripping SHADOWCATCHERS series. With over 200,000 in total sales, Sara has established a loyal following in the inspirational fiction market and her books have touched the lives of readers all over the world. Having lived in a variety of diverse locations from Georgia to Great Britain, Sara and her husband now make their home in Virginia with their two daughters. Sara enjoys hearing from her readers. You may write to her at the following address:

Sara Mitchell
%Bethany House Publishers
11300 Hampshire Ave. South
Minneapolis, MN 55438

Prologue

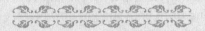

Landover, Maryland

She entered the ring again. Her hands tightened on the reins, automatically restraining an overeager Vesuvius. He would have preferred to attack the jumps at full gallop. The gun-metal gray hindquarters practically churned in anticipation.

"This is a jump-off, blockhead," she murmured to the restless stallion beneath her. "Speed—with finesse, remember? If you behave, I promise I'll—"

The announcer finished his introduction. She waited for the horn to sound, her gaze sweeping the audience. "Lively crowd today." She hoped she could keep Ves focused on the task at hand instead of the rowdiness, which was distracting him.

Her glance passed over a clutch of riders and spectators near the gate and settled on one man standing back, a little apart from the others. Hunter Buchanan! He'd come, after all, as he'd promised. Elation and fierce pride shot through her, but Sabrina concentrated on the brutal set of jumps for this final round as she guided Vesuvius into position. Even if they didn't win the President's Cup, her secret dream would be one step closer to reality. Montclair . . . and training with Hunter Buchanan.

They were off! *Easy, easy—not so fast . . . that's it. No! Quit fighting me, you stubborn firecracker . . . now!* That was close, but they'd done it! She could feel it in her bones—the soaring, exultant joy of merging with her horse seamlessly until they moved as a single unit.

You're an angel, you are! The best in the sport . . . in the world . . . in the universe. . . .

Only one more jump—the triple-oxer—raised another six inches for the jump-off. *Steady, boy, steady. You can do this.* He was straining, ears pricked, communicating back to her the confidence and intensity she fed him.

Suddenly—the instant his forelegs lifted from the ground—a loud noise ruptured the air. Alarmed, Vesuvius screamed, twisting violently, jerking the reins, all but tearing her arms from their sockets. She heard a splintering crack and felt the impact as his legs tangled in the fence, pitching them both straight downward.

Pain exploded in a starburst.

Then darkness, swift and stark.

One

Washington, D.C.
July, three years later

"No problem. I can have it ready by next Tuesday." Sabrina Mayhew held the phone at arm's length to avoid the torrent of effusive gratitude gushing through the receiver.

". . . and I'll pass your name along to all my friends. You'll have all the work you can handle!" the relieved county administrator finally wound down.

Sabrina grimaced. "I stay busy enough. Don't send too much my way, or you'll end up getting your report on Labor Day weekend instead!"

"I doubt it. I've heard too much about you—say, I got an invitation to this awards banquet a week from tonight, and I need a date. Would you—"

"Sorry," she cut him off politely. "I make it a policy never to mix business and pleasure. But thanks anyway."

After she hung up, she filed a copy of the administrator's report, flashed a quick glance at her daily calendar, then with a grateful sigh, shut down the computer. It had been a long day.

But she wouldn't be relaxing in front of the TV anytime soon. There was still an hour-long drive ahead, fighting the westward migration of Washington's infamous rush-hour traffic. For some reason Uncle Sebastian had insisted she spend the weekend at Woodleigh, his estate in the rolling hills of Virginia's Piedmont. Unfortunately, he'd caught her in a weak moment, and she'd agreed to come before she realized her wily uncle—true to his lawyer mentality—had out-maneuvered her again.

The old teddy bear! What was he up to this time? The last attempt he'd made to force her out of what he'd acerbically dubbed her "ostrich mode" had been a party. He had invited everyone in the equestrian world from three states whose names his beleaguered secretary could unearth at short notice. Sabrina had walked unsuspecting through the door, swept a resigned glance about the noisy, overcrowded rooms, then turned and walked back out. She'd spent the weekend in an obscure motel and hadn't called until late Monday to inquire sweetly how her uncle's weekend had gone. That had been five months ago, and he and her older sister, Renee, had been fuming ever since.

Sabrina went through her apartment now, making sure everything was turned off, garbage out, automatic timer for light switches set . . . *Poor Uncle Seb.* Why, she wondered, couldn't he and Rennie just accept her as she was—self-employed, fully independent (despite all her uncle's machinations to keep her under his wing), and perfectly content with her present lifestyle.

S.M. Services had officially been in business for less than six months, but already Sabrina was inundated with work. Her new vocation was respectable and lucrative; everyone should be cheering her on instead of singing Greek choruses about the past.

"The world won't come to an end if I never ride a horse again," she muttered, grabbing her weekend case and purse.

Typing masters theses, doctoral dissertations, undergrad term papers, professional resumés, and reams of reports was not thrilling, but it was satisfying. And on the days when she did research at various libraries, she actually got out of the apartment. You'd think Uncle Seb and Rennie would be pleased.

Of course, she had to admit it wasn't as exciting as competing at the Washington National Horse Show. But who said life had to be exciting? Life, Sabrina had learned, was meant to be endured. If one endured with grace and style, so much the better. She had also learned—painfully so—that caring too much was not cost-effective.

From the time Sabrina was a little girl, almost everything and everyone she'd ever cared about had been taken from her; the last time it had almost killed her. Well, she wasn't stupid. She wasn't a masochist, either. She would never be able to fathom God's reasoning, so she didn't try anymore. Instead, she accepted what she couldn't change and endured. Gracefully, she hoped.

On her way out the door she scooped up the day's mail, intending to read it when she got to Woodleigh. But the weekly edition of *Newsweek* momentarily diverted her attention. On the front cover was a photograph of Hunter Buchanan. *Hunter Buchanan*. What an odd coincidence. The rakish smile, crinkling blue-gray eyes, and burnt mahogany hair were the same as they had been another lifetime ago. A faint smile lifted the corners of Sabrina's mouth. How young and hopelessly idealistic that Sabrina Mayhew had been.

"May a thousand applications for Montclair land on your doorstep, all of them from Olympic-caliber riders," she told the photograph. Then she stuffed the rest of the mail inside the magazine, tucked it under her arm, and headed out the door.

The Friday afternoon traffic escaping from the nation's capital crawled along in its usual caterpillar pace. Unfortunately, it left Sabrina with plenty of idle time to berate herself for not severing *all* ties to the past. Even though she had moved into an impersonal apartment in a congested suburb of northern Virginia, she still lived in the same state. Maybe she should move to another one, preferably one with less traffic. Wyoming or Colorado, for instance ... *clear mountain air as pure, as irresistible as a newborn foal ... skies the color of Hunter's eyes smiling into hers. ...*

Don't do this, Sabrina. Turn it off, shut it down. Forget about that magazine—throw it away. Don't think, don't feel. Look at the cars—count the blue ones. Make up a story about the drivers ... how about the man ahead of you? Just another "beltway bandit," trudging home after a twelve-hour workday ... looks beat. Must like the heat, though; he's rolled his shirt-sleeve up to rest his arm on the window. "Be careful," she wanted to call out. "You'll get a bad sunburn that way."

"... and with skin as fair as yours, you'll need to be careful if you book a session in the summer. Montclair's a mile and a half nearer the sun than your southern-belle skin is accustomed to."

"Oh, don't worry about me. Nothing's worse than a summer in the South. Or—I could come in the dead of winter."

He'd flicked the end of her nose with the crop he was holding. *"Suit yourself. Regardless of the season, you'll be working too hard to notice the temperature ... or anything else."* The blue-gray eyes twinkled. *"I keep my students so focused they wouldn't notice if a sixteen-wheeler blasted its horn——"*

Sabrina jumped at the screech of an angry horn behind her and realized the car ahead had inched a good fifteen feet down the road. She also realized that her hands were clammy, with a death grip on the wheel that whitened her knuckles. Taking deep, calming breaths, she relaxed her fingers, one at a time, using a technique she'd been taught by the trauma psychologist. Then she turned on the car radio to a raucous country station and adjusted the volume so that the sound bounced around the air-conditioned interior.

By the time traffic cleared and she was able to accelerate to sixty, Sabrina was in control once more. The memories were safely locked away, and the past was once again where it belonged. In permanent cold storage.

༒

Unfortunately, Uncle Sebastian had other plans.

"*Why* won't you give it a try?" He slammed his palm down on the *Newsweek* magazine open to the feature article on Hunter. "Blast it, Sabrina . . . all you'd have to do is call him and explain. It's not as if you're a rank amateur. You were Rookie Rider of the Year! Your name was a household word; everyone expected you to make the Olympic team. In point of fact, you *were* accepted at Montclair——" He glowered at her. "I think he even wrote you when you were in the hospital, didn't he?"

"Maybe. I don't remember." Sabrina rested her head against the back of the chair and closed her eyes. When Uncle Seb chose to gnaw at an issue, a bull terrier came up short by comparison. "Even if I were interested—which I'm not—it would be a waste of time, not to mention money. Have you forgotten those other three trainers who failed after Glenn couldn't help me? Why should Hunter Buchanan be any different? Besides," she concluded with flat finality, "I told you I'm satisfied with my life as it is now."

"What a stinking load of garbage!" her uncle fired back. He hadn't yet changed out of his suit, though he'd unbuttoned the top button of his shirt and unknotted the discreetly patterned Burberry tie. In his aggravation, he'd also worried his neatly styled hair into a snarl, and when Sabrina opened her eyes to gaze across the room at him, she had to smile. He looked like a disgruntled Santa Claus in a Brooks Brothers business suit, even if his beard was salt-and-pepper instead of white.

"Calm down, Uncle Seb. You're going to give yourself indigestion."

"Don't take that tone with me," he growled, crossing the study to stand over Sabrina. "I know you better than you think." He dropped down beside her with a heavy sigh and patted the hand lying limply on the cushion. "Little Bit, what you're doing isn't healthy. Remember when your parents died? You wouldn't speak . . . barely ate. Just sat on the window seat in the library, staring outside at the horses." He pulled off his glasses and polished them with the tip of his tie. "You sat there—for *hours* at a time."

"I was only eight, Uncle Seb. I barely remember Mama and Daddy, if you must know, much less what I was like when they were killed. Stop fretting about me because I don't ride anymore." She turned a little, her gaze wandering over the deep furrows in her uncle's brow, the lines bracketing his mouth, and a pang of guilt stirred. "Uncle Seb, you weren't this worried when I was in the hospital all those months, trussed up like a mummy and dopey from all the pain medication. If I survived that—"

"It was horses that brought you back to us," he pursued doggedly. His hand was squeezing hers so tightly Sabrina winced. "You told me once, some years ago, that riding made you feel alive . . . free. You were *happy*, Little Bit. I just want to see that look on your face again."

Sabrina gently freed her hand. "Uncle Sebastian, I'm twenty-seven now. Horses were a childhood passion, but it's time to move on."

"You're lying." It was his dead-serious lawyer voice, the one Sabrina and Renee dreaded because it meant they'd pushed him over the line. "It might be a girlish hobby for some, but for you it was more. You haven't outgrown your love for horses, Sabrina. You've given them up because you're *afraid* to ride." The piercing brown eyes held hers in a level study. "The therapies you've tried in the last couple of years haven't worked, so you're quitting."

"You used guilt on me last year when I told you I wasn't going to waste time in another psychologist's office, remember? It didn't work then, either."

Suddenly restless, Sabrina stood. For some reason, she was unable to retreat entirely from her uncle's force-fed logic. Was she a coward? A trickle of doubt slipped through a crack in her defenses, worming its way inside her mind. Was it cowardly to try to avoid mental pain— even excruciating mental pain? She wasn't the same person she had been three years ago, but what was wrong with that? She'd coped with tragedy one way as a child; as an adult, she'd simply chosen another way to cope with her present loss. That time after her parents' death was still mercifully shrouded in a mist so deep and distant that she seldom thought of it or them.

Thanks to Uncle Sebastian, she found her memories of the fall surfacing with a vengeance—the agony of regaining consciousness to find Renee and Sebastian weeping over her, of begging them to tell her Vesuvius was all right. Of seeing the truth in their faces before they could hide it. . . .

She had submitted herself to the months of therapy because she knew that the best way to recover from the loss of Vesuvius was to begin riding again as soon as the doctors allowed. But then—

She wandered across the room to gaze out the window, not re-alizing what she had done until her shins bumped the cushion of the window seat.

Shut it down, Sabrina. Don't think. Don't feel. . . .

Hugging her elbows, she retraced her steps to the huge antique floor globe in the corner. It was here she and Rennie had spent many happy moments—one, spinning the globe and plunging an index fin-ger to stop its orbit; the other, concocting some wild adventure about whatever exotic country her sister had found.

Right now, though, Sabrina felt as though her world was spinning out of control, her carefully constructed reality collapsing around her. All because of a news magazine.

Because of a man . . . and the promise he had made to her.

"I've never met anyone—male or female—who rides like you. In-cluding myself." He'd taken a deep breath, and she'd waited—forever, it seemed. *"If you train here at Montclair, you'll end up at the next Olympics."* A little smile hovered at the corners of his mouth. *"That's not arrogance, Sabrina—that's acknowledgment of the tremendous gift God has given you. I'd like the chance to help you develop that gift to its fullest."*

After a long moment Sabrina returned to Uncle Sebastian. "Very well," she said, her voice cool, collected. "I can see you're not going to leave this alone until you call Hunter Buchanan. Go ahead. If anyone can talk someone into making a fruitless trip to Virginia, you can."

Sebastian was too wise to reveal any sign of triumph, but Sabrina knew his idiosyncrasies well. She lifted her brows in a gently mocking gesture when he stood, steepling his fingers to stroke his ugly bulbous nose while he arranged a suitably benign expression on his face. "I was hoping *you'd* do the calling."

Sabrina shrugged. "Sorry. I'm not the one wanting to fawn all over Hunter Buchanan—which you *do* realize is just how you'll come across, don't you? After that *Newsweek* article, every hopeful equestrian with even an honorary ribbon from a Pony Club show will be knocking at his door."

She casually gave the globe a spin. "So, dear Uncle Seb, if you want to risk your reputation by calling, have at it. *I'm* going to bed. It's been a long day."

Yawning, she moved to the doorway, turned, and studied her uncle across the room. She knew she shouldn't torment him this way, but—"I finished four resumés, a forty-page report, started a *very* poorly written term paper for a panicked senior wanting to graduate from George Mason at the end of the summer session, and accepted three new jobs. I realize what a disappointment this must be for you, but I'm actually quite *good* at what I do." She went back to kiss her uncle's cheek, feeling the tension quivering in his jaw. "Better than that . . . I *enjoy* it. That's more than I can say for the way I felt the last time I tried to ride."

And with that, she sailed out of the room in the wake of a deafening silence.

꧁꧂

Montclair Equestrian Center
Rocky Mountains, Colorado

It had been one of those patience-shredding days. Why, Hunter Buchanan wondered, couldn't disasters and crises happen at acceptable intervals instead of all at once?

He propped himself against the stall, absently stroking the velvety muzzle of one of his favorite schooling horses while the vet, Noah Dickerson, finished examining the gelding's swollen knee.

"He'll do in a month or so, Hunt," Noah finally said, rising to his feet and gathering his supplies. "But he can't be ridden until then."

"Tell me something I didn't know," Hunt retorted, grinning ruefully. Before the vet's diagnosis had come the unwelcome news from Charlie Waters, Montclair's garage maintenance man, that one of the Center's Jeeps needed a new transmission. And before that, Hunt's accountant had called to warn of yet another corkscrew in the latest tax laws.

The glow of a burnt orange sunset was fading as Hunt walked Noah back to his truck and waved him off. *What a day*, Hunt thought again, his mind replaying the events, particularly in the arena. Five of his twelve students had ridden with all the grace and style of orangutans. According to his two assistants, even the biweekly cross-country run had been nothing but a series of fumbles, falters, and downright amateurish hijinks. Stu had almost expelled one of the younger guys for smarting off.

To top it off, on his way out the door an hour ago, Elsa Menendez, Hunt's housekeeper, had thrust a copy of *Newsweek* under his nose. "They make you sound like some fancy prima donna movie star," she grumbled. "*Madre mia*, but the phone and mail will hound us even more now. I warn you, didn't I?"

"Right as always, Elsa," Hunt agreed, squeezing her shoulders. "Unfortunately, that's the whole idea." He'd found the entire interview process uncomfortable but had given in to intense pressure from both the teaching staff and his ubiquitous accountants. Hunt shook his head at the memory; he wasn't sure he could handle the final article.

"Señor Hunter! Telephone!" Elsa called, rolling her eyes, her imposing figure filling the doorway. "I *tell* this man you at the barn, but he refused to hang up."

"Who is it?" Hunt ran his fingers through his hair and warily eyed the smug housekeeper.

"A Señor Mayhew. He tell me he wait—no matter *how* long you take."

Hunt's brow lifted. "Well, I won't keep him waiting any

longer—" He broke off suddenly. "Did you say his name was 'Mayhew'?"

"*Si*. But he would not—"

Hunt left her standing, open-mouthed, in the hall. His thoughts whirled as he strode down to his study and shut the door, then firmly turned the lock.

Two

Bald Mountain, Colorado

Gabriel Wisniewski mopped his head with a filthy red bandanna that had faded long ago to a dingy pink. He was eight thousand feet above sea level, but the sun burning down on his thinning scalp was as hot as the sun on a Florida beach. "Nice cool Rocky Mountain summer," he groused, stuffing the bandanna back in the hip pocket of his jeans.

In his usual Boris Karloff imitation, Gabe limped along down the rocky trail below his cabin, no destination in mind. This afternoon was no different from any other—a worthless fifty-year-old wreck of a man killing time, wondering why he was still alive and lacking the guts to do anything about it. He had moved into the ramshackle two-room cabin the previous year, the final desperate move of a man one step away from either a jail cell or a padded cell, so tightly wound a growling dog would have sent him over the edge. Now, at least, his sanity was hanging on by a clothesline instead of a thread.

Something was moving below, in an overgrown gully formed eons earlier by the collapse of tons of jagged boulders. Gabe shaded his eyes with his hand and stood motionless on the edge of the track while he surveyed the gully. There. Definitely a large animal of some kind, probably a deer. And yet—

A soundless whistle escaped when a half-grown horse suddenly darted out from behind the scrub oaks and jutting rock. On first sight it was nothing special, except for those lines. Gabe made a quick assessment of the yearling from head to tail and realized with a flicker of rising interest that this was no scrubby mustang offspring. A moment later a second horse—in much worse shape than the youngster—ambled into view. Protruding ribs, lusterless coat, head hung low. The yearling turned to nuzzle beneath the larger horse's belly. Must be the mama.

What were two horses doing way up here in this lonely stretch of mountain? Gabe took a tentative step, hoping he'd be able to work his way down, see if he could get closer. But this cursed bum leg couldn't take the uneven terrain. He stumbled and lost his balance completely. Swearing, clutching wildly with his left hand, he managed to slither to a halt halfway down in a clump of prickly yucca. It beat falling into the gully, but not by much.

He heaved himself to his feet, angry and humiliated, just in time to glimpse the horses galloping down the dry stream bed, their hooves clattering on the loose stones. Gabe glared after them. "You worthless nags! Think you got me buffaloed, do ya? Me with this lousy bum leg and one stinking arm!" No way would he go chasing after two animals like some yodeling cowboy.

He made his way back to the cabin and spent the rest of the day reading a paperback on Zen Buddhism he'd bought the week before. Several hours later he hurled it across the room. Blasted piece of garbage wasn't helping his state of mind any more than the other books he'd read over the last two years. Nothing could give him back his arm, repair the damage to his leg, or provide him with some mystical insight that would allow him to hypnotize those two horses into following him home. Not a thing on earth!

⊙Ɫ∭⧵⊙

The next morning he was back, this time with a pair of binoculars. For two hours he waited near the gully, sitting without moving beneath the branches of a piñon pine, but the horses never showed. Gabe was disappointed, but he had nothing better to do. He'd wait it out.

Over the past year he'd spotted several bears, as well as a cougar, along with the usual assortment of mule deer and migrating elk and a coyote or two. Amazing how those two horses had survived this long, though from his one brief gander at them, they weren't making out all that much better than he was.

Next time he needed supplies, he'd ask around town. He did know a couple of the grocery store clerks by name now. He also knew there was some fancy horse center on the other side of the mountain—one of those snooty places where people wore stupid little black hats and rode in saddles the size of postage stamps. Gabe had no use for a sport that required two good arms and legs, but he'd always been fond of animals, and he hated the thought of a cougar making a meal of those two.

He'd definitely ask around town. Maybe he could claim and tame the two critters for himself. He'd never had much success with humans, but animals usually cottoned to him right well. He'd never know if he didn't try. . . .

Three

Woodleigh, Virginia

Hunter's flight from Denver had been smooth and uneventful. He was met at Dulles by a uniformed chauffeur, who held the door of a rental limo open for him. If Sebastian Mayhew had wanted to make an impression, he had succeeded, though the nature of the impression might be a bit of a surprise, Hunt thought with a trace of amusement.

Through the tinted window, he idly observed the tentacles of urbanization that were spreading into the Virginia countryside while he speculated on the two people waiting for him at the end of the drive. Until their phone conversation, he remembered Sebastian Mayhew only vaguely as a shadowy figure in Sabrina Mayhew's background. During her interview at Montclair, she had mentioned that he was her uncle, who had taken her and her older sister in after the tragic death of both their parents in a cruise ship fire when Sabrina was a young child.

Hunt thoughtfully scratched the bridge of his nose. It must have been difficult for the man, he decided, assuming responsibility for two orphans when Mayhew himself was a widower. No wonder Sebastian had dredged up every form of emotional blackmail in the book to persuade Hunt to fly to Virginia.

His thoughts turned to Mayhew's younger niece. He tried to picture the woman Mayhew had described over the phone—a cool, passionless automaton set to operate on overdrive. Nothing like the Sabrina Mayhew he remembered.

"We'll be there in about fifteen minutes, Mr. Buchanan," the chauffeur informed him.

"Thanks." Hunt shifted in his seat. Even with the air conditioning going at full tilt, he felt suffocated by the July heat baking through the enamel and chrome surrounding him.

Ah, yes . . . the South in summer. Green everywhere, the fragrance of honeysuckle and grass, the sound of crickets and cicadas. Humidity and heat waves shimmering in a hazy sunshine. The slow unhurried drawl of the people. A grin inched across Hunt's face. Back home in Colorado, he'd left a slate gray, fifty-nine-degree dawn, with winds whipping down the mountain slopes hard enough to peel the bark from a tree. Summers in the Rocky Mountains were as unpredictable as a yearling filly. The contrast between home and here, on the other hand, was about as dramatic as Sabrina Mayhew's alleged personality switch.

We'll just have to see, Hunt mused silently, focusing his gaze on the countryside instead of his uncomfortable memories of a vibrant young girl whose quiet self-possession ignited like a Roman candle when she was astride a horse.

A little over two hours after leaving the airport, the driver turned onto a winding gravel lane. It led to a stately antebellum colonial house resting with quiet dignity amid a stand of towering shade trees. The fences flanking the drive bore a coat of fresh white paint, and the grounds were as manicured as any English estate. A couple of grounds keepers glanced up from trimming the boxwood hedge surrounding the house, their expressions openly curious. Somewhere in the background he could hear the hum of a tractor.

A crisply uniformed maid stood poised at the front door, alerted no doubt by a timely call from the chauffeur's cellular phone.

Hunt thanked the chauffeur, nodded to the grounds keepers, and tried to ignore an unexpected prickle of disquiet. The maid smiled and led him down a mile of waxed wood flooring, covered at intervals by three-hundred-year-old oriental carpets. She knocked on a door halfway down a hall, then stood back when a muffled male voice called out a distracted "Come on in."

Hunt's first impression of Sebastian Mayhew—who was short, tending to portliness—was that the man resembled a gnome. His heavily lined face was partially softened by a neat salt-and-pepper moustache and beard. He was sitting behind a massive cherry desk covered with paper work. A pair of bifocals hovered on the end of his nose as he scowled at a document he held in his hands. The highly regarded lawyer he'd heard about over the last week looked about as powerful and intimidating as an irritable chipmunk.

"Mr. Buchanan, sir," the maid prodded, her sidelong glance at Hunter apologetic.

Sebastian hurriedly rose, throwing down both paper and spectacles. "Hunt! I wasn't expecting you for another thirty minutes." An expression passed across his face, so fleeting that Hunter wondered if he had imagined the look of guilt. "Come in, come in. Sit down over here in front of the window." He stepped with surprising agility across the room, waving his arm toward a couple of chairs. "How was your flight? Did the driver locate you without any difficulty?"

Hunt settled into one of a pair of overstuffed chairs. For some reason Sebastian was nervous. "Everything went like clockwork. But I—"

"Good. Good. Would you like something to drink? Non-alcoholic, of course!" He laughed, a little too heartily. "I read the article."

"Something cold would be nice." After the maid left with the promise of iced tea, Hunt turned to Sebastian. "All right. Let's have it. What's wrong? Has something happened to your niece?"

"Not exactly," Sebastian hedged, one hand stroking his beard. "She'll be along in a while." He steepled pudgy but powerful-looking fingers. "I told her you wouldn't be here until four. I wanted to talk to you—alone—before you meet Sabrina again."

"Why?" Hunt shot back, tired of the older man's evasion.

Sebastian turned to the low table between the two chairs and picked up a large envelope. "Here. Before I say anything else, take a look at these."

Hunt arched his brows, but he took the envelope, which turned out to contain half a dozen 8×10 black-and-white photographs. Sabrina, of course. In the first, she was standing beside a colt, her face pressed close against the animal's muzzle. She looked to be about twelve or thirteen, and an expression of excitement and pride shone out of the photograph. In the following three prints, Hunt watched her grow into the young woman he remembered from the old videos he'd studied the past week: a lithe, graceful figure whose phenomenal empathy with horses communicated clearly even through the medium of two-tone glossies. What the prints couldn't convey, however, was the serene, catlike aura of mischief and mystery that had intrigued Hunt from the very beginning.

He glanced up, dragging his thoughts back to the present. Sebastian had turned away, but an aura of tension hummed all around the man.

Hunt shook his head and flipped to the next-to-the-last photograph. This one was in color. The date on the back was three years ago. He stared; *this* was the Sabrina he remembered. . . .

Standing by a fence, one arm casually draped around the post, she was wearing a vivid turquoise sweater and long flowing skirt. Her shoulder-length hair was the color of sun-shot honey, an indescribable blend of colors ranging from chestnut to burnished gold. Hunt swallowed hard, then turned to the final photograph, also in color—an enlarged snapshot taken from an angle. He almost dropped it on first glimpse.

A man—Hunt recognized her long-time coach, Glenn Larson—stood at Sabrina's back, hands on her waist. He was obviously trying to help her mount a horse. Sabrina's entire body radiated rejection: hands like claws, stiff on the saddle, as though she couldn't bear to touch it; face glistening with perspiration, eyes scrunched shut. The pitiless photo had captured her fear as though she were a bug on a slide beneath a microscope.

Hunt stuffed the photographs back in the envelope and threw them down on the table. "She hasn't seen these?"

Sebastian winced. "Of course not. I'd like to burn that last one, but you needed to see, to understand, before you meet with her."

"Trying a little plea bargaining before the victim arrives?" Hunt murmured, annoyed with Sebastian—and himself. He knew he was being manipulated, and yet he could no more turn his back on Sabrina Mayhew's plight than he could have ignored an injured horse.

"Desperate men employ desperate measures." Sebastian walked over to the table, where the maid had left a tray with two pitchers and several chilled glasses, and poured himself a glass of tea. He looked as though he wished it were something far stronger. "I've made a lot of mistakes with Sabrina these last two years. She's not going to believe you care enough to help, Hunt, unless you're convinced in your own mind that she's worth salvaging. Not just as an equestrian . . . but as a person."

"If all I cared about was training Olympic riders, do you think I would have wasted my time coming here in the first place?"

"I wasn't sure. I've read—and heard—about your so-called Christian ideals. Asked around before I called you, of course," he admitted matter-of-factly. "You don't force your faith on others, but neither do you compromise just to avoid offending potential clientele. You tread a fine line, son, and I don't want my niece caught in the middle"—he waved his hand—"you know, some religious fanatic preaching that all she needs is to *believe* she's healed—that sort of thing. But I'm convinced you could help her overcome her fear of riding. Once past that, she'd be . . . Sabrina again . . . I hope." He set the glass down with a thump and mopped his brow again.

Hunt strolled over to the window and looked out, needing a moment to compose his thoughts, to sift through Sebastian's convoluted reasoning for the truth. "I try to live my faith," he eventually responded, turning back around. "But no, I don't use it as a club to browbeat anybody." He shrugged. "As to whether or not I could help Sabrina, only God knows . . . literally."

He paused, watching a flush slowly creep into the older man's cheekbones. "I'm a trainer, Mr. Mayhew—not a psychiatrist or psychologist. I can't promise you anything, especially if Sabrina herself isn't willing to try."

The older man massaged a spot on his right temple. "That's the problem. She . . . ah . . . you may as well know. She thinks I'm wasting your time. I can't even promise she'll show up here today."

"What?"

Sebastian removed his bifocals to polish them on his sleeve. "The last time I tried to interfere in Sabrina's life, she pulled a disappearing act. And after she called to let me know she was all right—and, of course, to firmly make her point—she refused to speak to me for two months." A corner of his mouth twitched beneath the moustache. "The girl hasn't much of a temper, but she's stubborn as a whole *herd* of Missouri mules when she has a mind to be. After she gave up horses, she took classes in computer and typing skills. Then she researched job markets, and more or less carved out a niche for herself, all in the space of eighteen months."

"Which is exactly why I tried to talk him out of calling you." Sabrina's light voice sounded from behind the two men. "But I guess stubbornness is an *inherited* trait."

Hunt swiveled about and watched Sabrina Mayhew walk across the room. He hoped the shock he felt wasn't reflected in his face. That final photograph of a terrified woman had been easier to stomach than the woman approaching him now. Her deadly composure masked any hint of emotion and life from her face.

"Hello, Sabrina," he managed, stepping forward to meet her halfway. "I've been looking forward to seeing you again. I'd wondered what had become of you—" He stopped abruptly, his gaze narrowing, then finished more slowly, "And I'm beginning to think I made a big mistake in waiting to find out." He held out his hand.

"Regardless of what story Uncle Sebastian has tried to sell you, I'm perfectly well," Sabrina insisted, taking Hunt's hand and giving it a brief shake. She turned to her uncle. "You look surprised to see me here so soon." A cool little smile touched her lips. "I called Cora, and she told me when Hunter was scheduled to arrive. If I hadn't gotten hung up in traffic, I would have been here half an hour ago." She glanced at the two pitchers on the sideboard. "Oh, good. I see she made some of her iced tea. I'm parched. . . ."

She lifted her gaze to Hunter. "I do hope Uncle Sebastian hasn't misled you too much. I did try to persuade him not to—"

"Oh, I'd say your uncle has pegged the situation fairly accurately," Hunt observed. He moved to the tray and poured her a glass of iced tea and held it out, casually brushing her fingers with his own. The second contact with her skin verified the truth he'd discovered from her reluctant handshake: Sabrina Mayhew might look and act as indifferent as an outcropping of windswept granite, but the cold, trembling fingers proclaimed another story altogether.

The knowledge was hardly comforting. A disquieting tingle feathered the back of his neck again as he picked up the gauntlet Sabrina had unwittingly thrown down. The lady had erected a whole battalion of barriers, but Hunt had never been able to resist a challenge.

Beneath the crushing load of denial and fear was a rare gift. He couldn't let it die, regardless of the cost to either of them. *You* will *come to Montclair*, he promised her silently.

Four

Bald Mountain, Colorado

Sweating and cursing, Gabe reminded himself hourly that he was a blamed idiot to torture himself this way. The rough planks he'd purchased weren't all that heavy, and any nincompoop should be able to build a crude corral. Still, two arms and a leg that didn't give out unexpectedly would have helped mightily. He *had* come up with a doozy of an idea for fastening the boards together with rawhide, using his one hand and his teeth. A man did what he had to do.

Mornings were spent down at the gully, where he sat for hours watching through the binoculars, waiting for the horses to put in an appearance. As the days dragged by, he still hadn't seen hide nor hair of those two. But on the tenth day his patience was rewarded. He felt like a kid on Christmas morning; he could barely sit still while he watched the horses pick their way down the gully. Gabe's hand began to shake, and he dropped the binoculars to dangle about his neck, wiping his hand on his dungarees.

The mare was limping badly. She had to stop every other step to test the air and rest her right hind leg. Younger and healthier, less inclined to suspicion, the youngster cavorted beside his mother, impatient with her exaggerated caution.

Gabe let out a long breath, lifted the binoculars again, and propped them on his knees. He watched for the better part of an hour before his foot dislodged a rock. The slight noise nonetheless stampeded the two horses right back where they'd come from. Stiff and sore, Gabe heaved himself to his feet, his mind made up.

That mare probably wouldn't survive the winter, and the youngster had little chance on its own. Whether they liked it or not, they needed Gabe, and no matter what it took, he planned to capture and tame both of them. He had no idea where they'd sprung from originally; around here ranches and homes with horses were as common as the acres of black-eyed Susans that danced across the meadows all summer.

Some feller had been up here several months back. Claimed he wanted to buy Gabe's piece of land, but maybe he just wanted an excuse to look for those horses. Didn't matter. Gabe had pointed the shotgun at the guy's belly and told him trespassers weren't welcome. He must've taken the hint because Gabe hadn't seen him since.

Gabe didn't think the horses had escaped from that fancy dude ranch Montclair, either. He'd had a bellyful of Montclair ever since making a few discreet inquiries in town a month ago. As far as the townsfolk were concerned, the head honcho over there—Mr. Almighty Buchanan—could all but walk on water. Well, he might be a dab hand with horseflesh, but Gabe was about to decide he hated the man's guts. It was like that, out there in the world. A few lucky bums had it all—looks, wealth, fame—while some, like Gabe, had nothing but a crummy hole-in-the-wall and a body kids openly ridiculed, while their parents whispered behind their hands.

His mouth tightened, and he viciously tugged a plank across the ground to the post he'd finally managed to sink deep enough into the dirt. Didn't matter what people said or thought. He owned this stretch of land, and he had a bankroll gathering interest in a Denver bank that would probably buy Montclair twice over.

And those two scrubby horses—they were *his*. He was going to catch them and tame them, and they would belong to Gabe Wisniewski.

⟨⟩

It took him a month to finish the corral. By that time the horses were growing accustomed to his smell. Fibbing a little—telling the feedstore owner he wanted to feed the deer come winter—Gabe stocked up on grain and hay. That was the easy part.

The hard part was dragging the heavy burlap sacks, a load at a time, down into the gully to leave under the animals' favorite scrub oak. Once he managed that, he retreated to the top of a boulder some fifty yards away.

By the end of the first week, the youngster gave in and snatched up both grain and hay, with Gabe in plain sight. On closer inspection, he could see that she was a filly instead of a colt, and that she was as curious about him as he was about her.

The mama, of course, was more skittish—snorting and pawing, nostrils flaring—but she advanced until she was in easy range of the goodies. Wouldn't be long now. From the looks of her, she couldn't hold out more than another day or so.

Sure enough, by the end of August both critters were eating their fill, ignoring Gabe as if he wasn't around, but galloping pell-mell back up the dry creek bed if he made any attempt to approach.

They were wild, they were scruffy, and some long-buried streak of humor had prompted Gabe to name them Janis and Joplin, after his favorite female rock star, light years ago, back in the sixties.

And though Janis and Joplin didn't know it, they belonged now to Gabriel Wisniewski. He might not be good for anything else, but those two animals needed him. Before the first snow, he planned to have them up in his corral, where they'd be *safe*.

Five

Washington, D.C.

Sabrina agreed to take Hunter out to lunch, then drive him to Dulles for his late-afternoon flight. Much to her relief, he'd spent only the one night at Woodleigh. She didn't mind admitting to herself that she was uncomfortable around the man, but she *would* mind if Hunter picked up on her edginess. Unfortunately, there was no graceful way to refuse Uncle Seb's logic. Why waste money on a hired limo when Sabrina was headed that way?

"I'm flying to Pennsylvania to check out a couple of Hanoverians at a farm a few hours out of Pittsburgh," Hunter told Sabrina after they'd been riding in congenial silence for a several miles. "One's a gelding. The other's a seven-year-old stallion. A real handful, so I hear. The owner's priced him cheap."

"I'm sure," Sabrina replied absently, her mind on the traffic. She didn't mind giving him a lift to the airport, which wasn't that far from her apartment. Lunch, however, promised to be a bit tedious, if all Hunter planned to talk about was horses.

"Want to come along? I could use another opinion."

She almost drove them into the roadside fruit stand they were passing. "Um . . . sorry. No. I've got too much to do," she managed, sneaking a glance at him. He intercepted the look and returned a bland smile. Sabrina's hands tightened on the wheel. So, he wasn't going to let the matter rest, was he?

"Has my uncle enlisted you, then?" she inquired, determined not to make a big deal over it. "You have the car ride and an hour over lunch to convince me of the error of my ways? Talk me into trying to ride again . . . and waste everyone's time?"

"I'll let the Lord do any convicting that's necessary, Sabrina. As for the rest, I figure the decision's yours. Not your uncle's. And not mine. I just thought you might be curious to see how you respond when you *look* at a horse, not ride one." He waited two heartbeats, then casually added, "*I'm* curious."

"Don't be. It isn't very edifying." She slowed, adjusting the car's speed for the steadily increasing traffic.

How she yearned for the uncrowded peace of rolling hills, where the roads were winding lanes and the only vehicles an occasional tractor. Quiet woods, with a whisper of wind and a bird call or two . . . *the muffled thud of Ves's hoofbeats on the spongy earth—*

"Sabrina?" His voice was sharper, as though he'd repeated her name several times already.

"Sorry. My mind was . . . wandering." She pasted a penitent smile on her face. "What would you like for lunch? Fast food? Politically correct cuisine? Ethnic?"

"Anything's fine with me as long as I'm at the airport by two-thirty," he said after a moment. "I'm very plebeian in my tastes, though. So I'll pass on the politically correct. Tell you what. You choose the restaurant, and I'll pay. Deal?"

"Deal. I never pass up a chance for a free lunch."

Hunter chuckled. "Yeah, I do recall that you were something of a moocher. Remember that charity show down in Richmond? It was the only time we competed together."

She didn't want to remember. It was far too dangerous. *Shut it down, turn it off.* "Vaguely. That was so long ago, I've forgotten most of the details."

"I haven't, Sabrina." His voice was very quiet, and a chill trailed ghostlike fingers down Sabrina's spine. "I've been remembering a lot about you this past week." He shifted, his arm stretching across the back of the seat, the fingertips mere inches from her shoulder. "And you know what I think?"

"What?" Sabrina muttered when it was clear he expected a reply.

"I think you remember more than you're willing to admit."

They were just passing the entrance to a fast food restaurant. Sabrina braked, whipped the car into the parking lot and into a vacant spot. Then she turned to Hunter. "I've made some decisions my family isn't wild about," she stated deliberately. "But for me, they were the best options available under the circumstances." She took a deep breath and pushed some irritating strands of hair off her face. "I'd rather not talk about the past or riding or anything to do with horses, Hunter. As far as I'm concerned, they hold about as much interest as last week's news."

"Hmmm. What *would* you like to talk about, then?"

Startled by the teasing tone, she turned her gaze from the windshield to stare across at him. Today his eyes were more gray than blue, and if his voice was teasing, his expression was not. He looked, she realized with an unpleasant jolt, like he used to look when competing. Intent. Determined. Utterly confident. What, she wondered uneasily, was he so confident *of?*

"Is this where you want to eat?" he asked.

"What? Oh . . . well, it wouldn't be my first choice. I just pulled in here because I needed to explain, and there's too much traffic." She was babbling, she realized, and pressed her lips together. *Shut it down.*

The remoteness returned, blanketing her, shielding her from Hunter's probing gaze and pointed questions. Sabrina glanced down at her watch. "It's a little before one now. It's another hour from here to the airport. There's a pretty decent Mexican restaurant a couple of miles farther down the road." She reached out to switch on the engine, and Hunter's hand whipped out, closing over her wrist.

"Just a minute." He removed his hand immediately. "Let's get something straight here and now, shall we? I flew out here to see you, and—if possible—to discuss ways to overcome your phobia, probably by bringing you to Montclair."

"Strictly speaking, it's not a phobia."

His hand slashed through the air in an impatient movement, quickly controlled. "Call it what you will. You're afraid to ride a horse, right?"

"Right." *That's it, Sabrina. Keep it cool, professional. It doesn't matter, remember. . . .*

"In your opinion, I'm wasting my time."

"Right again."

"I disagree."

"That's your privilege."

Suddenly he leaned forward, close enough that Sabrina instinctively drew back until her left shoulder bumped into the car door. "Well, I also think it's my privilege, as the man who took the time and trouble to fly all the way over here, to choose the topic of conversation. You owe me more than a polite brush-off, Ms. Mayhew, and I'm not talking about lunch and a lift to the airport."

"I wasn't aware that I was giving you the brush-off."

"That's the problem. You're not aware of a lot of things."

"I'm aware of time passing. Do you want to miss lunch or your flight?"

He sat back, crossed his arms over his chest, and settled back against the car door on his side. "I'll leave that up to you. Talk to me, and we can still have both. Keep stonewalling, and I'll likely miss out all around. I'm willing to risk it." He paused, adding levelly, "How about you, Sabrina? Are you no longer willing to take any risks?"

Sabrina's hands clenched in her lap. She could have easily stonewalled anyone else for the rest of the afternoon. With a little more warning, she might have managed the same tactic with Hunter Buchanan. But not right now. Right now she was fighting herself as well as the persistent trainer; deep inside, symptoms were stirring that she dreaded far more than Hunter's leading questions.

"Well . . . I wasn't very hungry anyway." He patted his trim abdomen. "Don't need all that fat. And there's sure to be another flight to Pittsburgh."

Sabrina's gaze fastened on a billboard advertising the development of a new subdivision—*Riversedge*. She began counting the number of letters, turning them around to form new words—anything to keep her mind diverted from the inner nightmare while she talked to Hunter. "I no longer take risks of any kind," she agreed, her voice satisfyingly composed. *Let's see now. There was verse, sieve, diverse, ridge . . .*

"Why not, Sabrina?"

"Why not? Well . . . mostly because it's not practical." *See, sever*— she had severed all feelings, amputated them like a gangrenous limb in order to save her sanity. What would Hunter say if she confessed *that*? Have her locked up as a certifiable nut?

"So you've decided to be practical, is that it? A conservative, competent career woman, secure in your paper world. Not a horse in sight."

"You got it. That's the new me."

"I see."

Time passed. A plane droned overhead, and a car pulled alongside, disgorging a group of noisy teenagers enjoying the hot summer day. The panic abated, receding into her subconscious. Gone, out of sight . . . she was safe. For now. . . .

"Okay," Hunter announced abruptly, slapping his thighs. Sabrina jumped. "Let's check out that Mexican restaurant. We still have time if we leave now."

"Ah yes. I suppose we do." At least there would be a rest room, where she could escape for a little privacy if she needed it.

"It's all right, Sabrina. I'm not going to rush any fences. You can relax."

His voice was gentle, and she froze, wondering if she had given herself away. If, somehow, he *knew*. She started to lift her hand to the ignition again, then stopped. "Hunter?"

He rumbled an encouraging sound.

"Thanks."

Over a marginally good meal of enchiladas and chili rellenos, Hunt maintained a low-key conversation with Sabrina in which they chatted on a variety of topics. All things equine were carefully avoided.

Hunt watched her while they ate, though he was careful to keep his scrutiny from Sabrina's notice. A challenging task, given she was as sensitive to his presence as a sunburn. What amazed him was that nothing showed on her face or in the controlled elegance of her movements. But he knew. He'd spent most of his life learning to tune his senses to others. As an equestrian, to horses; as a trainer, to people. His father used to tell him that he must have inherited his Scottish grandmother's fey abilities, so astute were his perceptions.

From the first time he'd met Sabrina Mayhew years earlier, he'd known that, for her, horses were more than a glamorous career or an expensive indulgence. Her fear now was understandable, given the circumstances. But her categorical denial of life "before the fall" was an anomaly, a contradiction to the essence of her personality, and he wanted to know why.

She intrigued him. Irritated him. Compassion was there as well, but Hunt wasn't about to reveal *that* particular emotion to Sabrina. Likely he'd have to call a taxi to take him to the plane if he even hinted at feeling sorry for her. He bit into an oozing conglomeration of tortilla, frijoles, and meat, grimacing at the bland taste.

"Normally the food's better," she offered apologetically. "They must have a new chef."

He took a sip of water and smiled across the table. "Sorry. Guess I didn't do too well hiding my reaction, did I?" The huge eyes flickered. Hunt deliberately prolonged the contact. Idly he tried to decide the color of Sabrina's eyes while he maintained his silence. By the time he'd decided that her eyes were an interesting blend of gray and brown and hazel, she had dropped her gaze to her plate and was placidly finishing the meal.

Irritated, Hunt speared another mouthful. She had withdrawn again, on every level. The connection had been broken, and he didn't like it. Well . . . Sebastian Mayhew had warned him that it would be difficult to change Sabrina's mind when it was made up, but that only solidified Hunt's decision. It was time to put into action the plan he had concocted over much of a sleepless night.

He signaled the waiter. After the plates were removed and a last cup of coffee ordered, he propped his forearms on the table. "Did you know," he began in a conversational tone, "that one of my worst character flaws is arrogance? Some of my biggest spiritual battles as a Christian have been keeping my personality out of God's way."

"I'd say you—and God—have done a pretty good job." She produced a tight little smile that didn't reach her eyes. "Montclair's world-famous, and so are you."

"That's His choice . . . not mine. Besides, you know as well as I do that God isn't interested in the trappings. He loves us for what we are inside, not—"

"Do we really have time for an in-depth discussion? It's quarter till two."

"Probably not." He grinned suddenly. "Hang on a minute, all right? I'll be right back." He left her sitting there, looking faintly bewildered, while he hunted down the public phone.

Several moments later he returned to the table, which had been cleared in his absence. Sabrina was turning the bill over in her hands. "Sorry 'bout that," Hunt apologized, sitting back down. "Took longer than I thought, but everything's arranged." He plucked the bill from her hands. "I changed my ticket to tomorrow morning at nine o'clock."

"What! Why?"

Satisfied, Hunt tugged out his wallet and extracted a credit card. He'd finally provoked a genuine response, cracking that Mona Lisa mask, if only momentarily. "Over the last hour or so, I've had to acknowledge that it's going to take more than a luncheon discussion to convince you that you want to come to Montclair." He smiled his most charming smile as he signaled for the waiter.

It was as though he'd blown out a candle. "That's impossible," she retorted. "I . . . told you. I'm not interested in that life any longer."

"Would you be . . . if you could still ride?"

"A moot point, since I can't." She waited until he signed the credit slip and the waiter left. Then she looked across the table, her expression blank, as remote and indifferent as a dead fish lying on a platter. "After I realized my . . . problem, I spent the next sixteen months visiting every psychiatrist, psychologist, and therapy workshop in the D.C. area in an attempt to be . . . healed. And before you bring it up, yes, I prayed, too. Talked to ministers. Read self-help books. For whatever reason, God hasn't chosen to heal me."

"The timing—"

"Is irrelevant." She gathered up her purse and stood. "Hunter . . . don't. I appreciate what you're trying to do . . . would give anything—" Her voice cut off as taut fingers clenched and unclenched on the thin leather strap of her purse. "Bad things happen," she quoted, almost to herself. "Either you rail against fate, or you trust God and get on with your life."

"Denial isn't getting on with your life." He ushered her between the tables and outside into the oppressive heat. "Denial is running *away* from your life."

"So everyone says. But it's still my choice to make, isn't it?" She fumbled for the keys, then started toward the car. "Would you like to go to a motel or spend another night at Woodleigh? I don't think Uncle Seb had any plans for the evening, but even if he did, Cora always keeps a guest room prepared."

He wasn't making any headway at all. She'd balked, ducked out of, and refused every opportunity to jump. If she'd been a horse, Hunt would have lowered the bar or dismounted and walked the animal right up to the obstacle to prove—

He stopped dead, standing on the burning asphalt as though his feet were stuck to the tar. It might work. It just might work. He offered up a hurried prayer, then waited until Sabrina turned around to face him.

"What is it?" she asked.

"I have a proposition for you," he began slowly, measuring each word. "If you agree to it, I can pretty much guarantee it will change your life."

"There's nothing wrong with my life."

"Stop lying to me and to yourself." Hunt's tone was hard, commanding. His famous teaching voice. "Look me in the eye, Sabrina Mayhew. *Look* at me—" He gestured toward his eyes with two fingers. "Tell me you're happy. Not the kind you turn on and off like a television sit-com, but the bone-deep kind of happiness born of the assurance that your life is a gift. That with God's help, you're enjoying it to the fullest. Can you convince me that's how you feel?" He pinned her with a look, challenging her with the considerable force of his will. "If so, you can dump me at the first hotel, and I'll get out of your life. Forever."

For a while, he wasn't sure she was going to answer at all. Heat rose in undulating waves, bathing Hunt in humidity and glaring sunshine. He didn't move, and neither did Sabrina.

"What's the proposition?" she said quietly, evenly.

Guilt pricked him, followed swiftly by grim determination. Her face was bloodless, and though her voice was cool and clear as a spring-fed lake, she was looking at him now. Looking at him, Hunt saw, through eyes that betrayed tortured uncertainties—and knowledge. *She knew.* Somehow she already knew what he was going to say.

He wiped the sweat off his forehead, then hooked his thumbs in the belt loops of his slacks. "I want you to fly out to Montclair." Why bother to dress it up? "Not to ride. Just to wander around, absorb the atmosphere." His jaw jutted forward, a warning sign to people who knew him well. "I want you to remember, in detail, every moment you've tried to wipe from your memory. If, after three days, you can still look me in the eye and tell me you prefer your new life, then I'll put you back on a plane for Virginia myself."

Her chin lifted. "What if I decide I want to resurrect the old life?"

He raised an eyebrow. "Then you move to Montclair for the du-ration."

"You don't know what you're asking."

"I'm not asking anything right now, Sabrina, except a yes-or-no answer to the proposition. And that's entirely up to you. I don't want you on my property at all unless you come of your own free will. The three-day proposition's a beginning, not the conclusion. If you decide to stay . . ." He watched her fiddle with the keys for a few long sec-onds. "Okay, take me to a motel," he said. "I'll be there until to-morrow morning, seven o'clock. You have until then to decide what you're going to do."

This time, the silence was even more strained and lasted so long Hunt was afraid they'd both suffer a heat stroke. But, like a hunter, he knew the value of patience. He was also determined to win. When Sabrina finally spoke again, he knew he had.

"All right. I'll call you later with my answer." She unlocked the car door, then glanced over her shoulder. Solemn, defenseless, a hint of defiance. "Don't worry. I'll call tonight. Wouldn't want you to miss your flight in the morning."

Six

Bald Mountain, Colorado

*S*now could arrive as early as September, Gabe knew. He'd been putting in eighteen-hour days, building a two-stall shed for Janis and Joplin. He couldn't very well leave them exposed in the corral, much less bring them into the cabin as if they were a couple of hound dogs.

The garrulous hardware store owner had shown him how to use the specialty hammer with a magnetic head to hold nails in place. He also suggested the electric drill to start the holes. It would have been nice, Gabe jibed to himself often that first week of work, if he'd admitted he needed help sooner. Then he wouldn't have had to struggle over the blasted fence.

Old man Henderson thought Gabe was building a storage shed. To keep it that way, he'd traveled all the way to Denver in his beat-up Chevy pickup to buy halters, lead lines, grooming equipment, and assorted other supplies he was assured no respectable horse owner could do without. Gabe also bought some books. It had been almost twenty years since his stint as a wrangler on a working ranch. He'd been told he had a way with horseflesh but, hotheaded lunk that he'd been, he'd thrown away the chance to make something of himself. Nothing new.

As the snug shed took shape, Gabe found himself feeling better about things. He had a reason to keep kicking now—make that *two* reasons. Janis and Joplin.

Every day he carried food and a bucket of water down to the gully, and each time he lingered a little longer, until both horses no longer shied away when they saw him coming.

"Brought your favorite—and you could have an apple if you'd come a little closer. No?" He pocketed the fruit and shaded his eyes against the glint of sunlight through the aspens. There was a hint of gold that told of a change in the season. "Haven't got all that long to win you over, now do I?" he muttered, making his way back to the house to keep after his hammering. "Nope. Not long till the first hard freeze."

Piece by piece, board by board, he worked to fashion a home for Janis and Joplin. And when the last nail had been driven home, the pride swelled up in his chest like a sunburst. For the first time in ten years, he was glad to be alive.

On a clear, calm day when the sky burned a deep blue and the aspens blazed molten gold among the evergreen, Gabe slowly made his way down the path he'd worn to the ravine. He had to be extra careful today because he was as loaded down as a donkey with extra supplies. Several times he paused, shifting the weight on his back, enjoying the fragrant smell of Douglas fir and ponderosa pine blending with the pungent odor of the kinnikinnick and bitterbrush that flicked his dungarees.

At the usual spot, he scattered the hay and filled one of the buckets with water from the canteen. But today, instead of retreating to the clump of Gambel oak, he dug out the bag of oats from his pack, then settled down ten feet away from the hay.

Ten minutes later Janis and Joplin appeared at the head of the canyon. They saw Gabe and stopped dead. Long minutes crawled by. Finally Joplin inched closer, the wariness in her big brown eyes gradually turning to curiosity. Janis hovered at the bend in the canyon, nickering to her wayward daughter and stamping a hoof. Gabe didn't move a muscle, though his gaze devoured the dusty yearling. This close, she looked closer to a two-year-old than a yearling. . . .

"What I wouldn't give to get my hands on you and that overprotective mama of yours." He kept his voice pitched low, soothing.

She was a beauty, all right—head well-shaped, neck arched, the deep chest of a Thoroughbred, and long, long legs. His hand itched to pull all the burrs and twigs from her mane and tail and brush the filthy coat until it shone.

Slowly, slowly he held up a handful of oats and extended it toward

Joplin. Janis neighed, the summons urgent. Joplin backed, ears flattening. Gabe didn't move, though sweat trickled down his forehead and his bum leg was on fire.

Joplin calmed, took another step toward the hand, nose outstretched, nostrils quivering at the scent of the oats. "C'mon, baby," Gabe whispered, his throat tight. "C'mon. Go for it. You can do it. I won't hurt you. . . ."

Janis whinnied again, the sound ringing off the walls of the narrow canyon. Joplin stopped, turned toward her mother—then swiveled back toward Gabe.

"Atta girl, Joplin," he crooned. "She's just a doting mama. But you and me—we'll show her, Joplin. We'll show her it's okay."

The filly took another step, close enough now for Gabe to feel her warm breath across his arm. She lowered her head, nostrils twitching, as she sniffed the oats. Ears pricked forward, muscles shifted and rippled beneath the dull coat. But her eyes were bright and lively as an inquisitive kid. Gabe froze, all his discomfort and pain suspended.

Joplin's velvety nose dipped, the whiskers tickling his fingertips. She nibbled at the oats, her teeth barely grazing his palm.

When she finished, she lifted her head, and she and Gabe stared at each other. Then, fire streaking down his arm, he slowly withdrew his hand. Joplin shied away, hooves skittering on the dry soil. Behind her, Janis neighed urgently.

Joplin swiveled about so abruptly her hind feet almost trampled Gabe's toes. Then she was gone, cantering down the gully with her nervous mama.

"Well, I'll be . . ." he muttered aloud, incredulous. "It's going to work. It's really going to work out."

Seven

Woodleigh, Virginia

Sabrina made the trip to Woodleigh faster than usual. It was late, a little past ten at night, and she had phoned ahead, warning Cora to tell Uncle Seb to go on to bed. Her fingers throbbed, her back felt as though a hot poker had been tied against it, and she'd eaten only a cup of yogurt and half a peanut butter sandwich in the past thirteen hours. On the seat beside her, a paper sack held a large order of the French fries she meant to nibble while she drove.

Thankfully, she had finished all her jobs and could try to relax the rest of the week. Maybe she could even achieve a little more balanced perspective about—everything.

The dark ribbon of road undulated in the moonlight, and the quiet roar of the car engine seemed to crescendo in Sabrina's ears. Already raw, her imagination conjured up the mental image of a terrified mouse cringing before a pack of hungry alley cats, their eyes glowing like the car's oncoming headbeams. *Stop it.* The stern command didn't work. An ominous wave of dizziness washed over her; she was alone, it was dark . . . on a deserted road.

The car slowed to a crawl, bumping to a halt as Sabrina somehow managed to steer it onto the side of the road. Hands shaking violently, she fumbled with the keys and switched off the ignition. She gripped the wheel, running her hands up and down the leather cover. *I can wait it out. Take control. Think, Sabrina. You're safe. Doors are locked. You know this road like the back of your hand; you've driven it since you were sixteen. Woodleigh's less than ten miles—give it a few minutes.* She was fine. She was—

The creeping terror suddenly pounced.

⟋⟍⟋⟍⟍

Time passed. Eventually, so did the attack. It had been one of the more unpleasant ones—intense, vivid. Crippling. Moving stiffly, like an arthritic old woman, Sabrina lifted her head from the steering wheel, wincing as she straightened her back. *Breathe in, breathe out.* Gradually her pulse returned to normal, and she became aware of the stifling heat, the stale odor of fried food mingling with the odor of her fear.

She'd been halfway anticipating an attack, ever since the night she'd phoned Hunter and agreed to fly to Montclair, in fact. Work had kept the dreaded episodes at bay all week, but the respite was only temporary. Wearily she fumbled for a napkin and mopped her clammy forehead. "Why, Lord?" she ventured aloud, gazing through the windshield toward the star-studded night sky. "I know—I'm not supposed to ask why. And you're not going to tell me, are You?"

She had been strong enough to build a new life for herself. Too late, she realized it was a new life built on sand.

Hunter Buchanan was responsible. He and his tempting three-day proposition. And he'd known just which of her buttons to push, too. Leaving the decision up to her. Taunting her with the subtle finesse of a fencing master. Backing off when his uncanny perception told him he had pushed too far.

It had taken Sabrina only three hours, that evening two weeks ago, to make her decision. She was strong enough, secure enough now to accept the proposition. She would prove it to herself and Hunter. Trust God to give her the courage to go through with it.

She apologized to God for her possible presumption, as well as what might be stubborn pride. But even if her decision brought on more episodes, she'd given her word. She wouldn't back out now. "Could have done without this last half hour, though, Lord," she sighed, restarting the engine and pulling back onto the road.

These past months, when the panic attacks seemed to be diminishing, she had foolishly interpreted the decline as divine affirmation. She was reborn and was getting better every day. More denial, of course. Denial wasn't facing life, Hunter had said; denial was running away.

All right, then. She was *going* to Montclair. True, only for three days, and with no intention of climbing on the back of a horse. If she was careful, she might just be able to carry it off without having another attack just from *seeing* a horse. The final attempt she'd made on her own, eighteen months ago, had triggered a doozy. Hunter would be too busy to hover, and Sabrina planned to spend most of the time either up at the big house, as it was called, or hiking in the woods.

At the end of the three days, she'd graciously allow him to drive her to the airport. She'd even pay for *his* lunch, and—if he wasn't too surly about losing—just maybe she'd refrain from saying "I told you so."

It was only three days. Sure, she could handle it.

⟨⟨⟨⟩⟩⟩

Montclair

". . . and he should be arriving in about ten days. Make sure you put him in the barn where we board the year-round horses, not Montclair's schooling mounts or the students' horses."

Jay, the Center's head groom, scratched a bristly chin, his expression puzzled. "But I thought you'd bought him for—"

"That information is *not* for public dissemination," Hunt interjected, softening the curt warning with a smile. "As far as the students and staff are concerned, he's just another boarder."

"What about training? I know you're not planning to start her out on a headstrong stallion, so who's going to put the lad through his paces? One of the students? Isn't Josh Silverstein scheduled to arrive next week?"

"You worry too much, Jay. I'll take care of it. That's all you need to know for now." Hunt himself would worry about the consequences if his plan failed.

He heard Stu Menninger's voice, calling for him, and met his assistant at the barn door. "I know, I know. It's five till ten. Time for my class. Thanks for covering for me the past couple of sessions." He shook his head. "It won't happen often, I hope. Too many excuses, and I'll start losing students."

It was the second time in a month other problems had had to supercede his training schedule. The past couple of days, he'd been up in Denver, speaking to his Congressman and a couple of sub-committees on the encroachment of land developers. For the last decade, the Eastern Slope of the Front Range had been staggering beneath an onslaught of people, all of them wanting to own a slice of Colorado. Now it was spilling westward. Hunt understood, but he refused to sit on his hands, watching the wholesale destruction of the wilderness. Not to mention the threat to his own heritage.

Stu's chuckle jerked him back to the present. "Which one's tying you up in knots now, boss? Winthrop and her latest scheme—or Sabrina Mayhew?" The morning sunlight bleached the assistant trainer's fair hair almost white, in startling contrast to his deeply tanned skin.

"Both," Hunt admitted with a wry grin. He dusted his hands on the breeches he'd worn this morning in readiness for an afternoon ride. "Come on, let's go. Impatient students await. How'd everyone do in the sessions I missed?"

"Well, they griped some. Let's put it this way. We're good, but we're not the incomparable Hunt Buchanan. Carla and I managed to get them out of Egypt, but Moses is going to have to part the Red Sea in order to deliver them to where they want to be."

"It was God who parted the Red Sea," Hunt pointed out, unruffled. He was used to the good-natured ribbing. Without missing a beat he began to interrogate Stu about the riders, listening carefully while Stu filled him in.

Unfortunately, Hunt's concentration today was not what it needed to be, mostly because he couldn't keep his mind off Sabrina Mayhew's imminent visit. He wondered what she was doing, if anything, to prepare herself and whether or not she'd actually show up. He'd replayed the scene in the restaurant countless times, wasting mental energy debating the wisdom of his actions. In the end, he'd concluded that he'd do the same thing all over again. It simply wasn't in his makeup to watch God-given talent go to waste.

When he and Stu reached the barn, they stepped from the bright sunlight into the cool shadows of the indoor arena. Hunt sketched a wave as they parted and forced himself to focus entirely on Joan Drummond, one of the contenders for Rider of the Year. "I hear you're all ready to win the National," he greeted her as he strode into the sand-covered arena.

A petite powerhouse of a rider, Joan's eyes lit up. "*Now* maybe we'll get somewhere," she said and returned Hunt's grin. "Not to mention that I've missed your good-looking face."

He steadfastly ignored the blatant hero worship—a constant bother—and listened instead to Joan explain what she hoped to accomplish in this session.

He didn't mind the respect of his students—even admiration was okay. He'd have to admit he needed some of that. But no man deserved to be treated as though he were some sort of idol. He'd realized almost from the beginning that he'd have to be careful. Since his father's death, Hunt had begun altering his teaching technique. His father had been low-key—a quietly powerful man in his late seventies, whose age and stature precluded much of the hero worship. At twenty-seven, Hunt had been fair game, especially for the young, impressionable females.

Those first years had been difficult, the experience costly. Not only had his pride—and Montclair—suffered setbacks, he had lost the woman he had planned to marry. She had refused to compete with Montclair and the unending stream of worshipful equestrians.

Unfortunately, the hero worship still intruded. But now, after nine years, at least his teaching style provided a shield of sorts. He stepped back and folded his arms across his chest, sweeping a comprehensive gaze over Joan. "Well . . . you ready?"

She nodded eagerly.

Hunt signaled, and she mounted. He took a deep breath, preparing himself mentally, and the lesson began. Eyes narrowed, he waited until she'd ridden halfway around the ring. "No, no, no!" he shouted, pitching his voice deep and hard so that it resounded off the arena walls. "I thought you said your seat had improved! You look like you're riding a plowhorse on the farm! I've seen better posture in a sway-backed mule. . . ."

⚬⚬⚬⚬⚬

The day before she flew to Montclair, Sabrina called Renee at her home in Charlottesville. "I'm going," she announced abruptly after her sister had filled her in on the latest antics of her three children. "I'm leaving in the morning."

"Hallelujah! It's about time," Renee crowed. "I just wish you'd made this decision two years ago. You'd probably be back in competition by now."

"You always did like to exaggerate, Rennie." Sabrina stared at the open suitcase on her bed. A pair of faded breeches lay on top, an afterthought. Completely unnecessary. And yet . . . "Look, I better go. Give my love to Evan and the other two musketeers. I'll see you when I get back." She started to hang up.

"Brina?"

Sabrina brought the receiver back to her ear. "Now what?"

"Oh, nothing much. I just thought . . . have you packed enough clothes? There's a possibility—teensy, I admit—but still a possibility, that you might end up staying at Montclair a lot longer than three days."

Eight

Bald Mountain

Joplin was a flirt.

She would eat out of Gabe's hand now, but she liked to put on a show first, prancing and priss-tailing her way closer and closer. Janis still didn't want any part of him.

In fact, the younger horse was letting him touch her—even run his hand down her foreleg. Gabe kept a halter in plain sight, dangling around his neck, so that Joplin was beginning to accept the contraption without snorting. The first time Janis had caught sight of it she'd disappeared down the gully and not returned for two days.

It was plain as his empty shirt-sleeve that some sorry scoundrel had taught the mare all about the viciousness of the human species. Every so often, he chewed over what he'd do to the scum bag, should he ever find out for sure who it was.

Gabe was determined nonetheless to teach Janis that *he* could be trusted. "Talk to your mama for me," he told Joplin every day. "Tell her to show a little horse sense for a change."

He'd made a joke. Not much of one, but a joke. He'd even found himself occasionally smiling, for no other reason than that it hadn't snowed yet, or over the feel of Joplin's whiskers on his hand. The lightening of his spirit was almost enough of a miracle to keep him from wallowing in despair over the ailing Janis. At least she was eating better, and in the past weeks had even put on a little weight. But he needed to get them both up the ravine and into their new home.

Fall—and cold weather—was coming. His bones told him that.

". . . so come on, baby. Help me out with your mama. We need to get the pair of you into your new home. It's nothing fancy, I know, but it'll keep you dry and warm. And safe."

Today, while he fussed over the filly, he casually allowed the halter to brush her nose, her cheek. Joplin didn't even twitch. Janis was munching hay a dozen feet away, one ear swiveled toward Gabe's droning voice. It was a cozy, domestic scene, and the longing swelled up in his throat for a real home.

⌇⌇⌇

That evening Gabe sat on the spring-shot old sofa, thinking while he watched flames shoot sparks and smoke up the chimney. What he really needed was a ranch. A ranch of his own, with plenty of land and a real barn. A place not just for Janis and Joplin but for any other broken-down nags nobody else wanted. Gabe figured he knew more than most about how it felt to be broken down and unwanted.

A ranch of his own, with horses to care for. . . . Now, that was something to do some serious thinking about. Maybe he oughtta look up that fellow he'd scared off with his shotgun. Give him another chance, if he was legit, that is.

Nine

Montclair Equestrian Center, Colorado

I'm really here.

Sabrina followed the line of passengers up the tunnel and into the concourse, too numb to notice much about Denver's controversial new airport. Waiting at the gate along with the crowd, standing a little off to one side, was Hunter Buchanan. Looking suave and comfortable in pleated khakis and a heather gray shirt. Confident. Relaxed.

Everything Sabrina *wasn't*. But she was determined not to betray her wobbling knees and roiling stomach. She adjusted her heavy carry-on bag higher on her shoulder and fixed a pleasant smile on her face. "You didn't have to make the trip yourself. I could have come in the Center's van, like I did—" *No, Sabrina.* No references to that first visit to Montclair, however oblique. The sooner Hunter realized the vast chasm separating the young Sabrina from the woman she was today, the sooner he would concede defeat.

Besides, even if she lost her marbles completely and asked to stay, he'd be wise to cut his losses. In her current condition, she could only generate unfavorable publicity for Montclair.

Suddenly she realized her mind had wandered again, and that Hunter had continued to stand there patiently, waiting for her to give him her full attention. Her smile wobbled.

"Tired?"

She nodded, grasping at the convenient excuse.

"I figured you would be." He lifted the bag from her shoulder.

"You haven't had enough fresh air and exercise lately—cooped up in your office all the time."

Sabrina nodded again. Her continued silence brought a raised eyebrow, but she couldn't think of a response that wouldn't betray her irritation. Cooped up in her office, indeed. But she had to admit . . . he was right. Deep inside, the sick anxiety stirred.

"Come along." Hunter put his hand under her elbow and turned her to face the opposite direction. "Let's grab the rest of your luggage and see if we can beat some of the traffic. We have a long drive ahead of us."

As they merged with the stream of passengers, he slanted her a faintly amused look. "Yeah, Ms. Mayhew, you're really here. It would help if you tried to look like you've arrived at the gates of paradise instead of purgatory."

Sabrina, raw and uncertain, retreated even further. "Well, maybe this wasn't such a good idea. It's not too late to change my mind."

"Oh yes it is. You're here, and here you'll stay for three days. Longer, if you'd only pull your head out of that sand trap you buried it in. Quit kicking against the pricks, Sabrina. It won't be as bad as you think it will."

No . . . Sabrina thought glumly. *It'll probably be a lot worse.*

⌥

He watched Sabrina out of the corner of his eye while he drove. As usual, on the surface she projected the placid calm of a mountain lake. But her hands rested stiffly in her lap, twined around her small leather clutch purse. And there was something about her expression, her almost frozen stillness that reminded him of a trapped animal.

Hunter moved in the seat, absently down-shifting the Jeep to maneuver another hairpin curve in the winding road leading up into the mountains. The first half hour he'd played the part of polite tour guide, agreeing that regrettably, traffic was almost as awful as northern Virginia. Pointing out the sites she might not have remembered in all the intervening years—Mt. Evans, bison. . . . He even touched on his favorite hobbyhorse: the ongoing battle between what, to him, was some of God's most magnificent handiwork, and man's encroaching civilization.

She responded with all the warmth of tepid water. Hunt would have been more aggravated if he hadn't been able to see her face. Aloof, yes. Quietly elegant in her plaid slacks, burgundy blazer, and matching sweater. Only at this close range could he detect the lines of fatigue shadowing her forehead. She was pale, taut from strain.

But she *had* come.

Fragile, but game, Hunt decided. It promised to be a challenging couple of days. After they turned off I–25, he lapsed into silence, and within three minutes Sabrina had dozed off. Hunt turned his mind to the multitude of tasks facing him when they arrived.

She slept until they turned onto the bumpy road that snaked its way through the pass to Montclair. Hunt hoped to persuade the county to pave it within a year. Horse trailers suffered grievously, and he'd fielded many complaints from justifiably irate riders. The jolts and constant turns eventually jarred Sabrina awake. Hunt waited until she stretched, blinked, then surreptitiously rubbed her temple.

"You might have a few altitude adjustment symptoms, remember," he commented. "Shortness of breath, dizziness, headache."

"I'll be fine." Her smile was fleeting.

Again she watched the scenery with little interest and less conversation. Now Hunt suppressed a stab of irritation. He hadn't wanted to force the pace, but Sabrina's almost otherworldly indifference to both her surroundings and her circumstances stung. She hadn't asked a single question about Montclair, hadn't expressed an ounce of enthusiasm or anticipation. Hadn't, in fact, even mentioned the three-day proposition or what he had planned for her.

He decided to push, just a little. "Got anything you'd like to ask before we arrive? Jody—she's my administrative assistant—sent you the info packet, didn't she?"

"Yes. Very impressive."

"Thanks. We just started sending them out year before last, three months before students who've been accepted arrive. Feedback's all been positive. I thought it would help reacquaint you." Also subliminally plant a seed and begin the process of retraining her brain. It was necessary before he had any hope of retraining the rest of her.

"I decided to let you stay in the dorm with the students. You'll have a better feel for things there, so you'll be able to more accurately evaluate your responses."

She stiffened imperceptibly. "I understood I'd be staying in one of the guest rooms in the house itself." Her knuckles whitened from their death grip on her purse.

"I know," he agreed calmly. "But after thinking it over, I decided the dorm's a better choice. Your suitemate's a realtor from Albuquerque—Amy Whitaker. She's training for eventing and will be here till the end of the week. Think you'll survive the loss of privacy, Ms. Mayhew?" he teased, deliberately keeping it light.

"I would have preferred staying at the house," she admitted, staring straight ahead. "But since it's only for three days . . ."

"Mmm. Look at it this way. If you decide to stay on, you won't have to transfer all your stuff a second time."

"Hunter, I don't think—" She half turned toward him, then withdrew again, only this time she kept her face completely averted. "What if I can't handle it?" she confessed, so low he barely heard the soft words.

"Don't let past failures steal the hope of success, Sabrina. You're *here*, aren't you? Doesn't that tell you anything? It sure tells me something." Still she didn't move. "It tells me," he persisted, "that you want to be here—not for three days, but for as long as it takes. The proposition I put to you was only a gimmick, and you know it." He shot her an exasperated glance. "Could you bring yourself to turn around? I don't particularly enjoy carrying on a conversation with the back of someone's head."

"Sorry." The word was grudging, but she did shift enough for Hunt to see her profile out of the corner of his eyes. "Stop goading . . . *pushing* me. You're not the first to try that tactic."

"Well, it worked, didn't it? I'd say the battle's already half won."

"Hunter, you haven't—" Once again she broke off.

"Haven't . . . what?"

Her hands fiddled more restlessly, twining around limp strands of hair, flipping the purse strap. Finally they balled into two white-knuckled fists and buried themselves in her lap.

Out with it, Sabrina, Hunter thought, every muscle tensing in expectation.

"You haven't seen me around horses!" she finally dragged out. Shame edged the words, haunted her face, her slumped shoulders.

The wave of compassion was so powerful he almost stopped the car so he could take her in his arms and rock her like a child. "Is that all?" he returned easily. "Your uncle's already explained, Sabrina. It's no big deal. We'll handle your fear one day at a time. One *step* at a time. You know, the way we're supposed to live our faith?"

"Don't, Hunter. Please."

The huge wrought iron gate appeared as they rounded a bend. Hunt took the hand control from the visor and pressed the button to open the gate, but after driving through, he pulled a little to the side and set the parking brake. "I wasn't trying to goad you—*then*," he admitted, watching her closely. "But now that you're here, I *will* do whatever's necessary to jar you out of your zombie mode."

"Insults won't work."

"That could be a problem when we start your retraining sessions."

Another bout of nervous hand movements followed before Sabrina murmured in a stifled tone, "I know. I probably shouldn't have come. It was a mistake."

"Take it easy, Sabrina. You're just tired right now. Look at it this way. Your condition is not a mortal sin." His voice gentled even more. Her face had turned the color of a pumice stone, and the skin around her rainwashed brown eyes looked bruised. "Everyone's afraid of something. So you have a little more exaggerated response—*phobia*, isn't that the term?"

She slanted him a bright, brittle look. "Not quite. Mine's much fancier, depending on whom you talk to. Post-traumatic stress syndrome, generalized anxiety disorder, panic disorder . . . or would you prefer the more old-fashioned anxiety hysteria and avoidance behavior? How about a dissertation on my coping style and repressed drives, my genetic predisposition. Or maybe you'd rather hear about the theories of exogenous versus endogenous behavior as related to—"

"I get the point!" Hunt growled. He released the brake and rammed the Jeep into gear. The rest of the drive was accomplished in grim silence. As they rounded the last curve and entered the valley, he tried to relax and absorb the peace he always sensed waiting for him at Montclair.

Located in a hidden valley, the Center stretched before them in stately splendor, bathed in the golden glow of the late autumn afternoon. Hunt never felt more content than when he made that last curve. The sprawling barns with their cupolas . . . freshly painted indoor arenas . . . horses serenely grazing in a pasture off to the right.

In one of the jumping rings Carla was coaching John Brenders, contender for a spot on the US Equestrian Team; beyond them, in another outdoor ring, Stu watched several riders longeing their horses. Hunt gripped the wheel tighter. The urge to compete never quite disappeared, and there were still times when he debated going back on the circuit himself.

Abruptly he realized Sabrina had spoken. "What?" he asked absently, still watching John take his horse Neptune through a series of jumps.

"Stop the car!"

His head slewed around, and after a rapid perusal of her face, Hunt brought the Jeep to a swift halt. Sabrina threw open the door, staggered over to a clump of aspen, then doubled over, violently losing the contents of her stomach.

It was not, Hunt observed sourly, a sterling beginning, and he was forced to accept the fact that the task of rehabilitating Sabrina Mayhew might not be quite as straightforward as he'd anticipated.

Served him right. Phobias, or whatever Sabrina suffered from, might not be a deadly sin. But pride—specifically, his own—*was*.

Ten

"Hi. How are you feeling?"

Sabrina jumped. She had forgotten to close the door to the bathroom, and her new suitemate had strolled into Sabrina's room without so much as a knock. Amy apologized for startling her.

"I'm not used to being around people, much less sharing a bathroom," Sabrina explained. She had, in fact, been sitting on the side of her bed, staring at the toes of her shoes and wondering how to gather the nerve to walk outside.

"A lot of us horse-lovers seem to prefer four-legged creatures over the two-legged variety." Amy tugged her sweat shirt over her head. "Didn't Hunt mention last night that you were supposed to meet him at nine? Maybe I better warn you that, for all his easygoing nature *out* of the ring, you don't keep our mentor and fearless leader waiting. Ever."

A nonstop talker, Amy didn't seem to care one way or the other if her listener ever made a response. The previous evening, the exhausting monologue had washed over Sabrina in a ceaseless flow, and she remembered little of what Amy had said.

Sabrina didn't want to think about her first day and night at Montclair. Denial again, perhaps—but then, she was so good at it, as Hunter had pointed out. She glanced across at the sturdy, brisk woman who finally headed back into the bathroom, her voice floating back through the open door.

The nondescript brick building that housed Montclair's students was similar in layout, if not size, to a college residence hall. It housed sixteen, with one end serving as a cafeteria. Sabrina shuddered anew, despising her loss of social skills. If only . . .

Amy poked her head back through the door, her round, no-nonsense face scrubbed clean, curly blond hair tousled and damp. ". . . and we're all making wild speculations about what he plans to do with you. Rumors are at the virulent stage. Say,"—she checked her watch—"did you know it's ten till nine? It'll take you at least that long to walk to the main house, if Hunt didn't tell you yesterday. He did at least tell you how to get there, didn't he?"

She came and stood over Sabrina. "You look like a puff of wind would blow you over. Don't worry, the mountain walks and the workouts will help. I've lost ten pounds since I arrived—not that *you* need to lose weight . . . did I tell you that's what started me riding? I needed to *do* something to shed extra pounds. Then, once I started riding, all of a sudden I was fired up to compete. When Hunt told me he thought I—"

"Better go." Sabrina scraped up a smile and a wave, grabbing her blazer from the bed.

Unoffended, Amy waved back. "If you missed breakfast, you can always get something at the field house," she called.

⌒WWW⌒

Sabrina would rather have faced a firing squad than the long walk up to the main house. And yet it was beautiful out here, with a fresh, invigorating atmosphere that tingled her nose and hurt her heart. For so many years, Montclair had been the pinnacle of all her dreams, the longed-for goal she had always hoped to achieve one day.

But not like this.

She trained her gaze on the massive bulk of the mountains, rearing jaggedly toward a sky so blue it shimmered. Thick stands of evergreens interrupted by clumps of slender white-trunked aspen crowded the slopes, while patches of red and purple wild flowers drenched Montclair's meadows in color. Splatters of gold dotting the aspens warned of the fast-approaching autumn. A gust of wind carrying with it the rhythmic sound of cantering hooves swayed the tree branches.

Sabrina risked a quick sideways glance. Someone doing flatwork, busily circling the ring while the instructor, a woman, watched from the middle. In another ring crammed with jumps of all types and heights, several riders were putting their mounts through their paces.

I can't do this. Acid rose in her throat, hot and bitter. The incipient headache intensified, pounding her skull.

Show a little backbone, Sabrina.

Her backbone right now resembled that of a jellyfish.

She was almost running by the time she reached the main house. An imposing brick mansion with two side wings and a columned portico, Hunter Buchanan's legacy stood in regal dignity, looking as impenetrable as the mountains rising behind it.

Sabrina stopped, bemused, amused, and terrified. *"The Center's offices are at the back,"* Hunter had told her. *"Don't use the front doors. They're for impressing visiting dignitaries and hopeful sponsors."* He'd smiled a deprecating smile. *"Commoners such as yourself come around to the back. You can't miss it. Jody's stationed right inside. She'll tell you where to find me."*

Sabrina stiffened her nonexistent spine and swiftly made her way to the back.

Buried behind a desk piled high with paper work was a petite black woman, whose long ebony hair was intricately styled in a multitude of corn rows. Hunt's administrative assistant waved Sabrina in, pointing to a chair while, phone cradled on her shoulder, she carried on a conversation and jotted notes with her other hand. A moment later she shoved back from the desk and stood. "Sabrina Mayhew? Nice to finally meet you." She stepped around to shake hands. "I'm Jody Stevens. Hunt's in an emergency meeting, though he promised he'd be done by ten. Until then you can wander around, take in the sights, whatever. . . ."

"I'll just wait here," Sabrina offered. "If he's free early, I'll be available."

Jody studied her a minute, then shrugged. "Suit yourself. Coffee and assorted teas in the butler's pantry, through there." She pointed to a partially closed door on the other side of the room. "You'll have to entertain yourself, I'm afraid. Until Hunt gives in and hires me some help, I'm busier than a short-tailed beaver in mud season."

Sabrina took in the clutter in a glance—stacks of folders on every conceivable surface, paper wads spilling out of a handsome leather wastebasket, pictures of several Montclair champions askew on the walls. . . .

"I wouldn't mind pitching in for a while," Sabrina volunteered.

It was Jody's turn to gawk, open-mouthed. "You? You're an equestrian . . . I mean, no offense, and thanks for the offer, but I need someone who knows their way around an office environment, not a barn."

"Um . . . I haven't exactly been much of an equestrian lately. As a matter of fact—" She paused in front of the L-shaped desk that housed a computer, printer, and an outdated electric typewriter, looking ancient and unwanted. Sabrina felt a certain kinship with the typewriter. "Where do I start?"

After Jody's initial wariness subsided, they worked in a silence that grew increasingly friendly. By the time an hour passed, she was chatting helpfully, filling Sabrina in on people and activities at Montclair.

"Who's this Kathleen Winthrop?" Sabrina queried at one point. She held up a letter displaying fancy real estate letterhead. "The date on this is almost a month old, and this woman needed an immediate response. Is Hunter buying property from her?"

Jody snorted. "Not likely. He and that Texas tornado strike sparks any time they're in the same room. Ms. Winthrop's some hotshot realtor. She moved here about five years ago, and she's been a big pain ever since. She likes to refer to herself as Kathleen, so Hunt calls her Kate. Really spools the woman up tight." She grinned over at Sabrina. "Sure is a fine-looking woman, though."

Curiosity piqued, Sabrina scanned the letter she had been about to retype into the computer's correspondence file. "Who's this Gabriel Wis-new-ski?"—she sounded out the name—"she wants Hunt to 'exert his influence over' so he'll sell his property to her?"

"Never met him. Neither has Hunt, probably because he hasn't even seen that letter. Where'd you unearth it anyway?"

"Inside a two-month-old copy of *Practical Horseman*. I guess Hunter hasn't read that, either."

For some reason the dry comment elicited a howl of laughter from Jody. She was still chuckling when Hunter came striding into the room. Busy at the keyboard, terrors firmly squashed in the security of a familiar environment and the unfamiliar warmth of companionship, Sabrina didn't even notice him.

"This is *not* what you came to Montclair to do, Ms. Mayhew."

Sabrina's fingers barely paused on the keyboard. "Has it been an hour already? Can you wait a few minutes? I've about finished here, and I hate to stop in the middle."

"Far as I'm concerned, that gal's wasted anywhere outside an office," Jody piped in. "Did you know she's accomplished more in two hours than I've been able to in as many months?"

"*Two* hours?" Sabrina muttered, astonished.

"And then some, I'm afraid," Hunter added from directly behind her. "It's after eleven. Save it or lose it all, Ms. Mayhew. Contrary to the wishes of my longsuffering assistant here, we have more pressing obligations." He waited until Sabrina, now muttering beneath her breath, exited the document. "Not that I'm downplaying your . . . astounding accomplishment." For a startling instant, his hand rested on her shoulder. "Thanks. You really didn't have to—what's this?" He reached past a disconcerted Sabrina and picked up the realtor's letter she'd been copying. "That woman! Sometimes I think her mission in life is to plague *mine*."

He sounded ticked off, and in spite of her rising nervousness, a smile tugged at the corners of Sabrina's mouth. "I'm sure she spends hours at a time plotting for ways to hassle you." She gestured toward the letter. "What will you do about this Mr. Wisniewski?"

"I'll do him a big favor and ignore this letter. Don't bother to transfer it to the computer—here." He took the letter, crumpled it into a ball, and tossed it into the overloaded trash can. "There. That's what I'll do about Wisniewski. One of these days I'll pay him a visit and tell him he owes me one." He grinned down at Sabrina. "You look shocked, Ms. Mayhew. Because of my response to that letter? Or my incompetency with paper work in general?"

Behind him, Jody's head was nodding vigorously. "Both," Sabrina admitted, and Jody gave her a mocking thumbs-up.

"Nobody's perfect. I hate paper work and everything associated with it, as Jody has no doubt been telling you."

"I enjoyed it," Sabrina admitted, scooting her chair sideways and standing. She rotated the kinks out of her neck, avoiding Hunter's gaze as she slipped beside him and crossed over to Jody. "If I have any spare time, I'll come back and give you a hand."

"You won't be having any spare time," Hunter drawled. "Starting now. Jody, did you unearth that order for those supplies yet?"

"Sabrina did. When she saw the date you filled out the order, she called FedEx. They came and picked it up forty minutes ago." The assistant was enjoying herself, but Sabrina wished she'd hush. "And, boss, Sabrina also agrees with me. Montclair needs to enter the information highway with a fax machine and modem. The supplies would have been here by now, if I'd had the right equipment."

Hunter's thick russet eyebrows shot up. He cocked his head in a manner Sabrina was coming to dread, and a wry smile twisted his mouth. "I might have guessed. Fair enough. Jody, take care of it however you please. Just spare me the details, and try not to buy the most expensive brand on the market." His gaze swept over Sabrina. "You wouldn't happen to have a twin sister, would you? Jody could use the help, as I'm sure she's already pointed out to you."

He ran a hand around the back of his neck, looking a little sheepish. "Come on to my office. We need to talk before I take you down to the barn and introduce you to Lady Fair."

"Before you disappear again, boss—"

Thankfully, Jody commandeered his attention, leaving Sabrina to recover from her rapid plummet to the unpleasant reality she'd been able to delay for over two hours. She wandered a little way down the hall from which Hunt had appeared and pretended to study the collection of photographs of various Montclair students. They spanned the past fifty years. Some of the names were famous enough to warrant listings in an encyclopedia. Montclair was a part of post-war Colorado history, and it was easy to see why Hunter and Kathleen Winthrop clashed at every turn.

"Sorry," he murmured at her elbow. "Paper work and bureaucracy remain one of the banes of my existence. As you saw, I'd rather be shoveling manure than dealing with it, much to Jody's everlasting frustration."

Sabrina shrugged. "It's been a nice reprieve, if you want to know." She paused, then added, "I could spend the three days helping her, if you like. I guarantee I could have Montclair's administrative affairs in order by the time I leave."

An indecipherable grunt was his response to that offer.

Hunter's office more resembled a study, with a comfortable grouping of sofa and chairs around a low center table, where a tray of sandwiches and a thermos and matching insulated mugs had been deposited. They sat down and spent a few moments eating, for which Sabrina was grateful. By the time Hunt poured her second cup of what had turned out to be hot spiced cider instead of coffee, she had steeled herself for the conversation she'd been dreading for weeks.

"You're feeling better, aren't you?" he observed, leaning forward to hand her the mug of cider. "Do you want to tell me what yesterday was all about now? Was it seeing the horses, altitude sickness . . . a combination . . . what?" He took a healthy swallow from his own mug. "Come on. Get it over with. If I can stand by while you're throwing up in the bushes, I reckon I can handle whatever it is you're having so much trouble admitting." The teasing drawl coaxed. But the underlying steel in his tone couched a command Hunter Buchanan wanted obeyed—now.

Time to fish or cut bait, Sabrina.

Eleven

Sabrina buried her nose in the mug. "It was a lot of things," she managed finally. Her heart began to pound in slow, heavy thuds.

Hunter sat back, legs stretched under the table, arm resting along the back of the couch. He looked relaxed, non-threatening. And indomitable. "I'm listening."

"I . . . don't know where to begin."

"Just tell me what's going on inside your head, for starters. Help me to understand. The woman I met in Jody's office is radically different from the woman I picked up at the airport. Tell me why, Sabrina. It's a little disconcerting, since I'm trying to convince you to become my student."

Sabrina spent several anxious seconds framing a response. "The office is . . . safe. It bears absolutely no resemblance to a riding arena. Classic example of avoidance behavior, of course." She shrugged. "But in the process, I discovered I'm good on a computer."

"You're good at *riding* . . . better than good."

"Used to be, perhaps. But now? You saw what happened last night. It wasn't the altitude, Hunter." Her hands had begun to tremble, and she carefully set the mug down. "That's not all of it. There's something you need to know about . . . my condition."

"Take your time, Sabrina."

She shook her head. "I should have told you before now, but I couldn't. I . . . I haven't told anybody, not even my family. But when I decided to come here for these three days, I had to face the fact that you deserve to know the worst. You've said you want to understand. It's just that . . . well . . ." She lifted her hands.

"You're doing fine. We're talking about your . . . let's call it your phobia? The fear is understandable, Sabrina. You don't have to be ashamed."

"I wish it were as easy as a simple phobia," Sabrina muttered. *Just say it, Sabrina.* She was sounding as melodramatic about the situation as Renee, for crying out loud. "Those words I flung out last night? They're all a fancy way to address the plain and simple fact that some months after the . . . after my fall, I started having panic attacks." She hurried to explain before she choked. "The exact interpretation of the diagnosis varies, depending on the training and philosophical bent of the specialist, but what it amounts to is . . . well, it's a toss-up between classic post-traumatic stress and panic disorder. It's difficult to pigeonhole every little hiccup of fear—"

"Slow down," Hunt interjected mildly. "Let me see if I'm following you. You're telling me that the fear isn't only present when you're confronted with horses? These attacks can be triggered by other situations? New territory? Unfamiliar people? What?"

He didn't sound angry. Yet. Sabrina scanned his impassive features, then shrugged. "I don't always know. I just know that, no matter how hard I try to control things—my environment, my emotions, my response—when one hits, I'm helpless." There. She'd finally admitted it out loud, to another person. "I've been to counseling, therapy. I know everything I'm supposed to be doing, everything I'm *not* supposed to be doing, and nothing has helped." She wiped her palms on her jeans.

"So you squirreled yourself away in a job that involves little interaction with other people and absolutely nothing to do with horses."

If she hadn't already been so sensitive, she might have missed the subtle undertone of censure. "That's about it in a nutshell," she returned coolly. "And regardless of your opinion, I'm good at my job. You said you wanted to understand, so stop passing judgment on my decision."

Tension crackled between them like a lightning bolt.

This time, Hunter backed down first. "Sorry." The word was terse. "I had no right to criticize."

"It doesn't matter. I just thought you deserved to know, even if

I'm here for only three days." Her mouth was dry, and the words emerging from her throat sounded strained, almost hoarse. "And if I decided to try to ride again, you needed to decide . . . in case you didn't want to—"

"Stow it, Sabrina. I don't want to hear any more about my wanting to back out." He sat up with a jerk, stood, and strode over to a wall crammed with books, trophies, and magazines.

If her legs would have supported her, Sabrina would have left the room, packed, and slunk out like the wimp she had become. She had known he wouldn't be pleased. Hunter Buchanan didn't have a cowardly bone in his body. Confidence and energy practically sizzled around him, along with a quiet determination evidenced in the set of his jaw.

"Come on," he ordered now, and Sabrina looked up with a start.

Hunter stood over her, arms folded, expression—yep, there it was again: that implacable force of will.

Reluctantly she rose to her feet. "I should have told you earlier, back in Virginia. I was wrong." With difficulty she met his gaze. "I'm sorry."

Something softened in his face, just for a moment. "It wouldn't have changed anything, Sabrina," he promised. "Except for the timing, perhaps, which we'll make up for, starting now."

"What do you mean?"

"If you'd told me this yesterday, we would have gone straight to the barn as soon as you arrived. I wouldn't have given you a day to adjust." He opened the door and waited for her to step into the hall. "All that served to do was deepen the anxiety. So . . . let's go meet your new charge, Lady Fair. Don't worry—you'll only have the one to care for . . . right now."

"Wait. What are you talking about? My *charge?*" Her hands clenched at her sides. "I haven't agreed to this, Hunter. You said I could do anything I felt like for three days. That was the deal. I only agreed to come for *three days.*"

"You're still playing mental games with yourself." He stepped right up next to her, so close Sabrina's skin crawled with an uneasy mixture of apprehension and resentment. "You want to stay here, Sabrina. You want to work with me, do whatever you have to in order to ride again. Don't you?" His hands closed around her arms, holding her still. "Don't lie to me. More to the point, stop lying to *yourself.*"

"How can you know what I want?" she whispered. She shivered in spite of herself, and Hunter released her, stepping back.

"You told me yourself just now," he said.

"I did not!"

An infuriating smile spread across his face. It made her itch to kick his shins. "Yes, you did," he retorted. "And you know it." One long finger tapped the end of her nose, then he was strolling across the room. At the door, he turned. "Do you need me to provoke you into a confession, Sabrina? Or will you be honest with yourself and save us both the time and energy?"

The man was maddening. How did he know that foremost among the tangle of emotions plaguing Sabrina at this moment was . . . anticipation. Hunter was right. She wanted to stay. Wanted it so desperately she had been unwilling to admit it, even to herself, until now. "I didn't bring enough clothes to stay longer than three days."

"No problem." He waited for her to precede him through the door. "After you gave me the date you planned to fly out here, I called your uncle. The rest of your stuff should be here by day after tomorrow at the latest."

By the time they were halfway down the path leading to the main stables, Hunt had regained his equilibrium. Hands stuffed in his pockets, he strolled along beside Sabrina and had to smile. Her spine was ramrod stiff, her strides brisk, almost defiant. She might not have a temper, but in spite of her self-inflicted character assassination the past few years, a woman of deep feelings was stirring back to life.

It was going to be interesting. What had seemed a rather ordinary rehabilitation project was turning out to be more complicated than he'd thought. The arrogance again. Well, God had always reined him in before, more often than not through unexpected venues. Looked like Sabrina Mayhew was the instrument this time.

He felt like a blindfolded juggler, handling lighted sticks of dynamite. His fingers were already singed from a couple of minor explosions. He hadn't anticipated the depth of her fear, nor what she had revealed about the panic disorder. He *certainly* hadn't expected to be impressed by her skill in an office environment.

But she wants to ride again.

He must remember that. Inside, buried so deep she still wasn't really aware of it herself, Sabrina's spirit cried out to be on the back of a horse. Iron determination settled inside Hunt.

They were surrounded by a breathtaking vista of mountains and deep blue sky; the evidence of his family's heritage swelled his heart with gratitude. But all he could see right then was the look of agonized hope on Sabrina's face, squeezing past the shame and fear.

You will *ride again*, he promised her silently. With God's help—and a little of his own—Sabrina was going to make it.

⧨

They were stopped three times before reaching the barn. As usual, the goldfish atmosphere at Montclair precluded most secrets: Everyone wanted to meet Sabrina Mayhew. Astonished, he watched her don the persona he was growing to hate. Except at moments like this, when her roots showed. She might not enjoy it, but Sabrina knew how to play the role of gracious southern lady. Poised, polite. Her low voice with its gentle drawl, responding to all the eager questions with charm and dignity. Yes, she was excited to be here at Montclair . . . and yes, she had completely recovered from that dreadful fall. . . .

Only Hunt realized that her answers were designed to shield and deflect while giving the illusion of conveying information. Everyone left convinced they'd met the *real* Sabrina. Reluctantly, his admiration for her grew.

He conferred with Stu about the new arrivals slated for the following week; listened to a brief update by Noah on an injured horse; watched both men covertly studying Sabrina, their expressions softening from neutrality to relief and protectiveness. He hid a smile behind his hand. His staff hadn't been shy in voicing their reluctance to involve Montclair with a troublesome student. The potential for negative publicity, possibly even a lawsuit—her uncle's a lawyer, right?—abounded. Hunt needed to concentrate on riders with better prospects.

One by one, they were falling for her as fast as the autumn leaves. There was something about Sabrina that made a man want to protect her. A fragment of conversation they'd shared at the restaurant returned. Hunt had asked why she wanted to live in an apartment, surrounded by people on all sides, when she could enjoy the privacy of Woodleigh.

"Uncle Seb and the entire staff treat me like I'm still six." Affection softened the frustration. "Besides, I needed to prove I could succeed at something, especially now. I don't want to be a . . . a parasite, living in what is, in fact, my uncle's home." She made a face. "I suppose being rich is most people's dream. Thanks to Uncle Seb's management of my parents' estate, I could sit on a French settee for the rest of my life."

"And be miserable," Hunt interpreted, relieved.

"Inherited wealth's more of a burden than people realize." Then she'd shrugged. "But I'll take it over being homeless. Everyone has a struggle, living life." After that, she'd changed the subject to a more neutral topic.

Several more students approached then, eager to speak with Hunt as well as Sabrina. By the time they finally left, Hunt had a feeling Sabrina Mayhew was inches away from bolting. Frankly, he couldn't blame her. Setting his teeth, he gestured toward the barn. "Shall we try one more time?"

"We can try." She darted Hunt a speculative look. "It's all right, Hunter. When I made the decision to come, I realized I might be regarded as public property. Actually, it wasn't so bad. Everyone was very nice."

"No reason why they wouldn't be." Not if they wanted to train at Montclair.

They reached the barn door.

"Well," she announced brightly, "I guess this is it, isn't it? My water jump."

Hunt looked down at her, his gaze taking in the rapid pulse fluttering madly at her throat above the collar of her sweater, the faint line of perspiration dotting her upper lip and temples. Determined she may be, but she was about to choke on her fear. "How long since you tried to touch a horse?"

"Eighteen months."

"Hmph. How long since you tried to mount one?"

"The same."

"Well, let's see how you do in the barn . . . with just the touching part, all right? Then we'll decide how to proceed." Actually, he already knew how he planned to proceed, but he had decided—based on the past twenty-four hours—that he would keep that little piece of information to himself for the time being.

He stood on the sidelines, waiting, giving Sabrina all the time she needed to walk through the door. Steeling himself as well for the unpleasant task of physically dragging her back if she *did* try to bolt.

Twelve

Bald Mountain

Joplin was allowing Gabe to groom her now, and he spent hours each day wielding a brush and a currycomb. It was the best part of his day.

Their relationship had progressed to true friendship, though Gabe knew he hadn't won her full trust yet. If he moved a little too fast, the filly would still shy away.

Janis had made some progress, too, much to Gabe's relief. She would eat hay and oats out of the bucket, then slurp noisily when he refilled it with water. But she still wouldn't let him any closer than six feet—not near enough to capture, so Gabe kept his worry under his belt and bided his time. At least she didn't startle at the sound of his voice any longer.

The mornings were nippy now. Fall was in the air. And at this altitude, winter wouldn't be far behind. He figured he had a month, maybe six weeks, before the first snowfall.

He'd been combing Joplin's mane today, and his hand tightened briefly, the impatience and fear churning close to the surface. Joplin snorted, her head slewing around inquiringly. "Sorry, darlin'." He rubbed the questing nose with the back of his hand. "Just in a hurry, as usual, and wantin' more'n I can have." He resumed picking out snarls with his one hand. "I got another letter yesterday from that real estate person." He spat on the ground. "Trashed it, just like the others. But you know, Joplin, they're so all-fired persistent. I'm starting to think maybe there's a gold mine on my mountain I don't know about. Whatcha think? Maybe the next time, I'll read the blamed letter." If they ever send another one. . . .

Joplin wouldn't care if the whole mountain was gold, as long as Gabe paid attention to her. Well, soon he planned to keep her close enough to do just that. "I think it's gotta be today," he announced some moments later. He carefully returned the currycomb to his backpack and withdrew the halter. When he turned back to Joplin, his hand was shaking.

Over the weeks, he had allowed the filly to see the halter, sniff it, even lip it. Gabe had draped it on top of her head, on her back, and had even put it over his *own* head while he brushed her. She was as used to its feel and presence now as she was to the blowing wind.

Gabe pulled a long breath, then casually lifted the piece of equipment. Joplin nosed it indifferently, then lowered her head to nuzzle at the breast pocket inside his jacket, where he tucked raw carrots for a treat. While she chomped in contentment, Gabe carefully slid the headpiece and noseband over her muzzle. Joplin blinked but kept on chewing. After a few agonizing moments, Gabe let out his breath.

"All right, girl . . . here we go." He removed the halter, then began to stroke her in a series of movements designed to ease her nervousness. The old geezer who'd taught him how all those years ago sure had known what he was about. Joplin stood quietly, eyes half closed. Gabe ended up slipping the halter in place and fumbling the throat latch closed so easily he almost burst into relieved laughter.

For two months he'd been working up to this moment, sweating through days and nights of near agony. And here he'd accomplished it with about as much fanfare as flicking a piece of lint off his shirt.

"Life still holds a few surprises," he decided, and Joplin's ear flickered in response. Gabe casually removed the halter, his heart thumping in his chest. "Tomorrow, girl, it's going to be *your* turn to be surprised. How 'bout if you whisper the word to your mama that you're gonna have a change of address."

That night, in front of the roaring fire, he tipped a bottle of grocery store whiskey to his lips, toasting the flames.

Thirteen

Sabrina halted at the stable's open entrance, trying to ignore a whole battery of disturbing physical symptoms. Her body wanted nothing to do with the barn. Her mind seconded the motion. But her *heart* . . .

"I want to do this," she announced resolutely. "Hunter . . . I really want to do this."

"Good. Prove it."

Stung by what seemed to be his indifference, Sabrina stepped forward. Smells and sounds enveloped her senses. Hay and grain. Leather. The pungent odor of manure. Horses snorting, an occasional nicker. A hoof stamping restlessly.

All as familiar as her own skin, and right now totally overwhelming.

"Shall I give you a push?" Hunter asked.

Sabrina wiped her damp palms on her jeans, giving him a sickly smile. "No. I want to do it."

"If you throw up, the floor's wash-and-wear. We had brick pavers installed last summer. They're rubberized, so if you're going to be sick, make sure it's in the aisle."

Chin jutting, Sabrina stalked stiff-legged into the cool, shadowed interior. She tossed a glance over her shoulder. "Well? Are you going to join me, or are you afraid I might mess up your boots?"

With a satisfied smirk on his face, Hunt followed.

Sabrina shook it off. Right now, all her attention was divided between controlling the fear and testing her limits. Her step slowed, then stopped. She forced her gaze to focus on her surroundings. *I'm in a stable, surrounded by horses, but I'll deal with it.*

The physical symptoms intensified: rapid heartbeat, skittering pulse, clammy hands, twitching muscles. *Good, Sabrina. Try not to leave anything out.*

"Lady Fair's stall is this way."

She jerked at Hunter's touch. "Oh, sorry. This way? Let's go." She took a deep breath. She wanted to do this. *Needed* to do this. Hunter was right, even if his manner was abrasive, almost cruel. She didn't understand why he was treating her this way, but she couldn't spare the time or energy thinking about it now. Strangely, his flippancy only fueled her determination. Right now, all she wanted was to grab the first horse she saw, leap onto its back, and trample the smirk clear off Hunter's face.

Hunt watched her fight what was doubtless an excruciating mental battle. He understood, to a certain extent, since he was fighting a few of his own. His protective instincts demanded that he sweep Sabrina into his arms, promise her that everything would be all right, and that he was going to help her through this.

But it was Sabrina's battle, not his.

Timing. It was all a matter of timing, instinct, and finesse.

Hunt shook his head at a couple of people who passed by, warning them to silence. Strange, he hadn't realized how susceptible to Sabrina's vulnerability he had become. Even now, he was taking her to Lady's stall in a roundabout way, down aisles vacated at the moment. Lady Fair would be shock enough; he didn't want to throw Sabrina more than she could handle.

"Hey, boss! Can you give me a hand?" Jay called, hurrying down the aisle, craggy face wearing a ferocious scowl. "One of the owners of a horse you're boarding has been trying for five minutes—oh. Sorry." The head groomsman glanced awkwardly from Sabrina to Hunt. "I . . . uh . . . I'll go find Carla or Stu."

He retreated, and Hunt finished counting to fifty.

"I hope you don't look at me that way when *I* irritate you," Sabrina said.

Hunt shook himself mentally and glanced down at her. "How was I looking?"

"Um . . . *quietly* steamed." The smile spread. "I'm okay, Hunter. Not great, but better than I thought I would be." She looked around. "Where are all the horses?"

"Oh . . . this block must be in the pasture right now. Don't worry, though. Lady Fair's just around the corner, at the other end." He made a mental note to skewer Jay if the mare had been taken to the pasture by mistake.

"Actually, I'm glad. It was enough of an effort just coming here."

"You're doing fine." He pursed his lips, inspecting her complexion. "A little green around the gills. But at least you're not—"

"I get the picture. Don't get too cocky. Things might change."

He shrugged. He *wanted* to tease her, coax some color back into her face. Light to the night-dark eyes. But he couldn't. Not now. Not yet. "What happened the last time you walked into a barn?"

"It was the barn at Woodleigh. My own horse—Sundancer. I made it to his stall. Then I ran—literally—out the door. It was . . . awful. I hated myself for being such a wimp." Her hand moved, a revealing, jerky little movement. "That's why I'm so determined. I mean, you've made me understand, and . . . I'm tired of running."

He held her gaze in a level stare. "Then shall we go meet Lady Fair?"

She nodded. Hunt silently led her down the aisle and around the corner, faintly astonished when he felt the acceleration of his own pulse. Sabrina might have thought walking inside the stables was her water jump—historically always a difficult obstacle both riders and horses dreaded. Hunt disagreed. Sabrina was approaching her water jump right now.

He stopped two stalls from the end. "Her stall is number twenty-eight. Go ahead. Introduce yourself. She's a lamb."

With only a slightly doubtful look, Sabrina sailed past and moved to the entrance of the stall. She still seemed a little uncertain, Hunt saw, but she approached without hesitation.

"Hello, Lady Fair. So you're the poor, unfortunate animal who's—" She halted in mid-sentence and stumbled back, hands thrown up in front of her face. A low, keening moan ripped from her throat. "No!"

Hunt reached her in two long strides. "Easy, Sabrina. Easy . . ."

She ignored him. "She looks like . . . looks like—"

"Like Vesuvius," Hunt finished. "I know." He took her arm,

intending to gently force her back up to the stall, where a puzzled Lady Fair stood watching, ears pricked forward.

Stiff-armed, Sabrina fought him, twisting to escape. Hunt grimly held on, knowing that if she freed herself and ran, chasing her down would result in a firestorm of gossip. "You have to look at her," he said, soothing her with his voice. "She looks like Vesuvius, but she *isn't*. Come on, now, I want you to meet her."

Sabrina shook her head violently.

He deliberately hardened his voice. "You said you were tired of running away." She flinched at his tone, then began to struggle in earnest. Gritting his teeth, Hunt shifted his hold to prevent her escape. "I'm not letting you go!" he finally snapped. "Cool it, Sabrina."

Her abrupt, total obedience threw him; for a second Hunt felt as though he'd stepped off a cliff. His hold gentled, and he opened his mouth to comfort her. Then he got a good look at her face, and a chill spiked down the back of his neck. Her eyes were open, fixed in a face stripped of color, as expressionless as a corpse. Hunt closed his eyes, swallowing hard.

"It's all right, Sabrina." he said, then cleared his throat. "It's all right," he repeated, murmuring the phrase in her ear, feeling the brittleness of her frame, smelling the faint fragrance of her shampoo in the tangled mass of hair. "You can face this. I'm going to help you, Sabrina. You're not alone." *God, help me to get through to her.* "It's all right . . . all right." As if with a mind of its own, his hand lifted to stroke her hair while his arm gathered her slack body closer.

Time passed. Lady Fair returned to the hay rack, the peaceful chewing sound blending with other mundane barn noises. Hunt heard indistinguishable voices and the occasional muffled clop of hoofbeats on the soft-cushioned pavers. The horses returning from the pasture. He held Sabrina, grateful at his foresight in having Lady moved to a stall in a deserted row.

For the first time, he wasn't sure if he could continue with the regimen he had concocted, even though he'd run it by the psychologist who had been recommended to him as a resource to use with Sabrina.

"Flooding, some call it," Dr. Rowan had told him, her kindly fortyish face thoughtful, hazel eyes studying Hunter. "There's another term, introduced a few years back, I believe, known as 'modeling.'

What you've described sounds like a variation of participant modeling, and I don't see why it wouldn't be worth a try. It's likely she's already tried it. But not, I daresay, with a look-alike horse."

"I thought of this particular mare right after her uncle called and I learned Ms. Mayhew was afraid to ride," Hunt had explained. "Not only does she look enough like Sabrina's horse to pass for a twin, she's calm and reliable—I use her to teach some of my less-experienced students."

Hunt lifted Sabrina's limp hand and checked her pulse.

She stirred, a wakening ripple moving along the slack muscles.

"That's it." Hunt began rubbing his hands up and down her arms. "Come on, Sabrina. Snap out of it. Reality's still pretty brutal, but it won't go away so you might as well face it. I'll be here with you every step of the way." It was a bold statement, and one he was doubtlessly foolish to make out loud. But it was too late now.

It had been too late since he'd looked at a set of photographs in Sebastian Mayhew's study.

"Sorry. . . ."

The faint whisper floated past his ear, and Hunt peered down into her face. Huge eyes, still dilated with fear, blinked once, then searched immediately for Lady. Her lips began to tremble. He had the uneasy impression she still didn't realize he was holding her in his arms in a close embrace. He murmured her name again, then slowly, slowly turned her so that her back was to the stall. "It's all right," he repeated, feeling like a parrot.

She blinked again. The trembling intensified. Her mouth opened, struggling to form a word.

"What? What are you trying to say?" Hunt asked. "Talk to me, Sabrina."

"Ve . . . Ves." As though the word released the last thread of control, her eyes flooded with tears.

Not knowing what else to do, Hunt wrapped his arms around her and let her cry. She wept soundlessly, her body lying heavy against him.

Carla appeared at the end of the aisle. His assistant instructor was notably reluctant to approach, but Hunt knew she would never have intruded if it hadn't been important. He jerked his chin, and Carla hurried down, concern battling with urgency.

"Need any help?" She eyed Sabrina.

"You'll be the first to hear," Hunt promised. "Now what is it?" Sabrina made an abortive effort to escape, but he pressed her face into his shoulder, gaze fixed on Carla.

Carla ran a hand through her short-cropped hair. "Linda took a spill just now—nothing's broken, but her ankle's twisted pretty bad, and—" She chewed her lip, looking aggravated—"her horse jumped the fence."

That was all he needed right now. "What's been done?"

"We've sent Stu and a couple of the grooms after the horse. Linda won't let us call the paramedics, and I confess I didn't want to press the issue until you looked at her ankle."

"Take her to the infirmary, elevate the ankle, and make an ice-pack. I'll be along in—" he glanced down at Sabrina—"as soon as I can. Thirty minutes, max."

"Sorry, Hunt." Carla hesitated. "I'll go do what I can for Linda." She gave Sabrina's shoulder a little squeeze. "Hang in there, honey. We're all rooting for you." Then she hurried off, boots thudding on the floor.

Lots of students had cried in Hunt's presence over the years. He had come to anticipate the emotion, especially given his *modus operandi*. Tears of embarrassment, anger, frustration, pain, even desperation. But never, either as competitor or trainer, had he deliberately pushed someone to the breaking point. Not only was it counter-productive, it violated his Christian ethics. Why mince words? It tore at his guts, this process of "tough training love." But in the world of competition, the toughening was necessary—to an extent.

Sabrina wasn't competing, yet he had brutally hammered away all her self-erected barriers. *God, help me*, he prayed silently. He couldn't go through this without divine guidance. Even then it was a toss-up as to who would suffer the most. Sabrina—or Hunt himself.

Keeping her face averted, Sabrina took several deep quavering breaths, then straightened her shoulders. "Oh, boy . . . I'm a mess." She stuffed matted strands of hair behind her ears and smiled a watery smile, a pitiful effort that caught Hunt totally off guard. "I hope I don't put either of us through this again."

"When's the last time you let yourself cry?" Hunt asked very gently.

The corner of her mouth twitched. "Three years ago, in the hospital, when Uncle Sebastian had to tell me about . . . Vesuvius."

Her voice cracked, and she clamped down on her lip, swallowed convulsively a time or two. "I knew I needed to cry, to mourn, but I couldn't." She shook her head. "Until now . . . thank you." She pressed her fingers against her temples. "I think."

Suddenly decisive, Hunt rubbed his palms together. "I need to go check on Linda's ankle, and you need to go back to your room and wash your face. Put on your walking shoes—we're going up to the mountain walk."

"But Lady Fair . . . shouldn't I—"

"Not yet." Not until he could give her his undivided attention again. He met the faint rebellion in her expression with calm inflexibility. "Trust me, Sabrina."

She ducked her head and for a long moment stared as though entranced with the toes of her boots. "I'm getting there," she whispered. Then she turned and walked rapidly down the aisle.

This time, Hunt let her go.

Fourteen

*T*wenty minutes later, Hunt hung up the phone connected to the barn and turned to Linda. "Stu radioed Jay. They found Honeybee and are bringing her in. She's fine. A little twitchy, skin abrasion on her right foreleg. Nothing serious." He sat down on folding chair by the cot in the infirmary. "Which is more than we can say for you, hmm?"

"I still can't believe this happened." Linda grimaced, glaring at her ankle propped on a folded pillow and swathed in bandages and an ice pack. "Stupid, stupid, *stupid*. I'll probably miss the Del Mar trials now."

Hunt patted her shoulder. "At least it isn't broken. But you're right about the trials, and I'm sorry. For you and for Montclair." He gave her shoulder a final squeeze and stood. "Things could be a lot worse, Linda. Just concentrate on taking care of that ankle, and be grateful for the good things." Like having a sound horse waiting for you. Like having a sound mind. . . .

He hurriedly stuck his head in the office to touch base with Jody, then grabbed a lightweight jacket. The mountain walk tended to be cool even on the hottest dog days of August. Halfway down the hall he swiveled on his heel, retraced his steps, and snagged a second one. In her present condition, Sabrina might not think about mountain weather.

"Señor! It's good I caught you."

"You haven't, Elsa. I was just on my way out." He kept walking.

"Whatever it is can wait for an hour."

"I do not think so." His imperturbable housekeeper launched into a stream of rapid Spanish, of which Hunt was able to interpret about every third word.

Unfortunately, he understood enough. A headache began to throb between his eyes. "Where is she?" he growled. "And why didn't you stop her, Elsa?"

Elsa drew herself up and subjected him to a frown designed to make him feel about twelve years old. "How many times have *you* told that woman not to bother you, *jefe*?"

When Elsa called him "boss" in Spanish, he'd learned it was better to listen than to argue. "I'm on my way." He might be the owner of Montclair, but after thirty years, his housekeeper pretty much owned the owner. To her way of thinking, anyway.

He stalked down the back hall and with little success tried to squelch an outpouring of highly uncharitable thoughts toward the woman waiting for him in the small room his mother had once dubbed the "ladies' parlor." "Kate. What do you want *this* time?" he greeted the realtor who had been a whole bush of thorns in his side for the past couple of years. "Whatever it is, the answer's no."

"Nice to see you, too, Hunter."

A striking woman in her early forties, Kathleen Winthrop radiated the confidence of success and money. After a bitter divorce, she'd moved up here from Dallas and bought a ranch fifteen miles from Montclair. She smiled a slow smile at Hunt. "Your housekeeper wasn't wild about letting me in, so I more or less ignored her." The Texas twang curdled his blood—which, Hunt knew, was why she always exaggerated it.

"Doesn't surprise me a bit, knowing you like I do." He swept a glance from the top of the short-cropped black hair to a pair of trendy lime green sandals that matched her blouse. "You look stunning as always. Sheared your head, though, I see. Can't say it does much for you."

She laughed, rising with sinuous grace from the chair where she'd been sitting. "It's a lot easier to keep, especially in the summer. Hunt . . . let's talk. Seriously."

"Kate, I'm busy right now, and—"

"*Kathleen*. My name is Kathleen."

"—if this concerns your grand scheme, nothing's changed. I'll fight you every step of the way."

"So I just found out. You spoke to that subcommittee at the state legislature. Thanks largely to you, a prime piece of mountain property I had in the bag was taken off the market."

A shaft of satisfaction stabbed through him. "Now, *that* piece of news was worth having you invade Montclair, Kate."

Annoyance flickered in the blue eyes. "Hunter Buchanan, you are the most *provoking* man when you want to be. Trouble is, you're also the most *honest* male I've ever met." She grimaced. "Sometimes you make me want to scream. My poor mother would have a spasm if she knew all the unladylike thoughts I've entertained about you."

He couldn't help it. A chuckle escaped, and a second later they were both laughing. "Since we're being so 'honest,' I'll admit to having similar unkind thoughts about *you*." Sighing, he glanced at his watch, then gestured to a couple of chairs. "All right. Have a seat. Five minutes tops. I've got another appointment."

"I'll take whatever I can get," Kathleen murmured, gracefully sinking back into the seat she'd vacated.

"That," said Hunt, "is the problem."

Without a word she reached inside a huge, soft leather portfolio and withdrew a sleek color brochure. "These just came back from the printer. I want you to take a look at them. Hunt, I promise you, I'm just as concerned about preserving the wilderness areas as you are. But my idea for a resort could *help*."

"By raping entire sections of forest to build your condos? Bringing in people by the car and busload, all of them thinking Montclair's an equestrian Disneyland? Try again, Kate." He handed the brochure back to her.

She shot him a vexed look and laid the glossy advertisement on a table next to the chair. "This is not priced for middle-class incomes, Hunter, any more than Montclair is a dude ranch for families." She waved a hand, flashing perfectly manicured nails. "I think half your problem is jealousy. Montclair's been the equivalent of Tara in this area for so long, you just don't want to share."

Hunt sat back, crossing his legs and folding his arms across his chest. Two could play the body language game. "If you're trying to enlist my support, your tactics are a little skewed. Montclair is not a tourist attraction. It's an equestrian training center for people who've dedicated their lives to the sport. And"—he met her gaze—"it's my home. I don't want a resort in the area. Period."

"Well, you're going to get one!" Their eyes clashed like a pair of dueling swords. "Since we're neighbors, I keep trying to cultivate a more neighborly relationship. You're making it awfully difficult, not even meeting me halfway."

"Your five minutes are almost up, Kate."

He watched her weigh her options, knowing after all this time exactly how her mind worked. She enjoyed the sparring, but she *hated* losing. Hated even more Montclair's powerbase: Everyone in a hundred-mile radius knew about Kathleen's plan to build a world-class resort, but they also knew Hunt was just as dead set against it. Unfortunately—for *her*—without Montclair's backing, she didn't have a hope of getting past the planning stage.

Or so Hunt hoped. After twenty-odd months of lobbying, she still hadn't managed to acquire enough land. But people and attitudes changed, and not always for the better.

"I sent you a letter last month," she said, irritation undisguised. "A letter you chose to ignore."

"The one asking me to brainwash some poor old geezer out of his little bit of land? You didn't really expect me to respond, now did you?" Silently he thanked Sabrina for unearthing the document. At least he knew what Kathleen was talking about.

"I just thought—since you're so highly respected and Mr. Wisniewski's property borders the southwestern corner of Montclair— you'd at least be willing to present my point of view. He has a right to make an intelligent decision based on full understanding of *both* sides, Hunt."

"Why don't you tell him yourself?"

"He despises women, or so Dale Spinoza, my executive assistant, told me. Nobody knows his story, other than he paid cash for that mountain, so he owns it free and clear."

"Too bad . . . for you."

"That's right, gloat." She drummed her fingers on the chair arm. "You and Mr. Wisniewski share more than a boundary—he never responds to written correspondence, either. So I sent Dale up there to talk to him in person. Dale came back shaking like an aspen leaf— Wisniewski chased him off with a shotgun."

"He didn't fire it, did he?" Hunt sat forward, concerned now.

Privacy was one thing, but he didn't care for threats of violence, even toward Kathleen Winthrop's egotistical assistant. "Was Dale rude?"

"He claims not." She looked Hunt straight in the eye. "I ordered him, specifically, to treat the man as he would any other prospective client. You know—your Golden Rule? Believe it or not, you don't hold a corner on the market of ethical standards."

Hunt shrugged. "They're not *my* standards, Kate. They're God's—for *everyone* to follow." He stood up. "All right. I'll find some spare time to pay Gabriel Wisniewski a visit. As you pointed out, we're neighbors—all three of us."

Kathleen stood as well, her relief evident. "Thanks, Hunt. I know—I'm not expecting anything. But . . . thanks all the same."

"Anytime—" He waited until she was almost to the door before he added, *"Kate."*

He listened to the furious staccato click of her heels as she strode across the slate tiles in the foyer. Oh well. It had probably been a mistake giving in to her. On the other hand, he really *had* been negligent. Wisniewski had moved up to Bald Mountain over a year ago, after all. True, he'd gained the reputation of a surly recluse who only wanted to be left alone, but common courtesy demanded at least a welcome visit.

Hunt ducked out the back door to avoid Elsa. By the time he'd reached the entrance to the dorm, he'd forgotten about Wisniewski and Kathleen Winthrop. A far more pressing need demanded his time and energy: Sabrina Mayhew.

The "mountain walk" was a five-mile, sand-covered path, located at the base of a smallish mountain covered with fir, pine, and a sprinkling of aspen, some ten minutes from the Center by foot. Two minutes by Jeep, if Hunter Buchanan drove you. Sabrina clutched the door as they bounced their way up a teeth-rattling two-track. "We could have walked!" she yelled at one point over the roar of the engine.

"I have a lesson in fifteen minutes!" Hunter yelled back.

Sabrina backed off. She was rapidly learning that, despite normal policy, Hunter was going to pursue an agenda of his own where she was concerned. The prospect, though daunting, also made her feel strangely . . . safe. Her mind skittered away from the thought. Hunter Buchanan was a lot of things, but she would find herself in serious trouble if she ever used him as a crutch. If she hoped to overcome her fear of riding, she would accept Hunter's help, but she wouldn't depend on him too much. He might change his mind.

Nothing in life was certain.

"You doing okay?"

His deep voice made her stomach muscles clench, though she wasn't sure why. Sometimes Hunter . . . unsettled her. When he pulled to a halt, Sabrina jumped out of the Jeep without waiting for him to follow.

So this was the famous mountain path, unique throughout the equestrian world. Over the years it had acquired an almost legendary reputation. She hadn't seen the path the first time she'd been here as a prospective student. She and Hunter had been too busy talking about—*Shut it down, quick. Don't think about the past.*

Sabrina hurriedly turned to stare at the walk. Covered with multiple footprints, the sand-coated path wound its way through the trees and out of sight. A stab of anxiety sparked through her. How many people would she have to face up here, away from the distractions of the stables? The eager questions . . . endless curiosity. The pity.

"Don't worry. People don't come up here to socialize," Hunter told her, almost as though he'd read her mind. "In fact, we've instituted a sign-up sheet in the field house—I'll show you where later—so that each person is assured of privacy. A group defeats the purpose."

"Why can't people just go for a hike anywhere on the grounds? Don't you own several thousand acres?"

He shook his head. "City slicker. This is the Rockies, not a walk in the park. I own the land, but so do the wild animals. Montclair's also a wildlife preserve. Didn't you know?" A bewildering look of annoyance darted across his face. "Lately, it's been something of a challenge to make sure it stays that way.

"At any rate, the path here is safe enough to be alone for a little while. But woe unto you if you forget to log back in before the end of an hour." The teasing tone had vanished now.

"People trip over a shoelace in the safety of their own homes," Sabrina pointed out with wry humor. "Nothing's a sure thing, especially . . . life."

"Which is why it's so important to cherish the one we have," Hunter returned. "Now. Pay attention. I'm only going to go through this once. Stay on the path, be aware of the time, but relax. That's the most important lesson to learn up here. While you walk, tune yourself first to your body, to the rhythm of your breathing, the swing of your arms and the beat of your steps. There's a whole lot more to these walks than aerobic exercise."

He took her arm, led her over to a healthy Douglas fir, and lifted her hand to press against the thick, corklike bark. "Feel this? It's alive, Sabrina. As alive as you and I. And that's what you're here to learn, as well. Tune in to nature, so to speak. The smell of the trees, the way the wind feels in your face. The sound of birds and the sounds of silence. Life is a gift from God."

A faint blush crept into her cheeks. "You don't have to lecture me. I know how fortunate I am to be alive."

"Sabrina." He shook his head and ran a hand around his neck. "Try not to be so sensitive. The 'lecture,' as you deem it, is standard issue around here. I don't force folks to agree with my Christian perspective, of course, but when they come here, they know that's part of the package. I assumed you remembered as much from before." He glanced down at his watch and muttered something under his breath.

Sabrina felt the familiar symptoms of her old insecurity. And a dollop of injured pride. "Sorry. Didn't mean to keep you from your lesson." She took a step toward the path. "I'll be careful. Don't worry about me. I'll walk back like everyone else and check in within the hour."

In a swift single movement, Hunter placed himself in front of her. Startled, Sabrina froze, skin prickling at his nearness, but she couldn't move away. Then his hand lifted, and his fingers brushed against her heated cheek. "I keep forgetting how vulnerable you are, Sabrina Mayhew," he said in a voice as soft as his touch. "*I'm* the one who's sorry." His hand dropped to his side, and he stepped back. "We'll work on that, too, shall we?" Then he strode across to the Jeep, folded himself back inside, and tore off down the track.

Sabrina went for her walk, and she swung her arms and listened to her footsteps and the sound of the wind. The experience was invigorating and somehow relaxing, but at the end of it, she was no closer to discovering what God had in mind for her here at Montclair.

Her cheek burned from Hunter Buchanan's casual touch. She told herself it meant nothing to her. But she knew that was a lie.

Fifteen

Warily, Sabrina slipped inside the square building known as the field house. A fireplace covered the wall at the far end; sofas and chairs and a couple of tables were drawn up in conversational clusters. Two drink machines hummed in a far corner, and another wall was lined with shelves covered with books, magazines, a television, VCR, and stereo. It was a little past three o'clock, and the only other people in the room were an older man reading a copy of *Practical Horseman* and a thin young woman writing a letter at one of the tables. They looked up, nodded and smiled, but went back to their reading and writing.

Sabrina was heading for the drink machine when the door flung open and a crowd of riders clattered inside, boots scraping on the plank flooring.

". . . and I thought if he shouted at me to keep my hands still one more time, I might tell him what he could do with his 'act.' I mean, enough's enough. It's not as though I'm a second-year novice."

"Yeah. Come to think of it, he *did* seem a little more vicious this morning in my session. . . ."

"Ah, you guys are whining like a pair of three-year-olds. . . ."

There was more good-natured bantering, and then the young man who had chided his two companions caught sight of Sabrina. "Hi. You new here?" He walked across the room, wiping his hand on a sweat shirt and extending it to her. "Steve Killea, local wonder-boy and newest darling of the grand prix circuit. You've heard of me, of course."

A wiry, loose-limbed youth with a mop of uncombed sandy brown hair, Steve Killea appeared to be no older than seventeen or eighteen, and Sabrina noted the rolling eyes of the others as she put out her own hand. "Sabrina Mayhew." She steeled herself.

An unspoken current rippled through the clutch of riders who had followed Steve over. After the morning, anonymity had been a pipe dream anyway.

"No kidding?" Steve asked. "The one everyone's been talking about? Junior Champion seven years ago, weren't you? Rookie of the Year when you had that fall?"

"Shut up, Steve. You're embarrassing her." This from a tall girl with slanting nut brown eyes. She freed her hair from the restrictive knot on top of her head, and a thick, curling mass of black waves tumbled about her face and shoulders. "I'm Lynn Powers, Willow Spring Stables, New York. Don't mind motormouth here. He likes to think he's something special."

"Probably because he is," the only other male in the group offered with a crooked-toothed grin. He also shook Sabrina's hand, releasing it slowly. "I'm Tim Jackson. We met a couple of times, but I don't know if you remember. It was back when you were—" He broke off, a flush staining his cheeks.

Tim Jackson. He'd been third in the rankings the year of her fall. Sabrina felt the perspiration gathering at the base of her neck, her temples; her pulse fluttered in alarm. Not now. Oh, not now . . . "I remember," she managed, fixing her gaze a little above eye level, retreating inwardly, back to the peaceful isolation of the mountain path. "Nice to see you again."

They tried to engage her in conversation, but all they wanted to talk about was the fall and why it had taken her so long to compete again. The words flew at her like missiles, each one finding its mark, wounding. She hadn't minded this morning, when she'd been charged with an adrenalin high induced by her decision to stay at Montclair. Then, too, Hunter had been beside her—

Sabrina brought herself up with a jerk, startling both herself and the others. "If you don't mind, I'd rather not talk about myself," she managed, hating the sound of the distance in her voice.

"Well excuse *us* for being interested." Lynn tossed her head. "It's just that nobody's seen hide nor hair of you in three years. Of course, since you're Hunt's student—"

"Is this throwing-the-Christian-to-the-lions day?" Stu Menninger called from the doorway. He strolled across the floor, hands stuffed in the waistband of his breeches. Sabrina flashed him a quick look of gratitude as he casually inserted himself in the group to stand next to her. "You've got Sabrina here pinned in the corner, and from the look of her, I'd say she's had enough."

"We're just getting reacquainted," Tim protested, looking at Sabrina with consternation. "Give us a break, man. The whole stable's buzzing. When a celebrity of the sport disappears for three years, then shows up again—"

"Whaddaya mean, 'celebrity'?" Steve cut in. "I'd never heard of her until two days ago."

"You were still riding ponies with a leading rein," Veronica Ashford-Smythe jibed good-naturedly, her British accent lending the words a subtle bite. "She tromped me more times than I care to remember."

Everyone started talking at once, a noisy group who had all grown comfortable enough with one another, both in and out of the ring, to let their hair down. Sabrina fought a needle stab of loneliness. Wanting only to escape, her darting gaze collided with Stu's.

He smiled encouragingly, but a slight frown puckered his brows. "Hunt's looking for you," he said. "I told him I'd check here. Did you enjoy your walk?" Deftly he turned so that his back was to the others, offering a human shield for Sabrina.

She nodded.

"Good. Hunt's big on that 'mountain walk' bit." He shook his head. "Guy's the best there is, and he's got a heart as big as the state, but sometimes, I wonder if he takes it all a little too far."

"You don't agree with his approach?" Sabrina asked, eyeing the distance to the door.

Stu shrugged. "I don't *disagree*, and it's hard to argue with results. On the other hand, I'm not much of a religious person myself, so tying the program into some grand plan to improve our relationship with ourselves, each other, and some invisible Supreme Being is a little too off-the-wall for me."

No it isn't, Sabrina wanted to shout. *It's the only way anything makes sense.* And yet . . . the words were glued inside her head, and all she could do was smile feebly and suggest that she'd better go ahead and look for Hunter before he was forced to come looking for her.

"Hey, Sabrina!" Lynn called when Sabrina was halfway across the room. "Good luck with your trial-by-fire. You *do* know what to expect, don't you?"

Everyone laughed, and the panic, still curdling in the pit of her stomach, rose into her throat, choking off her breath. She and Hunt hadn't even discussed the training regimen. They hadn't discussed *riding* a horse at all.

"Be sure to invite us to your pity party afterwards," Tim added. "Everyone has one after the first session."

"Don't worry," Steve went on, "if you're half as good as everyone says you are, you won't feel a thing."

Sabrina fled, with Lynn Powers' parting sally destroying what was left of her composure. "Just don't fall for Hunter!" she jibed. "Stick to falling off a horse—it's safer!"

⌒◍◍◍◍◍⌒

Hunt finished helping Carla set up a series of jumps in the indoor arena, working with absentminded skill. He hoped Stu had located Sabrina, because he didn't need to waste any more time searching for her.

"That one needs to go a notch higher," Carla suggested, dusting her hands on her breeches as she crossed the ring to help. "How's Sabrina?"

"I took her up to the mountain walk. Haven't seen her since, though that's where I'm headed next." He glanced across at the unsmiling Carla. "Why?"

"Everyone's talking about her. You know what it's like here, Hunt, so wipe the scowl off your face. Everybody knows what everybody's up to—and if not, they're going to find out." She made a face. "I'll do what I can to quiet the gossip, but—"

"What, Carla?"

"You might do Sabrina a favor and just go on and formally introduce her at supper or whatever. Explain things. Bring the situation out in the open. You're not going to be able to keep this under wraps for long, Hunt."

"So you and Stu and half the staff keep reminding me." He stared unseeingly at the whitewashed post. "Sabrina's a very private person, and she's struggling with a lot more than the fear of riding."

"You'd never know it. She's got that look, you know? Class, culture, cool? When I first saw her, I thought she must be a first-class snob, oozing that southern old-wealth aristocracy. Maybe just a less obnoxious version of Kathleen Winthrop. But this morning in the barn . . . well, I've never known anyone to cry like that. I didn't even cry that much when my mother died two years ago."

"Your mother's death was a blessing—or so you told me—since she'd been wasting away with cancer for months. Sabrina's horse was in his prime, his death a complete shock and needless tragedy." Hunt worked in silence for a few moments. "Sabrina's uncle also gave me a copy of her medical report. She was a mess—broken ribs, crushed pelvis, concussion, both collarbones snapped. She had a struggle just to survive her physical injuries, so it's not that surprising that she's never adjusted to the death of her horse."

Hunt paused, then added, "Her parents both died in a shipboard fire on a Mediterranean cruise when Sabrina was eight. Kids cope with that kind of loss in different ways. For Sabrina, it was horses. But when you first lose your parents, then the anchor you clung to after their deaths—" He stopped, disturbed by the depth of his own feelings. Compassion was still there, but admiration and respect were growing, along with a dangerous spark of tenderness. *Hunt, buddy . . . you might be in trouble here.*

"When you think about it, I suppose the fear isn't all that out of proportion either, is it?" Carla looked him straight in the eye. "Do you think you can heal her after all this time, Hunt?"

For a moment, the daunting task hovered above him like the Sword of Damocles. Hunt lifted his head, his gaze absorbing the protective bulk of the mountains, always present, solid and invincible. A slow smile tilted the corners of his mouth. "I'll have some help," he said.

"I don't know how much help Stu or I'll be, but—oh." Carla punched his arm, shaking her head in fond exasperation. "Never mind. You weren't talking about us, were you?"

"Nope." Hunt gave Carla a quick hug. "See you later."

"Good luck!"

Hunter waved an acknowledgment, although it wasn't luck he needed with Sabrina. He prayed all the way to the barn for the wisdom of Solomon, the patience of Job, and the towering faith of Daniel. Every cliché in the Book, he mocked himself. . . .

⟨∞⟩

Sabrina was waiting for him just inside, next to the long row of lockers used by riders who permanently boarded their horses at Montclair. They studied each other in a moment of strained silence. She looked just as Carla had described: remote, reserved, collected—except for her eyes, which were dark with fear, betraying the inner turmoil.

"I . . . enjoyed the walk, but could we please . . . get on with it? I need to see Lady Fair."

"That's what we're here for," Hunt returned equably. He gestured for her to precede him down the aisle. "Let's go."

This time, even with the other horses back from the pasture, Sabrina marched along the aisles with grim determination. Shoulders squared, she kept her gaze straight ahead, and her steps did not falter. But three yards from her destination, Sabrina came to a dead halt when Lady poked out an inquiring head, stretching her neck forward in welcome.

Standing at Sabrina's side, Hunt looked on as she made a futile attempt to lift her hand, to take a step. Her fingers twitched, her foot shuffled, but apparently she simply could not bring herself to touch the mare.

Quietly he moved in behind her, so close he could hear her rapid, uneven breaths. "You're doing fine." His voice was low, intended to soothe. "Just fine. Let's try this, shall we?" He clasped her shoulder and began stroking her upper arm, up and down, until the shock of his touch abated. Then he slid his hand down to her wrist. "All you have to do right now is touch Lady, Sabrina. That's all. Just touch her. Feel how warm she is, how satiny smooth. How alive. She's alive and warm and loving—the new picture I want you to fasten in your brain. Vesuvius is gone, but Lady is here. Easy . . . that's it. Come on, now. Just relax. Relax your arm, Sabrina. That's it. You're doing great. Just great."

Hunt pressed close against her back, his arm outstretched, parallel to hers, holding her wrist and pressing the palm of her hand against the mare's neck. Quiescent as an old tabby cat, Lady stood still, head lowered, snuffling at Sabrina's hair.

"That's it. Rub her—scratch her ears, if you like. She loves that. She'll love you when you let her get to know you." His voice dropped to a whisper as he continued to hold Sabrina, spinning a cloud of safety, of warmth so encompassing that he was vaguely astonished at himself. *Watch it, man. You're over your head.*

He ignored the flicker of warning. His hand slid in a caress back up her arm to her shoulder, allowing her to continue patting the horse on her own. He lowered his head so that his mouth brushed against her ear. "That's it," he breathed again. "You're on your own, Sabrina Mayhew." Then he stepped back, retreating with the silence of a shadow.

For another endless moment, Sabrina stood, moving her hand in stiff, uncoordinated strokes. Then Lady snorted, butting her head against Sabrina.

Sabrina jumped. This time, Hunter squelched the impulse to step in. The road back *must* be a personal discovery.

Once again she reached out, unaided, and laid her hand against the mare's neck, then pulled away. Looking bemused, she stared at her hand, then turned to search for Hunter, a dazed look blooming in her face. "I did it . . . I really did it."

Hunt grinned. "Yep, you did it." Elation swelled; unwisely he allowed himself to be carried away with it. "Believe it, Sabrina. You're on the road to recovery. This time next year, I'll have you back in competition, and who knows? Shall we aim for the 2000 Olympics?"

All the tentative joy illuminating her face faded. "Competition?" She strangled on the word. "Hunter, I . . . I don't want to compete again." She backed away, stuttering. "What if I fail—what if I fall again? No. No competition. *Ever.*"

Sixteen

*I*t was around mid-September when Gabe made the decision to look for a new place to live. Trouble was, he didn't quite know how to go about it. The shack he lived in now had been advertised in the back of a magazine, and he'd bought it over the phone, sight unseen.

"Reckon I better use a real estate agent this time," he told Joplin late one afternoon. "Still need to figure out a way to haul you and your mama up the hill and into your new stalls. But they won't do for the long haul."

Joplin playfully nipped at his empty sleeve—the only living creature Gabe permitted to touch him. He shoved the questing nose aside. "Hey, cut it out. I'm serious, here. I've been thinking about going to town first thing in the morning. Ask around for a good realtor—one that won't try to sell me the Brooklyn Bridge or some swamp in Florida." He squinted up at the bright blue sky. "'Course, that person probably doesn't exist. But I'm gonna try." He grabbed a fistful of Joplin's flowing mane and gently batted her neck. "You and Janis—you deserve it."

He looked across at the mare, nosing at the load of hay he'd brought. Janis tolerated his presence now, but he'd still never managed to get any closer than a dozen yards away. "But don't you worry," he told the indifferent horse. "Things are different now. Wherever you were before doesn't matter. I'm going to fix us all up so you'll never be afraid again."

Rain was falling in a cold drizzle the next day when Gabe drove into town.

"A realtor?" The hardware owner stroked his double chins while he gazed up at the ceiling. "Well, now, most of the real estate people I know of are in the larger towns. We don't have any hereabouts." A strange look crossed his face. "Well, there *is* one—nah. Never mind."

"What—who?" Gabe asked irritably. "If you got a name you're willing to share, spit it out. Otherwise I'll quit wasting my time."

"You planning on selling Bald Mountain or something?"

"None of your business. You going to tell me his name or not."

Unoffended, the man studied Gabe a moment longer. "It's a woman, Gabe."

Well, dadblame it all. . . . "What about the other towns?"

He shrugged. "Most realtors nowadays seem to be women. I'm real sorry, Gabe, but Kathleen Winthrop's the only one I know of locally—and I'm not rightly certain she can help. She's more into purchasing land herself, so if you're not planning on selling Bald Mountain—"

"Forget it," Gabe snapped, tugging his Stetson lower on his forehead. "I'll ask somewhere else."

He'd rather hunt down a ranch on his own than have any truck with some female who'd take advantage of a disabled man. Either that or she'd treat him like a half-wit and refuse to look at him, much less work with him. Like Trina. Gabe stomped out to his truck, feeling the burning shame as raw as if thirty years had not passed. Nope. "Might only have one good arm, but when I learn a lesson, you don't have to tell *me* something more than once," he muttered.

Trust a female? A female *realtor*?

No way, man.

⌘

Montclair

Hunter popped a throat lozenge in his mouth and pocketed the package. He was tired today. Drained not only from the effort required in his training sessions, but also the past weeks of waiting and watching Sabrina Mayhew. Patience, he had learned years earlier, was a fruit of the Spirit, but *practicing* patience often consumed a tremendous amount of mental energy.

With Sabrina, he was having to cultivate even more than usual.

September was half over, and he still hadn't been able to work with her in a private session. She'd been spending the past few weeks reacquainting herself with horses—but only in the stable. She also spent hours every day holed up in the office with Jody. The place had never looked so uncluttered, so well-organized. But Sabrina was here to become reacquainted with *riding*, and Hunt itched to get on with it.

It wasn't time yet. Sabrina still wore that haunting expression of wariness, like a half-tamed wild horse. Yearning for the security offered, but too deeply bound by fear. She was no longer afraid to be *around* a horse, but she categorically refused his daily suggestions that she needed to work on feeling comfortable astride one.

"The more you push, the more panicky I get," she'd told him just yesterday. "I don't think you understand how hard it's been for me just to groom Lady."

"I know." He'd laced his fingers on top of the stall door and propped his chin on his hands. "I also know that the longer you postpone the inevitable, the more it preys on your mind. Sometimes, you just have to get it over with."

"I will." She'd tossed the currycomb down, giving Lady an affectionate pat on her withers. "But since you promised to give me time to readjust and grow comfortable in this world again . . . you're just going to have to trust *my* judgment, for a change."

"I can do that, as long as you don't delay until the Last Judgment." At least that little joke had brought a wan smile.

Hunt glared morosely at his image in the bathroom mirror. " 'How long, O Lord,' " he quoted. A sheepish smile spread. All those people who marveled over his "strong Christian faith" should see what he looked like right now.

"Señor Buchanan? You in here?"

"Yeah, Elsa. I'm here." He left the bathroom adjoining the large workout area that fifty years ago had been a ballroom. "What is it?"

"There is a . . . very rude *person* on the front steps." She drew herself up and folded her arms. "I would not let him inside."

"So why is he still hanging around? And if he wasn't expected, how did he get here?" The gate across the road deterred most curiosity-seekers, though all a determined person had to do was abandon his car and walk the rest of the two miles up the drive.

"He's a *reporter*." She spat the word.

Hunt stilled. "What's he after?"

Elsa pursed her lips and returned his glare with one of her own. "Señorita Mayhew. He claims he heard you'd persuaded her to return to the grand prix circuit."

"And how," Hunt inquired in a deadly soft tone, "did he happen to hear that, I wonder?"

He stalked down the hall, his mind tormenting him with the picture of Sabrina's face when he'd blurted out his future plans for her. They'd both meticulously avoided all mention of the future ever since. The *last* thing either of them needed was a nosy, insensitive reporter shoving a microphone under her face. By the time Hunt yanked open the front door, he was smoldering.

The stranger jumped, whirling about. He'd actually been trying to peer through the frosted beveled glass panels flanking the two front doors. "I understand you've made a long trip for nothing," Hunt observed in a deceptively pleasant voice.

"Hunter Buchanan?" Undaunted, the stoop-shouldered thirty-something reporter thrust out a hand. "Gil Babcock." He named a prominent magazine that covered the horse world. "Is it true? Sabrina Mayhew's training here?"

Hunt glanced at the sky. Billowing white clouds with soot-covered bases were creeping over the mountains to the southeast. "You know, if you start back immediately, you should be able to make it to wherever you stashed your car before the storm hits."

Babcock's head whipped around, and he eyed the sky, then Hunt. "Looks to me like I've got plenty of time. I can make it to my car in thirty minutes." He flashed a crocodile smile. "C'mon, Buchanan. Give me a break, and do yourself and the Mayhew chick a good turn. This is big news—especially with someone like me to play it right. It'll generate even more interest in this place than that article you did for—"

"Tell you what"—Hunt started down the steps—"you tell me where you got your information, and I'll tell you if it's true." He returned the reporter's smile.

"Aw, you know better than that." Babcock shifted the heavy camcorder and equipment on his back. "I have to protect my sources. Confidentiality and all that—you know."

"Ah. I'm glad you understand where I'm coming from." Hunt clapped the other man's shoulder and began urging him down the path to the road. "It's refreshing to find a member of the press who understands the necessity for keeping some things from coming to light."

One of Montclair's stable staff was approaching in a dust-covered black pickup. Hunt waved him down. "Mickey, would you mind giving Mr. Babcock here a lift back to wherever he left his car? Near the road outside Montclair, wasn't it?" Flummoxed, Babcock nodded. Hunt turned back to Mickey. "Take good care of him. He's a widely respected reporter, and I'd hate for something to happen to him out here in the middle of nowhere."

"Be glad to, boss," Mickey chimed in, flashing a sunny grin. Big and burly as the muscle truck he was driving, the stable hand leaned across and opened the passenger door. "Hop on in."

Fuming, Babcock climbed in with ill grace. "I'll be back," he promised.

"We'll be here." Hunt kept his face impassive until the truck was out of sight. Then he retraced his steps to the house and swiftly made his way to the offices at the back. "Jody, I have a little job for you. Don't worry, it won't take much time. Just a phone call or two, and a letter. Here's what you say."

⁂

By the time Hunt made it to the barn twenty minutes later, he was under control again. At least he hadn't given in to the urge to send Babcock back to wherever he came from—in pieces.

What was happening to him?

He was known throughout the industry as low-key, unflappable. More than that, he tried to *live* his Christian convictions, yet for a little while there he'd felt stirrings of a temper he'd never known he possessed.

Sabrina. What was he going to do about Sabrina?

On his way to the barn, Hunt chewed over a lot of things but had only resolved one issue by the time he turned down the aisle to Lady Fair's stall: Over the next weeks, possibly months, he was going to need an extra portion of grace.

He ducked inside, nodding casually to riders and stable hands, all busy at their work. The place was always a beehive of activity, except for the almost deserted row where Lady Fair was stabled. Hunt took a long, deep breath as he approached. Down near the end, Sabrina waited, one hand stroking Lady's muzzle. She looked calm. Resolute. And terrified.

"Hi," she said, a nervous smile flickering and dying. "Guess what? I'm ready." The offhand tone didn't fool Hunt for a heartbeat. "I'd like to . . . I want to try to ride." Her hands knotted together, but she kept her chin up and her gaze steady on him.

An upswell of protectiveness caught Hunt completely off guard. He throttled back the uncharacteristic emotion and managed a tight smile. "Is that so?" He glanced at Lady. "You're sure? Because once we're in that ring, I'm not going to let you change your mind."

"Yes . . . I'm ready. Are *you*?"

Hunt's lips thinned. "I've *been* ready." He scratched Lady's forelock. "But we'll need a bridle. You remember where the tack room is? The bridles are on the back wall, and they're labeled. How 'bout if you fetch Lady's and meet me in the small arena." He smiled at her then. "It's going to work, Sabrina. Trust me."

"I don't know if I can." She kept her gaze on Lady. "Now that I know you expect me to—that your purpose is . . ." She swallowed hard, and he saw the muscles of her throat quivering with tension. It was the first time she'd brought it up.

"Why don't we table future expectations for now," he offered. "Let's think in terms of a day, a week at the most. Right now, my only goal is to see you on Lady Fair's back with a smile on your face." He waited, then persisted gently, "Relax, Sabrina. Just fetch me the bridle, and let's worry about the future another time. Sufficient unto the day, remember?"

"I . . . all right. I'll meet you in the arena."

Five minutes later Hunt watched her walk toward him across the smaller of Montclair's two indoor arenas, the one used principally for flatwork. Lady Fair was tethered to a ring in the wall, waiting patiently. Sabrina approached stiffly and thrust out the bridle.

"Just hang it on that hook there," Hunt said, pointing. He waited until she obeyed. "Did you do your exercises this morning at the gym?"

Sabrina nodded, glancing nervously at Lady.

"What do you think of James? Does he still work with you on the Nautilus equipment?"

A headshake and a quicksilver smile.

"He used to play pro football, you know." Pity and tenderness battled with determination; Hunt plied her with more questions. Had she gone on the daily mountain walk today? What did she think of Montclair's cafeteria? Who was her latest suitemate? Finally, with a rueful shrug, he gave it up. "Okay, Ms. Mayhew," he announced, rubbing his hands together. "It's obvious conversation isn't going to do the trick." He took her shoulders in a light clasp and turned her away from Lady. "We'll try this. Give me three laps around the ring—jogging. No walking."

"What? Why?" She looked from him to Lady. "I thought you'd want me to mount."

"I do. You will." He took her arm. "In a little while. Come on. See if you can keep up with me."

He was frankly amazed when she did, and even more amazed because she wasn't breathing hard. Even after the second lap, she had barely broken a sweat.

"Time out. Tell me about the last time you tried to ride."

She blotted the faint dew of perspiration on her brow and breathed in deeply. "Glenn worked very hard to help me. But by then I was so . . . afraid that I—well, I just . . . froze. After several tries, he got impatient . . . and—" She hunched her shoulders and stared blindly across the arena. "Well, he just grabbed me and tossed me into the saddle."

Hunter stifled his response to that little stunt. There was flooding—and then there was *flooding*. "What happened after that?" he asked.

Her eyes flashed momentarily to meet his gaze. "I fainted," she answered, her voice clipped, defensive. "Passed out cold. Scared the daylights out of Glenn and Uncle Sebastian and spooked the horse. The next day, after the doctor and psychiatrist assured Uncle Seb it was emotional rather than physical, I packed up my riding clothes. And until a month ago, I didn't *look* at another horse."

"Well, things are going to be different this time." He smiled a crooked smile. "You're working with *me*."

The corner of her mouth barely twitched. "I know. I . . . that's the only reason I scraped up the nerve—Hunter, if you yell at me, I don't know if I can handle it!" she burst out. Then she clapped a hand over her mouth, gaping at him. "Sorry! I have no right to ask for special consideration . . . I'm sorry."

"You know, right now there's only one thing I'm after, and that's for your promise to quit apologizing every third breath."

She stared, blinked, wry acknowledgment lighting her eyes. "Sorry," she murmured without cracking a smile.

Relieved, Hunt laughed out loud and lightly punched her shoulder. "Touché." He paused, sent a quick prayer upward, then nodded toward Lady Fair. "Shall we?"

Sabrina swallowed hard, lifted her chin, and stepped up while Hunt retrieved the bridle and swiftly fastened it in place after removing the halter. He kept up an easy patter of conversation, talking off the top of his head about everything from the storm building in the south to how the Broncos were faring this season.

"Okay, then, since we're working bareback today, how about if I give you a leg up?" he suggested, still in the same easygoing style. He moved close to Sabrina and stooped a little, cupping his hands for her foot so he could boost her onto the mare's back.

Sabrina nodded. Hands poised on Lady's neck, her left foot twitched . . . and froze.

Hunt glanced up. All the color in her face had fled, along with the glimmer of life. Glassy-eyed, she gripped Lady's mane so tightly the mare turned her head as if to inquire, though—well-trained animal that she was—she didn't move or even snort. Sabrina tried again to lift her foot; Hunt could see the ripple of effort as her muscles strained and balked. Droplets of perspiration broke out on her forehead.

Hunt straightened. "No problem," he murmured. "Tell you what. I'm going to put my hands on your waist and lift you up. But I won't let go, Sabrina. Okay? I won't 'throw you in the saddle' like Glenn did. And I'm not going to yell. Look at me, sweetheart." The unprofessional endearment slipped out, but he hoped Sabrina was too deep inside her fear to notice. He waited, ruthlessly suppressing any hint of impatience or urgency.

Finally her head moved jerkily, and terrified eyes the color of a rainy November morning gazed up into his face. "That's it," Hunt encouraged. "Okay now, Sabrina. You'll have to help me here. Nod when you're ready for me to lift you onto Lady's back. I'll keep my hands on you—I won't let you fall. If you start to faint, I'll be here to pull you off. Easy . . . easy." She had stiffened, backing away as Lady shifted her hindquarters slightly. Hunt's hands tightened on her waist, and he tried not to notice its supple slenderness or how she was all but plastered against him in her terror.

He wasn't sure he could follow through. What an arrogant fool he'd been, proclaiming he'd be able to cure her, confident that a few phone calls and a single visit to a clinical psychologist had armed him with sufficient knowledge to deal with Sabrina's problem. That his well-honed patience and perception were equal to the task. If he'd had a whip, he would have used it on himself.

"Please . . . have to . . . try." A shudder shook her rigid frame. "Please? Help me?"

No way could Hunt ignore that display of raw courage. "I'll help you, Sabrina," he promised. *Lord, You'll have to help us both. Neither of us can accomplish a miracle on our own.* He lifted her up onto Lady's back, noting in a distant part of his brain that, even trapped in her terror, Sabrina's natural instincts took over so that she landed with the grace and lightness of a snowflake.

Hunt kept his hands on her waist, kept up the ceaseless flow of conversation, but it wasn't doing any good. Sabrina's instincts might be intact, but the fear still ruled. She sat, but she wasn't *there.* He sensed that in her spirit she had fled to some distant place. Her eyes were open, fixed, her body as responsive as a mannequin. "Sabrina?" He gripped her waist, speaking softly. Nothing. He gave her a little shake, spoke more sharply. Still no response.

Give her time, Hunt. Calm, sustaining, the counsel sank in, giving him the strength to momentarily concede defeat. He lifted her down, his heart squeezed in a vise of frustration and pity. "It's over, Sabrina," he told her, all but dragging her away from the horse. "Come back. You're safe." His grip shifted, and he lifted his hand to brush strands of hair from her face. "You did great," he told her, and though his heart railed against him for the lie, a fleeting sense of approval warmed his insides.

Sometimes God's mysterious ways were more mysterious than others. Hunt shook his head and relaxed enough to smile a bit. It wasn't much but, as always, the grace was sufficient.

Seventeen

$\mathcal{E}$ven after an entire week of daily sessions with Hunter, Sabrina woke every morning with a contradictory blend of anticipation and dread. So far, he had been nothing but kind and understanding. He never yelled at her, never lost patience, never acted like he was discouraged or frustrated. He didn't lecture her about her lack of faith, either, or try to shame her into false declarations of renewed hope.

Hunter Buchanan made her *very* uneasy. Restless, too, with a strange sensation inside that was not quite pleasant . . . but not *un*-pleasant. He confused her. For years, the international circuit had buzzed with opinions of Hunter's style. Bluntly, *in* the ring, he was an ogre. Constant yelling and verbal abuse accompanied clipped instruction during the lesson. Outside the ring, however, the man's kindness and gentleness provoked almost as much comment as his coaching technique.

Everyone understood the rationale and knew what to expect: Riders tough enough to handle his teaching style were better prepared to deal with the stress of competition. If, after three lessons, someone was still unable to cope, Hunter refunded half their tuition. Those riders, Carla had told Sabrina dryly, seldom lasted on the professional circuit very long.

"We don't get many of them coming through here anymore," she'd finished. "Actually, there's an unofficial competition among whatever group's here at the moment—whoever Hunt yells at the most wins."

"Those are probably the ones he thinks are the most capable."

"Bingo." Carla gave her a quick hug. "Don't look like that, honey. You'll get there. Look at it this way—I've been working here ten years now. In all that time, Hunt has never allowed a student to remain at Montclair longer than two weeks—until *you*."

That distinction offered little comfort. Especially when Hunter treated Sabrina exactly the opposite of the way he treated the others. During his sessions with Sabrina, he was the soul of Christian compassion. At all other times, Hunter's attitude toward her was . . . disturbing. Especially when he reminded her, in varying tones of voice, that fear was *not* of God.

Panic—she knew the symptoms so well. Instant and hurtful, forcibly subdued. Sabrina watched a tractor trundling a cartload of straw toward the barn as she fought off the sensation. She had managed to confess the depth of her disorder to Hunter, but she had yet to summon the nerve to share her loss of faith.

"Mornin', Sabrina. Enjoying the lovely fall?"

"Autumn in the high country of Colorado is a little different from autumn in Virginia." Sabrina smiled back at D.B. McCann as he joined her on the walk to the barn . . . through two inches of wet, new-fallen snow. She'd learned—the first time they met—that the initials stood for Dexter Bromwell, and she understood why he preferred "D.B."

"This'll be gone by noon," he promised with the comfortable knowledge of experience. He'd been coming to Montclair the first week of October for the past four years, Sabrina now knew. She also knew he was tied for second in Rider of the Year standings, though he didn't make a big deal over it. "It's already close to forty degrees, and with the sun shining . . ." He shrugged, matching her shorter stride. "So how ya doing? I saw you yesterday afternoon, leading Lady like an old pro."

"Some old pro," she jibed, keeping her gaze on the snow-dusted peaks. She still didn't like being on display, having her every action analyzed as though she were a lab specimen. And yet, most of the riders seemed to genuinely care, though—like D.B.—they persisted in picking her brain every time they got a chance.

"How are you handling Hunt's Jekyll-and-Hyde routine?"

"Just fine." She lengthened her stride. *If they only knew. . . .*

"Hey, slow down! Where's the fire?" He jogged around in front of her, still grinning. "I know, I know. All of us are an obnoxious crowd of busybodies, and I'm the worst. But you bring a lot of it on yourself, you know."

"That's ridiculous."

"You're as aloof and mysterious as a Siamese cat, and about as talkative. Hunt always coaches you in the *indoor* arena and—contrary to normal procedure—threatens immediate dismissal to anyone foolhardy enough to try to sneak a peek or two."

Sabrina halted, gasping. "He wouldn't!" Hunter hadn't mentioned a word to her. She knew that, while all of the riders received private instruction, spectators invariably wandered over at odd moments to observe from the fence or the bleachers. She had been relieved not to have any onlookers, but she hadn't realized the reason until now.

D.B. was studying her, a small frown between his brows. "You're blushing. Is that because of Hunt's meddling . . . or are the two of you up to something? You're planning to beat the socks off me at the Ramtap Trials in Fresno come November, and Hunt's trying to keep it a surprise?"

"Oh, don't worry. I won't be competing in November, or any other time!" Sabrina snapped, thoroughly disconcerted now. Fortunately, when they reached the barn, the inquisition ceased.

D.B. lifted a hand and disappeared inside the storage room, though Sabrina knew she had inadvertently fueled the flames of gossip again. A twinge of panic threatened, then subsided. She was better now, after six weeks of unrelenting exposure; Hunter was right about that as well. One evening he had appeared in the cafeteria, hauled her up front, and in a couple of sentences shared her pathetic circumstances. Sabrina had been mortified, but resigned. Because she had been given no choice, irrational as the concept may seem, she was coping better . . . and slowly but steadily creeping back into a more gregarious lifestyle. Or at least, more so than she'd been for the past few years.

"Howdy, Ms. Mayhew. You look purty enough to shame a sunrise."

"Hi, Charlie. The heater in Hunter's office acting up again?"

"Yes'm. Contrary as my old grandma, but she's humming along right now." The bow-legged mechanic tipped his grease-smeared cap as he stood aside to let Sabrina pass.

"Hey, Sabrina. How's it going?"

"Sabrina! You're looking good today. What do you think of Montclair's first snowfall?"

She smiled and spoke, a strange sensation of camaraderie slipping beneath her skin in spite of the curdling shame. Even though she still couldn't so much as sit by herself on the back of a placid "schoolmaster"—the term designated for trustworthy older show horses retired from the circuit and used primarily for teaching inexperienced riders—everyone treated her as an equal.

After gathering a grooming box, she spent a leisurely half hour with Lady, cleaning and brushing the thick gun-metal gray coat until it gleamed. *Like Hunter's eyes when he was concentrating.*

She dropped the hoof-pick into the straw. Where on earth had *that* unwelcome thought sprung from? *Don't start this, Sabrina. You know better.* Every female at Montclair vied for Hunter's attention—from the tart-tongued admin assistant Jody to the openly worshipful Cherisse Taylor, a talented eighteen-year-old amateur who'd arrived the previous evening. Even Elsa Menendez, in spite of her ironclad dignity, softened when Hunt turned on the charm. The men weren't a whole lot better. In fact, *everyone* all but fought duels to merit a word of praise from Montclair's riding master.

There's a difference between coveting his respect as a world-famous trainer and nursing an infatuation.

"Don't be more of a mush-head than you already are," Sabrina muttered, snatching up the hoof-pick and forcing her attention to the task at hand. She had to be in the arena in fifteen minutes, and she still needed to clean the mare's hooves.

Perhaps today would be the day.

Yeah, right. She was going to march in there and calmly tell Hunter she was cured, leap onto Lady's back, and demonstrate a faultless dressage routine . . . bareback.

In your dreams. Even after six weeks, she hadn't made near the progress she had vowed to achieve. She was still nothing but a coward.

She wanted to trust Hunter. He'd promised to help her.

God also promised to help anyone who asked.

Asked in faith, *Sabrina. Don't forget* that *little detail.*

No wonder she wasn't riding yet.

"It's time to try again, Hunter. To ride, I mean. I've been taking care of Lady for weeks now, and twice a day you watch me work her on the longe line and trot beside her around the arena . . . it's time."

"Mmm. I'll think about it. Warm her up for a few minutes first. Have you been to the gym today?"

"Yes." Sabrina wanted to shake her fist at him. Hunter was as demanding as a drill sergeant, as gentle and understanding as a mother, and a bewildering enigma during her twice-daily sessions. "Hunter—"

"Warm the horse, Sabrina. Then we'll see."

When he used that uninflected, quiet tone, *nobody*—including Sabrina—argued. It was even more effective than his cultivated shouts. Without a word she clasped the line just below Lady's jaw and turned away. For some reason, today Hunter's attitude really stung.

Ten minutes later he signaled her to bring Lady to the center of the ring. Sabrina obeyed, then waited silently while Hunter scrutinized her. "So you want to ride today."

A thrill of fear shot up her spine, then disappeared. "Yes. I do."

"How badly do you want it?"

"Enough to risk passing out again," Sabrina retorted just as quietly.

He was silent so long she felt as though her paddock boots were cemented to the arena floor. The tiny spurt of courage she'd mustered fizzled out. Perhaps she should have lied.

"All right." He smiled a little. "Don't look so astonished. Did it ever occur to you that I'm as uncertain about this as you?"

Open-mouthed, Sabrina searched his face, marveling that he had even let her glimpse this hint of weakness. "You're not sure it's going to work anymore, are you?"

"It doesn't matter how *I* feel about it." He moved beside Lady and cupped his hands. "It doesn't even really matter how you *feel*. What matters is how much you're willing to trust in what you *know*. But for whatever it's worth, I believe I can help you, Sabrina—if you let me. Now come here, and let's give it a try. That's it, put your boot here. *Do* it, Sabrina."

Recklessly she lifted her foot and all but threw herself up onto Lady's back before the fear swarmed again. Automatically she adjusted her seat, legs tightening, one hand moving to clasp the mare's short prickly mane. "There." She glared down at Hunter. "You see,

I—" Lady shifted her weight, and terror swooped down, engulfing Sabrina in a choking black veil. Cold. She was so cold.

"I've got you, Sabrina. Hold on. I've got you—I won't let you fall."

She tried to focus on the voice, the words, but the darkness roared in and around her, suffocating her, robbing her of sight, of breath.

"Easy. It's all right. Lean back, Sabrina. Relax and trust me. I'm holding you—you're safe. I won't let you fall."

Over and over the words were repeated, until the warmth and reassurance at last seeped into her benumbed brain. Hunter. She could hear his voice in her ear, and yet . . . she was sitting on a horse. *She was sitting on a horse.* She gasped.

"Shh. Shh. I've got you, Sabrina."

Gradually she became aware that she was being held, supported in sturdy arms, and that they belonged to Hunter Buchanan. "Hunter?" she whispered. "You're . . . we're . . ."

"Riding double. So you noticed." His breath gusted past her right ear in a soft laugh. "And guess what? You didn't pass out. How 'bout that, Ms. Mayhew?"

She stared down at Lady's mane, so baffled by Hunter's extraordinary behavior that she scarcely noticed the fear. "We shouldn't be. We're too heavy for Lady."

"Don't worry about Lady. Come on, now. Let's try something. Relax a little—lean back against me. That's it." He began stroking her arms and shoulders, his voice maintaining a soothing litany, forcing Sabrina to focus on the words—and his touch.

"That's it, that's good. All you have to do is let go of your fear and trust me. I am *not* going to let you fall. Do you trust me, Sabrina?"

After a moment, Sabrina realized Hunter was expecting an answer.

"What?" Her throat hurt, and she had to wet her lips and clear her throat. "I didn't—what did you say?" She was distracted by the touch of his hands, by the unfamiliarity of being held so closely. By the thrilling, terrifying truth that she was actually on the back of a horse. And that she felt . . . safe.

"Will you trust me, Sabrina?"

Hunter lifted his hand to cup her cheek and turned her head so that she met head-on the blazing blue eyes. They glittered like sunlight sparking off steel, she thought. And there wasn't any gray in them at all. The longer she gazed into them, the darker—yet brighter—they blazed. It didn't make a bit of sense.

What had he asked her? If she trusted him?

Sabrina searched her heart, and the realization drifted upward as softly as a sigh. "I do trust you," she said, and a slow smile began at the corners of her mouth. "I don't understand why . . . but I do."

"It isn't always necessary to understand," Hunter replied. "Sometimes you just take the risk . . . and let go of the fear."

Somehow she knew he was talking about more than her present circumstances.

But it was enough, right now, to savor the moment.

She might not be riding, but she *was* sitting on a horse, and Hunter Buchanan had chosen—whatever the reason—to single her out for his personal attention.

Oh, my.

Eighteen

Bald Mountain

*E*arly on a gray October day that smelled of snow, Gabe reached the bottom of the ravine with the horses' morning feed. Only Joplin was waiting for him. In between snatching mouthfuls of food, the filly glanced nervously back down the gully.

A cold fear, as raw as the bitter wind blowing up a storm, chilled Gabe's guts. "Where's your mama, girl?" he asked Joplin. "Where's Janis?"

He set off searching, Joplin prancing ahead of him all skittish and high-strung. A half mile down, they came upon the older mare. From the look of it, she'd fallen, and one hind leg was wedged between two boulders. Gabe didn't know how long she'd been trapped, but her sides heaved from panic and exertion, and white lather coated her flanks and neck. Her head had dropped down between her forelegs, too. A bad sign.

Gabe swallowed his panic and grimly set about the task of rescuing her. Slipping and swearing, he hurried back up the ravine, fetched the bucket of oats, and slung the halter and lead line over his shoulder. By the time he reached the horses again, the first snowflakes had begun to fall from the leaden sky. He scooped out a handful of oats and slowly approached the terrified Janis.

Squealing in fear, the mare renewed her struggles to escape, then stilled, quivering, her breath billowing in harsh groans. Gabe continued coaxing and pleading, while Joplin anxiously circled her mother. After several moments, he took another step toward the older horse, struggling to keep his balance on the rocky, uneven ground.

It took him a good forty-five minutes, and both he and Janis were sweating buckets, but at last he was close enough to touch the glistening neck. Snowflakes coated the ground and swirled in thickening spirals from the sky. His bum leg was on fire, while the hand inside his glove was cold enough to freeze boiling oil. But he didn't give a rip. If he couldn't free Janis and somehow lure both horses up to the barn, she would end up slaughtered where she stood by some hungry cougar.

The fear in the mare's eyes was painful to see, and Gabe's throat tightened. "C'mere, Joplin," he called to the filly. "Show your mama I'm here to help." But when he extended his hand, palm downward, Janis flinched as though he'd laid a whip across her flanks.

To Gabe's vast relief, the months of patient handling paid off. Joplin approached with little hesitation. Gabe patted her, running his hand over her head, her withers. "See, Janis? See, baby? I won't hurt you. Joplin knows that—you'll see, too. You gotta trust me. I won't hurt you."

He shrugged the halter off his shoulder so that it dropped into his hand. He held it toward Janis, who shied away. Then, abruptly, her head lowered, and she stood in utter defeat. Too exhausted to fight waiting dumbly, Gabe saw, for the killing blow.

The mare didn't move as he fastened the halter in place. "No way am I gonna let you die," he told Janis, the words thick with emotion. "No way. Come on, baby. Let me help you."

Up close, he could see her pitiful condition. Her nostrils, flared wide and blowing hot steam clouds, were caked with blood and mucous. The eyes were dull and feverish. For the first time in over twenty years, Gabe almost wept. Tears stung his eyes, but he told himself it was the wind. Fumbling in his haste, he clipped the lead line to the halter, then stroked the stubbled muzzle. No reaction. No attempt to bite. No pulling away. Nothing. He held a handful of oats to her mouth. Still Janis didn't respond. Grimly determined, Gabe turned to the task of freeing her leg and saw immediately why she had been unable to move. The trapped hoof around the coronary band was swollen, oozing with an infection already at the abscess stage. He wondered if she could even walk.

Gabe blistered the frigid air with a few searing words. There was no way he could get Janis up that hill by himself—not a man in the shape *he* was in. But if he didn't, she'd die. If there really *was* a God, as his war buddy Yancy used to claim, then Gabe reckoned it was about time to ask for some help.

"So if You're there," he mumbled defensively, "You can see we're a couple of losers. How about lending a hand?"

He took a deep breath and carefully began to chip away at the rock that had snared Janis's hoof. Joplin crowded behind him, nosing her mama, all but trampling Gabe's toes. Janis didn't even flinch at the touch of his hand any longer; she just stood there, shivering and spent. Gritting his teeth, Gabe kept digging.

When she was free, he rocked back on his heels, his breathing ragged, and held his hand under his armpit to warm it. Janis didn't move, probably because she was in too much pain. After a while Gabe resumed talking, his voice hoarse now, while he ran his hand lightly over her body. Time she was getting used to a man's touch again.

The brief snow shower had momentarily ended, though the air was so cold it sawed back and forth in his lungs like a rusty machete. Now, if the weather would just hold up until he managed to get the horses to shelter. . . .

Ultimately, it was Joplin who turned the tide. Gabe had cajoled and tugged on Janis's lead line to get her moving, all to no avail. The cold and exertion had sapped his own strength, but just as he was about to curse aloud in despair, Joplin turned, trotted up the gully, then twisted back and nickered to her mother.

Janis took a feeble, tottering step.

A fresh surge of energy swept through Gabe. He watched, holding his breath, as Janis took two steps, then stopped, sides heaving, head sunk. "Come on, baby. You can do it. Come on, now. I got a stall waiting for you, all cozy and warm. Come on, Janis. . . ."

⟨୭୶୶⟩

It took almost three hours, but they made it. Gabe was weak as a kitten, and from his hip down, his leg was on fire. He was soaked with snow and sweat and rank-smelling as a polecat, but Janis and Joplin were safe inside the barn. He'd done it! He'd really done it!

Janis ended up limping into the stall without hesitation, as if she welcomed its sanctuary; it was Joplin who eyed the enclosed structure with jittery reluctance. But with a little more persuasion and a few carrots dangled just beyond their reach, he finally had both horses locked up safe and snug inside their stalls.

It was nothing short of a miracle, and he'd accomplished it without another uppity soul spitting out orders and claiming credit.

Gabe sprawled in front of the flames that night, his half-finished drink forgotten on the floor beside him. He should have been celebrating; he'd sure enough accomplished what he'd set out to do. Instead, he sat there staring at the fire, fear eating his insides. He might have finally led his two charges to shelter and safety, but it wasn't good enough. He needed a better place, with a real barn. Supplies to last the winter. . . .

He needed himself a ranch.

"Reckon I can even risk having a go at the female realtor, since it's for Janis and Joplin." He fumbled for the glass, took a sip, then suddenly threw it across the room, shattering the glass and splattering the cheap whiskey on the rough plank walls.

Who was he kidding? Restoring Janis's health would take a lot more than he had to offer. He could yammer out pleas and curses to heaven all he wanted, but if he couldn't persuade a vet somewhere to check Janis out, she'd probably end up dying anyway.

What good would a ranch be then?

Montclair

As often as possible, Hunt tried to join the riders on a cross-country run. The half-day excursion freed his own soul as much as it strengthened skills for the riders and horses. During the winter months, of course, the treks weren't possible. On this particular October morning he eyed the snow-covered peaks with regret. Looked like winter would be early this year.

For some reason his gaze wandered southwest, toward Bald Mountain. He never had made it up there to visit Wisniewski. Kate had called twice and left messages, neither of which Hunt had returned.

Well, he'd make sure Jody sent Wisniewski an invitation to Montclair's annual Thanksgiving dinner, if he didn't find time between now and then to visit the man. Beyond that, if any more reports of Wisniewski brandishing a shotgun reached his ears, he'd let the county sheriff handle it.

Stu approached, tugging on a pair of riding gloves. "Everyone's ready and wondering where you are."

"How many ended up coming along this week?"

"Seven." Stu hesitated. "Sabrina's lurking around in the background somewhere, trying to remain invisible." He tapped his crop lightly against his thigh. "She's failing miserably. And every time someone tries to console her, she gets this look on her face. . . ." Shaking his head, the assistant trainer watched some horses frolic in the paddock outside the barn. "It's been almost two months since you started working with her, Hunt. What's going on? Has she made any progress at all?"

Hunt gave Stu a sidelong glance. "Yesterday she made it twice around the arena. At a walk." And riding double, with Hunt holding her close and talking in her ear the whole time, teasing, distracting her . . . encouraging her. He clenched his fists, then forced himself to relax. "She's coming along, Stu. It's just going to take time."

"Well, at least she's opening up with the other students a little better, though not as much as Pete Galioto would like."

"Pete?" His response was too quick, too sharp, and Hunt wanted to kick himself. Galioto was a superlative eventer, but he was an accomplished flirt, and Hunt wasn't sure Sabrina would know how to handle him.

And it's your business, Buchanan?

Stu quit tapping the crop against his thigh. "Yeah. Says he goes for a woman of mystery like Sabrina. That's one deep lady, boss. Wonder what she was like before. Right now, for the most part, she's still as buttoned down and zipped up as any female I've ever met."

"I know." His voice was curt to the point of rudeness.

Stu threw up a hand. "Well, let's go before the horses get too wired." He turned back toward the barn entrance.

Hunt followed after a moment, but the fizzling anticipation of the ride had gone flat. He led his horse down the aisle, subconsciously searching dark corners for Sabrina. He knew he wouldn't see her; for the last week she'd begun avoiding him outside their sessions. Hunt knew it was because she was responding to him—and she didn't like it. She liked even less the fact that *Hunt* knew. What irritated—and scared the boots off him—was how easily he seemed to be able to read a woman who remained such a closed book to everyone else.

He joined the other riders just outside the barn's southern entrance and mounted up. "Remember to stay together as much as possible," he reminded them as they started down the road. "I'm not in the mood to track down lost riders today."

"You're never in a mood to track lost riders," Carla called over her shoulder, and everyone laughed.

"When are you going to let Sabrina do a private show for us?" Cherisse had urged her mount closer. Beneath her crash helmet's visor, bright, curious eyes were fastened on Hunt.

Her question might have been foremost in everyone's mind, but Hunt resented it anyway. "She didn't come here to entertain the masses."

"Hey, isn't that Sabrina? Over there, starting up the path to the mountain walk?" Another rider pointed with his crop, and all heads swiveled to the distant figure.

"Nice walk," Pete observed with undisguised admiration.

A strange tightness wound about Hunter's chest. He had no claims on Sabrina outside that of coach, yet Pete's interest bothered Hunt. His gaze remained glued to the poignant sight of the graceful figure making her way up the mountain path—all by herself—while a group of laughing, eager riders headed in the opposite direction for a day of fun and exercise.

Her fear had destroyed a whole lot more than her riding skills.

⌒∭⌒

An hour later Hunt called for a rest stop in a secluded grove of Douglas fir and ponderosa pine near the top of a smallish mountain behind Montclair. Sometimes they rode longer, particularly when several eventers were testing the stamina of their horses. Today, however, he himself needed some time to unwind, enjoy the view, and think.

He should have known better.

"You look like a lion, all sprawled out enjoying your kingdom." Carla dropped down beside him, shoving aside a couple of pine cones.

The other riders had wandered off in groups of two and three; Ed Sanger, the oldest in the group at forty-two, was lying with his arms above his head, eyes closed. Hunt smiled. Looked like a good idea to him, but he could tell from the glint in her eye that Carla had something on her mind. "What's up?" he went ahead and asked to get it out of the way.

Carla reached over and ruffled his hair. "If I didn't know better, I'd think you were able to read my mind. Sometimes you make me very uneasy, always having this uncanny awareness—"

"Carla. . . ."

"Oh, all right. It's a couple of things, actually." She picked up one of the cones and ran her thumb over the prickly spines. "You remember your reservations about letting John Brenders come back for a second session right now? You might have been right. He's pushing too hard, and it's affecting his judgment. He won't listen to me." She sighed. "I'm not sure he'll even listen to you, but I thought I'd warn you. I'm afraid Neptune is going to peak too soon."

"I'll talk to him." Hunt looked out across the valley, through the trees, to the rugged peaks that surrounded them. They stretched in jagged waves as far as the eye could see. *God . . . how I love this land You created.* "What else, Carla?"

She sighed again. "Wynn Baker's been Sabrina's suitemate this past week. She talked to me this morning—wanted me to tell you that she thinks Sabrina must be having nightmares or something. She heard her cry out a time or two in the middle of the night, but Sabrina absolutely refuses to discuss it."

"What are the pair of you discussing over here, anyway?" Wynn herself strolled up then, looking windblown and red-cheeked. "You both look as serious as a couple of morticians."

"We thought, for starters, that it might be a good idea for you to volunteer to clean everyone's tack when we return to the barn," Hunt returned lazily.

Wynn snorted and kicked the sole of his boot with her toe.

"I told Hunt what you said about Sabrina's nightmares," Carla explained. "Hunt, you can't let her hide behind you or this wall of silence any longer. She *knows* everyone is talking about her, and the more we all pretend that nothing is wrong, the more she withdraws."

"You ought to see her in the field house," Wynn commented, sinking gracefully onto the ground on the other side of Hunt. "She never joins in the discussions or the card games. Even when we're all watching a horse show on ESPN or something, Sabrina sort of crouches in a corner. She wants to fit in, I think, but for some reason she seems to feel—" Wynn hesitated, as though searching for the word, then shrugged—"*inferior* is the only word I can think of. Both Pete and I have tried to draw her out, but we're leaving soon."

"It doesn't help that you won't let anyone *near* her sessions," Carla observed with dry humor.

Hunt suppressed a groan. "All right. All right. I'll talk to her. But the decision will be Sabrina's. If she's not ready to step into the spotlight, then the wall of silence will remain unbreached." He stood, stretched, then added softly, "So you two pass the word."

After Wynn left, Carla lingered, though she avoided looking at him. "Be careful with this one, Hunt. She's not like any other student you've ever coached."

"And what is *that* supposed to mean?"

"Sabrina's pretty private. Real sharp, but about the most vulnerable person I've ever met."

"I know that, Carla. Why do you think I've been so careful to shield her as much as possible?"

"You've shielded her from other people, but what about from *yourself*? I don't know what you do with her in those sessions, Hunt. But lately Sabrina seems to go out of her way to avoid you everywhere else. I suppose *you've* noticed that, too?"

He'd noticed, all right. He snatched up his crash helmet from the ground and crammed it back on his head. "I . . . don't yell, Carla, if that's what you're worried about. In fact, that's one of the reasons I refuse to let anybody watch. Might ruin my reputation."

"Well . . . I had wondered." Carla glanced around, obviously seeing as Hunter had that the other riders were restless and ready to leave. "Hunt," she began hurriedly, "just be careful. I've seen Sabrina's face when she looks at you and she doesn't realize anyone's watching. She's falling in love with you, and she doesn't strike me as a woman who loses her heart to a man but once."

For the rest of the ride, Hunt committed the cardinal sin of a horseman: he lost his concentration. Fortunately his mount, a surefooted gelding born and bred at Montclair, did Hunt's job for him, so that they both returned to the barn in one piece.

Sabrina, Jay informed Hunt after the others had trooped by with their horses, had returned from the mountain walk, then spent an hour working Lady on the longe line. The head groom hadn't seen hide nor hair of her since. Hunt listened grimly while he cared for his horse. Then he loped up the path to the house.

He had a gut feeling he knew *exactly* where Sabrina had disappeared.

Nineteen

*A*nyway, Rennie, I just don't know what to do. I know *why* he's doing it, but it doesn't seem to make any difference."

"What makes you think Hunter's only trying to take your mind off your problems?"

Sabrina leaned her head back against the sofa cushion and closed her eyes. "What else would it be?" she asked painfully. "Renee, he wants to rehabilitate me, so to speak, for one reason only. He wants me back in competition. It would be such a coup for Montclair. 'World-class Trainer Hunter Buchanan Takes Former Olympic Hopeful to the Top Again.' Can't you see the headlines?"

"It's not like you to be cynical." The criticism wasn't lost on Sabrina, and she winced. "Has it ever occurred to you that Hunter's a *man*, as well as a professional trainer? I wonder what *he's* feeling, sitting behind you on that horse, and you about as responsive as a fencepost."

"Come on, Rennie. He's trying to keep me on the horse, not make a pass."

"Ha. How would *you* know? If you haven't talked to him about this, then I'd say it's about time for a little honesty."

"He already knows how I feel."

"He knows you're afraid to ride," Renee shot back impatiently. "I'm not talking about that, and you know it. I'm talking about the way you feel about *him*."

Even sitting alone on the floor of Montclair's library, surrounded by nothing but books and videotapes, Sabrina felt the hot color wash up through her in a burning tide. For weeks she had shied away from examining her feelings toward Hunter Buchanan.

"Sabrina? I can hear you breathing, so I know you haven't dived under a convenient piece of furniture. Why can't you just admit you're attracted to the man? You're a grown woman, and he's a great-looking guy—and unattached. Even better from *your* perspective . . . he shares your faith. You've been fascinated with him and that place for years anyway. So. . . ?"

"If you start playing matchmaker again, I'll hang up and not call back. I might even refuse to come for Christmas."

Renee laughed. "Don't worry. I won't invite any more of Evan's bachelor friends to join us this year." There was a pause. "Paul wasn't *that* bad, was he?"

An unwilling smile took the edge off Sabrina's defensiveness. "He could have been worse, I suppose. But he did remind me of a clumsy puppy."

"Well, you wouldn't say that about Hunter now, would you?"

Her sister never had bothered with subtlety, much less diplomacy. On the other hand, Sabrina had had enough. "I have to go. Give my love to Evan and the two munchkins, with a special kiss for the dumpling."

"Okay, okay. I'm sorry, already."

"Tell Uncle Sebastian I'll call him next week."

"Sabrina, don't do this. I promise not to—no. I'm *not* going to promise, doggone it. It's time you poked your head out of that infernal shell and acknowledged that you're *alive*. Other people care about you, and they're not all going to die and leave you. If Hunter Buchanan—"

Very gently Sabrina hung up the phone. Hot and cold prickles raced along her veins; she hadn't actually meant to cut her sister off in mid-tirade, but the reaction had been reflexive.

Behind her the door, which had opened just as Renee waded into her, shut with a soft click. A lamp was turned on, then came the sound of booted feet, striding deliberately across the waxed wood flooring, straight toward Sabrina. Heart pounding, she scrambled to her feet.

"Jody said you wanted to call home, and she'd told you to use the library extension."

"I . . . used my credit card," she explained breathlessly. "It won't cost Montclair anything."

Hunter kept walking until he was standing close enough for Sabrina to feel wrapped in the delicious aroma of horses and leather. "She also told me that you spent the last three hours helping her with paper work." His expression was inscrutable, the quiet voice bland. Sabrina fought the urge to bolt. "But she also told me that you slipped up and confessed," he continued even more softly, "that you were thinking of leaving. That you'd . . . *wasted enough of my time*, I believe you told her."

"Well, it's the truth," Sabrina muttered. Then, defiantly, "Stop being a bully. Why can't you just admit this isn't working and let me go?"

"Hmm." His hand lifted abruptly, and before she could help herself, Sabrina jerked back. For a long tense moment Hunter studied her. In the soft golden glow of the lamplight, his face looked harder, somehow sterner. "That's interesting," he finally murmured. "You don't flinch at all when we're sitting together on Lady Fair's back. Makes me wonder."

"You startled me. I didn't mean to—"

"Ah." He lifted his hand a second time, brushing his finger along her cheek, then lightly cupped her chin. "I appreciate the office help. But don't tire yourself out. I mean it." He dropped his hand and stepped back.

Her blush had probably scalded his fingers. Sabrina gazed up into eyes the color of an impending thunderstorm and tried to gather her scattered wits. "You know I enjoy helping Jody."

He half smiled. "Probably not as much as she enjoys having your help. But you came here to work with horses, not papers. Since you seem to find yourself with so much spare time, perhaps you need a few more chores. The hands can always use help mucking out the stables."

She nodded, not trusting herself to speak. Was he *angry* with her? There wasn't any blue in his eyes.

"Maybe it's time to start observing some of the other riders." His head tilted sideways. "Everyone wants to observe *your* lessons, of course. But I don't think that's a good idea yet, do you?"

He *was* angry. Each soft word flayed her spirit. Sabrina withdrew mentally, struggling to marshal her unruly emotions. Hunter was her *coach*. He was a world-famous personality, a devastatingly attractive man whose private life remained a mystery. She knew he'd been engaged once and that the foolish woman hadn't been willing to share him with Montclair. But surely he didn't want the emotional quicksand of an even *more* foolish woman, who had nothing to offer but a trunkful of insecurities and an uncertain future.

A woman who had so little faith in God's love that her spiritual life was nothing but a greasy blob of doubts and fears and guilt.

A coward who had no intention of ever riding competitively again, even if by some miracle the rehabilitation actually worked.

"When you look at me like that, do you know what it makes me want to do?"

Jarred and wary, Sabrina stiffened her back. "How am I looking at you?"

"Like I'm either about to attack you—or kiss you." His voice, like his eyes, became smoky and intense. "Since there's no way I'd ever attack you—or any other woman—that leaves the second alternative." His hands lifted to settle warmly on her shoulders, and his thumbs began a slow rotation on either side of her neck. "This is *not* a good idea," Sabrina heard him whisper as his head lowered.

She had time for a quick intake of breath before he kissed her—a brief, soft kiss that nonetheless destroyed all her defenses in a single swipe.

Then his head jerked up, his hands tightening almost painfully on her shoulders. He thrust her away. "God, help me," he muttered hoarsely.

Their eyes met, held. "Oh, I'm sorry," she gasped out. Then, "I . . . I didn't mean to say 'I'm sorry,'" she stammered, so nonplussed she couldn't control herself. She clapped her hand over her mouth. She had an IQ of 140, the unflattering reputation of a passionless, professional female, and the survival instincts of a currycomb.

Incredibly, a rueful grin kicked up the corner of Hunter's mouth. The stormy gray eyes began to twinkle. He shook his head, ran his fingers through his hair until it resembled a windblown haystack, and took a deep breath. "*I* kissed *you*," he reminded her. "Don't you think I'm the one who should apologize?" He turned abruptly and stared up at the ceiling. "There's no help for it now, is there?"

"No help . . . for what?" Sabrina ventured. Her lips tingled. Dazed, she touched them with trembling fingers.

"It looks," Hunter replied as he turned back around, "like I'm going to have to take a different approach with you." He met her bewildered gaze, his own expression resigned. "The trouble is, I don't know where it's going to end. For either of us."

A knock sounded on the door. Three firm raps, followed by Elsa's commanding voice. "Señor? I must come in, please."

Hunter walked across the room and opened the door. "What's wrong, Elsa?"

"She is here again. That woman. When I saw who it was, I would not even open the door." The black eyes flashed. "She has gone around to the back, Señor."

"And now she's right behind your amazon of a housekeeper," Sabrina heard the thick drawl and watched in bemusement as a tide of red spread across the bridge of Hunter's nose, into his cheekbones. Seconds later a strikingly beautiful woman strolled around Elsa into the library.

"Sorry to barge in," she murmured in a husky contralto. Sky-blue eyes framed by incredibly thick, dark lashes honed in on Sabrina. "Very sorry."

"Kate, what on earth—"

"Now, Hunt, don't lecture me on manners." She sailed by him and walked over to Sabrina, thrusting out her hand. "Kathleen Winthrop. I'm Hunt's neighbor, even if he refuses to acknowledge my existence. I apologize for the intrusion—"

"Gross invasion of privacy—"

"—and I'll only stay a minute, but the only way to talk to the man is by resorting to guerilla tactics."

Sabrina almost smiled. In her ivory-colored wool slacks and cashmere sweater, Kathleen Winthrop looked about as much like a guerilla fighter as a Thoroughbred resembled a zebra. The woman was a clotheshorse, and she had a good eye. Thanks to Renee, Sabrina recognized the lines of a famous designer when she saw one, right up to Ms. Winthrop's matching half boots and leather satchel purse.

By contrast, Sabrina felt about as sophisticated and attractive as a dirty stall. "I was just leaving," she murmured politely. "Nice to meet you."

"Please don't go. If you do, Hunt and Elsa will skin me alive and use my coat for a rug." Her hand caressed the buttery-looking front of her suede parka. "And I *do* love my coat."

"Kathleen—"

Both women turned to Hunter. Sabrina wasn't sure about Kathleen, but if she was smart, she'd listen up. Real close. Hunter didn't have to raise his voice to command attention; in fact, that deadly soft tone could peel the bark from a tree a hundred yards away. At the moment, Sabrina felt sorrier for Kathleen than she did for herself.

Some of the brassy confidence faded from the other woman's face. She gestured awkwardly with one hand. "I *am* sorry, Hunt. Please believe me. I was just in the neighborhood—believe it or not, I was actually on my way up to Bald Mountain. I—" she laughed a little— "I was sort of hoping to talk you, or one of your . . . ah . . . *male* staff members, into coming along with me."

An indefinable look softened some of Hunter's controlled anger, Sabrina saw with rising curiosity. "I haven't kept my word, I know," he replied after a long moment. "I apologize. But I can't spare anybody right now, Kathleen. If you'd called—"

"How could I? You never take my calls, much less answer your mail."

"Guilty as charged." He glanced across at Sabrina. "You wonder if you've lost your senses, right? Well, don't worry—you haven't. Kate and I—"

"Kathleen."

"—have what I suppose amounts to 'a history.' " He propped his hip against a library desk and crossed his legs. "She wants to build a high-class resort hotel, freely capitalizing on Montclair's fame, and—"

"I offered you a percentage of the profits in return for carefully arranged tours."

"—I oppose her on every hand. With every weapon at my disposal. So far, I'm winning. Right . . . Kate?"

So *this* was Jody's "Texas tornado." The fine-looking woman Hunter baited by using her nickname? Sabrina looked from one to the other, wondering if they realized that sparks filled the air between them. Something deep inside Sabrina, born in those few tender moments when Hunter had kissed her, shriveled up completely.

Pain waited. Sabrina expected it, didn't even try to fight it. "Excuse me. I need to go." She willed a smile. At least she still had the ability to command her voice and limbs. Nobody would guess that her heart had just disintegrated into dust.

"You can wait. We'll be through in a minute." Hunter's hand closed around her wrist as she started by. His grip was gentle but unbreakable.

Sabrina's gaze slid from his hand to his face. She wondered why he looked so grim all of a sudden. "I need to go."

"No, *I'm* the one who needs to go," Kathleen spoke up, her drawl more pronounced. "I truly didn't mean to intrude, as I obviously have. Never mind, Hunt. I'll go beard the lion of the mountain in his den. I'll stay in my car and wave a white flag or something. Hopefully, he won't actually shoot me. There *are* laws about that sort of thing, aren't there, way up here in the mountains?"

"I wish you'd wait." Sabrina moved, and Hunter's thumb began caressing the racing pulse in her wrist. "You don't know anything about this man, Kathleen."

"I do know that his property is all that stands between me and enough acreage to finally apply for the building permit," Kathleen responded. In a graceful move, she slipped by them, leaving in her wake the scent of expensive perfume. "I'll keep you posted . . . through your housekeeper." The startling blue eyes rested momentarily on Sabrina, an expression of sympathy causing a blush to creep into Sabrina's face. "Nice to meet you, honey," she murmured. "Take care, y'all."

"What's wrong?" Hunter asked the moment Kathleen was gone. "Sabrina? You're pale as a salt block, and your hands are like ice." He began rubbing them between his own. "You having one of your attacks?"

"Don't patronize me. No, the emotional retard is *not* having one of her attacks."

His gaze narrowed. "Hmm. Sarcasm. I begin to see . . ." The corner of his mouth twitched.

Sabrina went very still. "You don't see at all," she said, her voice low, cold. Very deliberately she removed herself from his grasp. "Don't touch me again. Ever."

"Sabrina, there's nothing . . . romantic between Kathleen Winthrop and me." All of a sudden he laughed. "Never has been. Call me old-fashioned and a chauvinist, but she's a good ten years older than I am. She's smart, intelligent—and yes, beautiful. But, Sabrina, I've never been tempted to kiss her."

"Your loss," Sabrina whispered, then fled.

Twenty

*I*t took four nerve-frazzling phone calls on the pay phone outside a convenience store before Gabe found a vet who agreed to trek up the mountain to see Janis. Worry gnawing at his bones, Gabe had blistered the hides of the first three sawbones who couldn't be bothered; the fourth, an old codger with the unlikely moniker of Hiram Tubbs, sounded over the phone as though he'd be willing to commit murder if the price was right. By that time Gabe didn't care, as long as the vet made it up to his shack first thing in the morning.

He bought himself a soda in the store, then stomped outside and climbed into his truck. The weather matched his mood—cold, bleak, drizzling rain. Gabe glared out the water-streaked windshield. Why had God created human beings anyway? The bulk of them were shysters and sleazeballs. The women were the worst, batting their eyes and promising anything and everything, then sticking the knife in deep, and laughing while they did it. Yep, he'd had his fill of females. Never again would he be dumb enough to believe their lies.

He'd take Janis and Joplin over a human being, anyday.

"That vet better know what he's about," he snarled aloud. But all the way back up the mountain, he couldn't quit fretting over it.

When he arrived at the top, he found a car parked in front of his shack. A rich man's car, painted a deep wine color. What was it doing here on *his* mountain? Gabe's temper sparked to near exploding, and it was all he could do not to ram his truck into the gleaming metal grill.

A head poked briefly out of the window on the driver's side—a *woman's* head. He knew it was a woman even if her hair was sheared off till it looked like a man's, because he could see her face. Cursing, Gabe brought his truck to a screeching halt beside the car, slamming the door so violently the vehicle rocked on its axle. Furious, he stomped around the hood, cold rain dribbling beneath his Stetson and down his collar.

"Get out 'fore I fetch my shotgun!" he snarled. "You're trespassing on private property."

"Mr. Wisniewski, I'd like to talk to you, if I could." She had a low, smoky voice, with a drawl that reminded him of his war buddy Yancey, who'd hailed from Mississippi. "Will you give me five minutes?"

"I'll give you five *seconds* to drive this hoity-toity set of wheels off my mountain. I don't have anything to talk about with the likes of you."

"I'd like to buy Bald Mountain." She named a figure that halted Gabe in his tracks.

"You're crazy. That's twice what I paid for it." It was out before he could call back the words. He squinted down at her, then at the discreet panel fastened to the side of her car. " 'Mountain Dreams Real Estate,' " he repeated, slowly. "You're that realtor who's been bugging me for months."

" 'Fraid so." She smiled a smile full of white teeth, and he saw that her eyes were as deep a blue as any pair of eyes he'd ever seen. Probably colored lenses. "You chased my executive assistant away with that shotgun, but I'm hoping that you'll—"

"Nope. Don't do business with females."

She didn't bat an eyelash. "I know. I'll send Dale back if you promise not to shoot him. Mr. Wisniewski, I know you bought Bald Mountain outright. Either you spent every penny for it and now live very . . . simply—or you stash your wealth somewhere out of sight. Is there anything I can say or do to persuade you to sell, if money doesn't appeal to you?"

He'd already opened his mouth to shout a definite no, but something stopped him cold. He wanted to buy a ranch, didn't he? Wanted one so bad he'd even been considering talking to a female realtor. *This* female, come to think of it. He glanced toward the barn, anxious to check on Janis, but suddenly torn by temptation.

It would take time—time away from Janis and Joplin—to find another place to live. Time he didn't have to spare right now. He stared down at the woman. She was a smart one. Instead of yammering away at him like a woodpecker, she'd stated her case, plain and simple. Then she'd shut up and let him think.

Blamed if he didn't appreciate that.

"Tell you what," he heard himself say, "you find me another ranch that suits me, and I'll consider selling Bald Mountain."

"Done," she whipped back so fast Gabe didn't have time to change his mind. "You want to tell me what you're looking for?"

He scowled, wary all of a sudden. She was smart—and she was sneaky. And very pushy. "Don't have time to talk right now."

"Tomorrow, then? Or, better still, *you* name the time."

Cornered, he tried to think, but Joplin let out a whinny just at that moment. "Uh . . ."

"You have a horse, Mr. Wisniewski?"

She sounded interested, but Gabe wasn't fooled. "Naw—that's a blasted goat you just heard bleating," he growled. "Yeah—I have two horses, not that it's any of your business."

"But it *is* my business," she retorted promptly. "You'll be looking for a ranch with proper stabling, I imagine. That's something I'd need to know." She gave him another one of those blinding smiles. "Don't snap my head off again. I'll come back in the morning and we'll discuss it in detail. I'll go ahead and bring some preliminary offerings, show you what's available. You do want to stay in this area?"

Head spinning, Gabe managed a curt nod.

"Great. I'll go now. I have a feeling I need to prove that I'm willing to meet you more than halfway . . . how about ten o'clock tomorrow morning. That all right with you?"

Anything to get her out of here before that honey-smooth drawl had him inviting her inside his wreck of a shack, out of the rain. "Fine," he muttered. "Now go on. Get off my mountain. I gotta take care of my horses. Don't have time to stand out here gabbin' in the rain."

It wasn't until her car bumped sedately out of sight around the bend that Gabe remembered the vet, who had also promised to show up in the morning. Gabe unloaded another round of expletives as he limped hurriedly toward the barn. Might as well be living in a bus station.

ᏟᎳᏉ

Montclair

On the bulletin board was a message directing Sabrina to observe four different riders during their sessions with Hunter that day. The first one, Sabrina noticed, began in thirty minutes, allowing her barely enough time to clean Lady's stall, much less feed and groom her. *Drat the man.*

Hunter Buchanan was as crafty as Uncle Sebastian when it came to manipulating her into doing something she didn't want to do, she grumbled to herself as she hurried through her morning chores. The summons might as well have been announced over a loudspeaker. Somehow Hunter had known that if Sabrina didn't show up for every one of those wretched sessions, she'd be plagued with questions from all sides.

Forty minutes later she crept through a side entrance to the large indoor arena. It was raining today, a dreary, bone-chilling drizzle that threatened to turn to sleet any minute. It matched her mood exactly. She brushed water from her jacket and face, counted to fifty, then moved out of the shadows toward the bleachers. Since the rider in the ring was Edward Sanger, the top three-day eventer in the world, a handful of other students were already there, clustered halfway up. Above them, near the top, Stu Menninger was taking notes.

Sabrina sank down on the bottom bleacher at the end, but heads swiveled her way almost immediately, and Stu waved at her to join them. Sabrina shook her head, then resolutely turned her gaze to the ring. The glass panels had been pulled shut to minimize the noise, but Hunter's non-stop spate of abuse was still easily discernible. He was, of course, shouting a whole arsenal of unflattering remarks. Ed looked like a glob of cold spaghetti . . . he wouldn't last ten minutes on the course . . . if he didn't learn how to guide his mount better with leg pressure, Hunter was going to skewer him with a branding iron. . . .

I must be insane. I'll never be able to endure that. Transfixed, Sabrina stared unseeingly through the glass, self-doubt eroding her already lacerated confidence. She knew what Hunter had up his sleeve: He wanted her to understand what was coming, that her present state was *unacceptable*, and that he had only been coddling her.

It wasn't time to give in and give up. It was time to move on. He'd been patient long enough . . . Sabrina was a big girl . . . she'd promised to do whatever he dictated—

So . . . why had he kissed her?

Ed cantered slowly past her—right in front of her nose—guiding his horse into position to make the series of five jumps arranged in the ring. He appeared intense, focused—but relaxed, as though he were having the time of his life. Apparently he *thrived* on Hunter's insults—taking the jumps with an easy confidence that shook Sabrina to the bone. *I used to ride like that.* Hunter Buchanan's controversial methodology was being proven on the spot. Ed—in fact, all of Hunter's students—bloomed in the ring. Every one of Hunter's students . . . except *her*.

A hot, hard lump squeezed up into Sabrina's throat, nausea swirling sluggishly. She shifted on the bench.

"Come on up, Sabrina." Stu appeared beside her, and his arm dropped around her shoulders. "There's a better view from there."

She resisted, shaking her head, but Stu persisted, the low-pitched whisper as insistent in her ear as the arm around her shoulders. When she realized he was going to risk distracting Hunter, she gave in. Cold prickles joined the queasiness. Oh, well. If she barfed all over Stu's boots, he had no one to blame but himself.

Couldn't he see that she was *here* at least?

Stu sat her down next to Pete Galioto, who smiled, then ignored her, his gaze fastened on the ring. Stu settled beside her and squeezed her arm. "Ed's looking good today," he murmured in a matter-of-fact undertone.

"I plan to beat his socks off in Fresno anyway," Pete quipped, still intent on watching what was going on in the arena.

Sabrina sat without moving, pressing her hands against the cold metal bleachers while she took slow, deep breaths. She absolutely would *not* succumb to an attack now. *Remember what you were taught. You're not helpless. You can control your body, and you can learn to control your emotions the same way.* Well, she wasn't having much success in *that* department—at least, where Hunter Buchanan was concerned. . . .

"You okay, Sabrina? You don't look so hot."

"Leave her alone, Cherisse, and keep your voice down unless you want Hunt on your case."

"You just missed Ed executing a perfect vertical jump. Why don't we *all* leave Sabrina alone and watch the show?"

The voices flowed over and around her, forcing a level of awareness she really wasn't ready to handle. Unfortunately, Sabrina wasn't given much choice, as Wynn and Cherisse clambered down to settle in front of her, so close her knees brushed Wynn's spine. Surrounded on all sides, she abruptly gave in with half-hysterical abandon, and the sucking black hole of despair evaporated in a single swoosh. Sabrina blinked, then cautiously turned her head to meet Stu's concerned brown eyes.

"You okay?" he asked again.

The amazing sensation of togetherness, of support, swelled. Warming. Affirming. She was part of the group. She was, if not precisely equal, at least being *treated* as one of them. It felt good. It felt freeing, as though God himself had actually warmed the cold bleachers.

A smile blossomed deep inside Sabrina. Slowly it began to inch across her face. "I'm . . . fine, thanks to you and everyone else," she whispered back. She wasn't quite prepared to thank God yet. Her mind might still be playing tricks on her.

"Shh!" Wynn hissed. But she glanced over her shoulder and wrinkled her nose affectionately. Stu chuckled, and as naturally as sunlight, everyone's attention returned to Ed and Hunter.

Fifteen minutes later the lesson ended. Ed dismounted next to Hunter, who clapped him on the shoulder and grinned. They began talking, Hunter's voice and stance once more that of good-natured coach.

With a satisfied grunt, Pete stood, turning to Sabrina. He wrapped a friendly arm about her shoulders and hugged her. When Sabrina stiffened, he dropped his arm instantly. "Easy to see why Sanger's number one," he commented casually. "Makes me wonder if I might as well hang up my hat and boots and sell insurance."

"Hunt's doing a good job of training that reckless streak out of him," Wynn observed. "I remember last year, he and I ended up being here together. Ed had just purchased Jellybean and kept trying to impress everyone. He got thrown twice, and on a cross-country, he and the horse parted company about five miles from here."

"I heard it took three hours to find him," Stu added.

"Jellybean, on the other hand, didn't have a bit of trouble finding his way back to the barn!"

Everyone laughed, except Sabrina, who didn't contribute anything more than a nod. Stu gave her hair an affectionate tweak. "Watching Ed's an experience, isn't it? Both he and Pete here are leaving day after tomorrow for Fresno, and Hunt's been sweating horseshoe nails to get them ready for the trials there."

"He's . . . good," Sabrina ventured. "You're both good." Her mind scrambled to remember something about Ed's lesson. As though a window had blown open, the information clicked back into place. "But he still comes a little too far out of the saddle when he jumps, I think."

"Good point," Stu said into the stunned pool of silence while everyone gaped at Sabrina. "You ought to tell Hunt, since Ed could argue that the sun rises in the *west* until you agreed with him just to shut him up." He beamed at Sabrina. "You have a good eye, Ms. Mayhew. Thanks." He looked as if he wanted to say more, but with a little cuff to her shoulder, he hopped down from the bleachers and headed into the arena.

The others teased her good-naturedly, then drifted away one by one until only Pete lingered, his gaze wandering over Sabrina's face. "Later this morning I'm working with a green horse for Hunt. Nothing exciting—all flatwork—but you're welcome to watch," he said, then added with a half grin, "in fact, I'd downright enjoy it. Both you and your opinion. Stu's right, you have a good eye."

"Thanks, Pete. I'll try to make it."

He finally left, but Sabrina stood at the bottom of the bleachers a moment longer, hugging the moment. It was a small step, to be sure, but she had learned to savor the random flickers of confidence wherever and whenever she found them. If only she could apply the same principle to her feelings about Hunter. . . .

Twenty-One

*Y*ou came. Good. I wondered if you would."

Sabrina started, whipping about. Hunter stood not three yards away, studying her with that intent look she found so disconcerting. Her heart turned a somersault, but she managed a composed response. "Your strategy was flawless. I have a feeling half the students and staff would have dogged my every step if I *hadn't* shown up. It seemed easier to give in gracefully."

A muscle twitched in his jaw. "It would be nice if you conceded to *all* my strategies as gracefully." A strange look crossed his face, and he amended sheepishly, "Well . . . maybe not all. One of them seems to have taken a direction I wasn't expecting."

Could he mean—? Sabrina dropped her gaze to the dusty toes of her Wellingtons, unable to maintain eye contact. "Um . . . Ed Sanger seems to thrive on your teaching style, doesn't he?" Inwardly she groaned, disgusted with herself. Well, why *not* pretend she didn't know what he was talking about? More denial—just what Hunter expected from her. After all, she'd already proved to him that she was a coward, with no mental discipline at all.

"The best riders tend to go along with it," Hunter returned agreeably. "I've never met anyone who didn't need to learn how to better prepare themselves mentally for competition." He studied her a minute. "What did you do? To prepare for competitions, I mean." Casually he reached behind her to pick up a crop one of the riders had accidentally left behind. The movement caused him to brush against Sabrina.

Rattled, she answered automatically, "Talked to Ves a lot. Walked the alphabet . . ."

"*Walked* the alphabet?"

An involuntary smile trembled on her lips. "It was better than walking in circles. I'd walk an 'A,' then a 'B,' a 'C' . . . all the way to 'Z.' Sometimes I'd do it backwards, if it was a really tough show, like the Washington International." Her head lifted as the smile turned to a light laugh. "Once, I was so focused on what my feet were doing that I didn't hear the announcer calling my name. I was nearly eliminated."

"I hope that taught you to mind your p's and q's."

Sabrina rolled her eyes, relaxing into a peal of laughter. "That was awful." He hadn't teased her before, as he did everyone else. She was torn between enchantment and self-consciousness.

"I agree. If I promise not to make any more bad jokes, will you come to my office with me? The one here, not back at the house." His voice altered. "We need to talk, Sabrina."

"I—all right."

She followed him out, down a freezing, rain-scented alleyway, then waited while he unlocked a door and ushered her inside. His "office" consisted of a small room with a single window overlooking the western pasture. A beat-up metal desk and chair overflowed with magazines, papers, and videotapes; a small loveseat covered with a faded plaid fabric was pushed against the wall. In the corner a portable refrigerator hummed next to a butcher block table holding a coffee maker. Several folding chairs were stacked against another wall.

"Sabrina, try not to look as though I'm about to toss you over my shoulder and carry you off into the night."

She froze, hot color storming into her cheeks. "I'm not!"

"Maybe," he conceded. He walked across the floor to stand in front of her, rocking a little on his heels. Then he heaved a sigh. "I shouldn't have kissed you yesterday. But I did, so we're going to talk about it like two rational adults." He muttered something beneath his breath. "Forget it. There's nothing 'rational' about what I'm feeling right now, especially when you look at me like that."

"I can't help the way I look." She forced the words past numb lips. *I shouldn't have kissed you*, he'd said. For the first night in months her dreams had not tormented her, because they had all been of Hunter. And now he was *sorry* he'd kissed her. "But go ahead," she added flippantly. "Tell me how I look today."

"Bruised," Hunter snapped. He swiveled on his heel and stalked across to stare out the tear-streaked window. "Do you have any idea—no, of course you don't." He turned back around, breathing deeply, looking almost dangerous in his intensity. Then he relaxed and ran his hand around the back of his neck. "Would you believe that I've been praying about this encounter since yesterday? Somehow, I don't think I've received whatever message the Lord has been trying to give me." His voice was whimsical.

"I'm not a child," Sabrina retorted and glanced longingly at the door. "You're sorry you kissed me. Fine. I agree. It was a mistake. Now, obviously you've decided that coaching me would be too awkward, but you don't know how to tell me. I'll make it easy for you. I'll—"

"Whoa there, lady. Back up a moment. I think we've crossed a few wires." He started to walk back over, then veered in his course and dropped down on the loveseat. "Come and sit down. Let's get something clear, here and now."

Oh, boy. That tone again. *Keep your cool, Sabrina.* All she needed to do was pretend she was back in her apartment in Virginia, far removed from Montclair . . . and Hunter. "Sure." She sat as far away from him as possible, perched on the edge of the seat, and stared at a crumpled-looking wall poster advertising the Del-Mar Two-Day Horse Trials.

Undaunted, Hunter calmly took her hand, forcing the clenched fingers to relax inside his. "You're a student at Montclair. Center policy frowns—heavily—on pursuing any kind of personal relationships between staff and students, though needless to say, sometimes human emotions are like a runaway horse." The corner of his mouth lifted. "So . . . there have been lapses. Until yesterday, however, I admit I always felt a little superior. Maybe that's because I'd never been tempted—" he stroked her fingers, waiting until Sabrina finally met his unwavering gaze—"until yesterday."

She quit trying to recapture her hand and searched the blue-gray eyes. A faint band of red stained the rugged cheekbones—he wasn't as controlled as he was pretending, either—and the pulse in his throat visibly throbbed. "You're saying that I . . . that I—" She couldn't finish.

"Yes." Suddenly he smiled, and twin blue flames shot through the murky gray of his eyes. "The look on your face! Sabrina, has a man ever told you he's attracted to you?"

She began sputtering. "Well, yes. Several. I just never believed them."

"Why?"

"My older sister, Renee, was the one with the looks. With me, it was easy to see they were after the money and the power that goes with our name. Or maybe it was just that I was a challenge, this naïve little rich girl so caught up in horses she wouldn't recognize a come-on if one slapped her in the face." Renee's words to that effect surfaced, and Sabrina almost choked on her embarrassment.

"Well . . . you didn't." Hunter picked up her other hand, holding them both between his in a warm, unnerving clasp. "You do a good job of hiding your feelings, sweetheart. Except for your eyes. They show your suffering and your strength. They show—" He stopped, and wry amusement flickered briefly. "I don't want to take advantage of you, Sabrina. You deserve better."

She shook her head. "Hunter . . . I need—you have to let me go."

"I probably ought to let you go." Instead he tugged, pulling her closer, the gentleness belying his considerable strength. "But if I do, you'll never overcome the fear, and I—" he shifted, stroking the damp palms of her trembling hands—"I would always wonder what God really intended for the two of us."

"God doesn't have anything to do with this," Sabrina blurted. She felt as though flames were licking her hands, but the sensation was as far from pain as sunrise from sunset. "You're trying to confuse the issue. You're trying to confuse *me*. Well, it won't work. I don't know what you—mmph."

His lips stopped the panicked flow of words. This time the kiss lingered, though he was beguiling her instead of storming her defenses. Gentling her to his touch, as though she were an untried Thoroughbred. *I won't let this happen . . . won't be foolish enough to believe he means any of this.*

But the firestorm of feeling exploded inside, engulfing her in its heat. She may have fooled herself before, but Hunter had destroyed her last flimsy pretense.

Sabrina was in love with the man, and she was as helpless against the overwhelming emotion as she was against the fear.

Bald Mountain

"Yer horse is in bad shape," Hiram Tubbs announced. He scratched his oversized belly, the bloodshot gaze indifferent.

"So *do* something. That's what I'm paying you for." Gabe hung on to his fraying temper, fearing that Janis would sense his anger. He continued to hold the quivering mare's halter, wishing he could plant a two-by-four in the sawbones' fat belly.

"Animal don't like humans much, does she?"

"Can't say as I blame her," Gabe growled.

"Well . . . your mare's in a bad way. Cold and cough, possibly influenza. Left foot's badly infected; should've had that shoe removed a long time ago." He wiped his pudgy hands on his jeans. "Frankly, she ain't worth your money and my time. If she were mine, I'd just—"

"She's not yours." A red mist swam before his eyes, and Tubbs hastily backed out of the stall. Gabe followed, his hand clenched in a fist.

"I'll . . . uh . . . how 'bout if I leave you some antibiotics and ointment," the vet offered. "That'll help. And keep the leg wrapped." He scuttled out of the shed into the cold, windy morning.

Gabe was inside the barn, staring blankly down at a handful of pills, a large tube of ointment, and a rolled-up bandage, when he heard the purr of an engine coming to a stop out in the yard. A car door slammed, and a feminine voice called his name.

That realtor woman! With a low growl, Gabe hurled the medicine into an empty water bucket and stepped over to the entrance. Sure enough, she was marching toward the door of the shack like a general, a fancy leather briefcase clutched in one hand. Gabe put two fingers to his lips and whistled. The woman turned, waved, and strode across the yard until she caught sight of Joplin, who was cantering across the paddock in response to Gabe's whistle.

"Good morning, Mr. Wisniewski. Beautiful horse you have there. What's her name?"

"Don't have time for chitchat," Gabe muttered rudely. "Or for you, either." He patted Joplin's head and pulled her ears when she butted her head against his chest.

"This isn't a social call," the woman calmly reminded him. "I've brought a number of properties. Give me fifteen minutes of your time to fill me in on what you're looking for, and I'll be gone."

"You'll have to wait." He eyed her warily. She just stood there, looking as spiffy as a model in a lady's magazine, even with the wind ruffling strands of her short black hair all over the place. The level gaze never faltered. "I gotta take care of my other horse," he finally admitted. "She's sick, if you gotta stick your nose in it."

"Oh, I'm sorry. I used to have horses myself." The bold smile flashed. "Well, I used to ride. The place I bought here included a stable with half a dozen horses, along with a horrible man hired to care for them." Her gloved hand reached out and patted Joplin's questing nose. "Oh, you're a sugarplum, aren't you, darling?" she drawled.

Gabe snorted. "You'll get those fancy duds dirty, lady. But if you wanna hang around, I won't stop you." He limped off toward the barn.

"My name's Kathleen Winthrop." She appeared at his side, matching her steps to his bumbling gait. "Call me Kathleen. May I call you Gabriel?"

"Only if you want me to fetch that shotgun."

She laughed. "Gabe, then?"

"You're as pushy as any female I ever met." They reached the shed, and without hesitation she followed him right inside. "Uh . . . yeah. Call me Gabe. Now stay out of my way."

Kathleen peered into the stall. "Uh-oh. She's really bad, isn't she? Was that the vet I passed on the way up?"

The unexpected sympathy caught Gabe off guard. "The sorriest excuse for a vet on the planet." His voice roughened, and he kept his head turned, busying himself with the medicine and bandages. "Gotta get these pills down her somehow," he muttered beneath his breath.

"I'll help."

"Sure ya will." He looked her up and down, a sneering look designed to set Ms. High-and-Mighty back on her heels. "All the blood and puss and dirt'll look real nice on those realtor clothes."

She shrugged, glancing around. "Got an old shirt I can borrow?

No? Oh, well." And with Gabe standing there dumbstruck, she shucked her gloves and coat and draped them over the stall door. "You better go in first. He doesn't know me."

"*She's* a mare."

"What's her name?"

Slowly, he opened the stall, torn between disbelief and unexpected gratitude. "Janis," he croaked, then cleared his throat and spat. "Her name is Janis."

"Janis? Janis and Joplin." The blue eyes swam with merriment. She choked off a laugh when Janis started. "Sorry, girl," she murmured. "Oh, Gabe, she's trembling! Is she in pain?"

"She's scared of you," he said gruffly. "Scared of humans. Some useless snake worked her over good before I—before she was mine." Inwardly he swore. Put him around a woman, and he started blabbing like one of *them*.

Kathleen was gently patting Janis's quivering flank. "There's a lot of snakes around. The man I told you about who kept the horses at the estate I bought? I found out he was abusing the animals, so I fired the scumball. Found out later several horses had run off, but by then it was too late to—" She stopped, staring over the mare's back at Gabe, who felt as though his tongue was permanently stuck to the roof of his mouth. "Gabe, who sold you the horse? Wasn't a man named Ned Truro, was it?"

"No. And how I came by my horses is none of your—what do you think you're doing?"

This time she'd sidled up to Janis's head, her hands stroking, gentling the frightened mare. "The Edgehills—the people who sold me their estate—told me they tattooed their horses' lips for identification."

"You accusin' me of being a horse thief?" At the savage fury in his voice, Janis shied, throwing Kathleen against the stall.

Kathleen never broke eye contact with Gabe. "I'd never accuse anyone of stealing without knowing all the facts," she returned, those blue eyes shooting sparks that singed his scalp.

"Get away from her," Gabe snarled. "I only got one arm, but I can still—"

"Shh. You're frightening Janis." The long slender fingers were spreading the mare's lips now. She dipped her head to better examine both upper and lower areas. Then she patted Janis, soothing her, and her eyes met Gabe's in a level stare. "Why don't you tell me the whole story?" she asked. "Because this animal is tattooed—and it matches exactly those on the other horses I sold off a couple of months after I fired Truro."

Twenty-Two

*A*fter the last of his lessons for the day, except for Sabrina's, Hunt checked the mountain walk list. Noticeably blank, probably due to the weather. No matter. Signing his name in a hurried slash, he took time only to shrug into a wool-lined, waterproof anorak, then headed for the mountain.

He needed some time alone. Moses, wandering atop Mt. Sinai. He checked himself. That thought was perhaps subtly blasphemous, since it wasn't divine mandates for the human race he was seeking.

He should have kept a tighter rein on his emotions. His boots squished through puddles, spraying out icy rivulets of muddy water, but Hunt didn't notice. The sky had lightened and the rain had moved on, though the peaks to the north and west remained shrouded in clouds.

The silence was overwhelming, yet curiously comforting. Except for the faint hollow whisper of a breeze and the occasional splatter of branches shedding raindrops, he might have been the only living creature on the planet. *I needed this. Thanks.*

Halfway up the path, his furious pace slowed. Surrounded by the serene watchfulness of the trees, dwarfed by the mountains, he allowed God's presence to seep inside, reducing his problem to manageable size. Notably, the problem of Sabrina.

He had scrupulously avoided singling her out, though his awareness of her presence always seemed to tug at his consciousness. In spite of his fierce concentration during teaching sessions, he had somehow always sensed when Sabrina was watching from the bleachers. Stu, along with several other students, had remarked on her astute commentary. Of course, they'd had to drag the words out of her.

"But when she says something—it's worth listening to," Stu observed. "Don't give up on her, Hunt. That gal needs to be back in the ring."

Thanks to the disastrous scene in his stable office, Hunt had wondered if she'd show up in the stands to observe any of the sessions. Once again Sabrina had surprised him by appearing for not just one, but all four. By the time Cherisse sashayed into the arena an hour ago, his discreet sidelong glances had assured him that Sabrina's fear, as well as her embarrassment, had been successfully averted. She hadn't panicked at the sight of horses jumping. She'd toughed out the smothering concern of staff and students. Had seemingly returned to her acceptance of Hunt in his professional persona, though Carla had confided that by the end of Cherise's session she couldn't escape fast enough. "She avoiding you again or something, boss?"

Hunter's step slowed even more. In forty minutes, he and Sabrina would conduct their next lesson, which was why he'd escaped to the mountain walk beforehand. He had an uncomfortable presentiment that his feelings for her would spill into their sessions. *That can't happen. Lord . . . You know that doesn't need to happen.* He couldn't afford another breach of professional ethics, not to mention *Christian* ethics.

Of course, Sabrina showed little awareness of the temptation she presented. Her tightly controlled reserve challenged him; her rare flashes of self-deprecating humor so like his own made his skin prickle.

"That's the problem," he announced out loud. Sabrina Mayhew had gotten under his skin. He couldn't see her as a student anymore. Couldn't even label her as a troubled woman in need of his help as a professional coach. Somehow over the past months she had become the elusive prize he'd sought most of his adult life.

He barely remembered Danielle, his first love, when they were students together at the university. She'd gone on to pursue a master's in botany, and he'd traded the academic world for the equestrian world. As for Margaret . . . he shook his head. Their engagement had been long and stormy. Stormy, at least on Margaret's part. In fact, Hunt reminisced with a faint smile, one of the reasons she'd lost her temper with him so often was because Hunt never lost *his*. In fact, until Sabrina, Hunt had felt pretty confident of his self-control. "You'd think I'd learn, Lord."

Sabrina's stubborn resistance to accept God's help was another constant frustration. He could have handled his growing attraction to her, even the complications arising from flouting Center policy, but he didn't have a clue as to how to handle Sabrina's rejection of God's place in her life. And so, Hunt had come to the mountain walk.

After verifying landmarks, he stepped off the path into the darkening forest, quietly maneuvering between rain-wet trunks and low branches until he reached an outcropping of boulders. The wind stung his cheeks, and the air was frosty enough to escape from his lungs in puffs of vapor. Hunt sank down on an age-worn rock, ignoring the dampness that penetrated his breeches, and bowed his head.

Bald Mountain

"Your mama's a tough old lady," Gabe told Joplin as he refilled her water bucket, then ladled a handful of oats into her feed trough. "But between you and me, I'm a little worried about her." Actually, it was more like a heavy foreboding that lay in his belly like a plateful of cold beans.

Joplin playfully nudged his chest, almost knocking Gabe down. After his struggles with Janis the last two days, his leg was about useless. "Cut it out, ya big lummox." He scratched between the filly's ears; she loved that. He could have taken the Winthrop woman's offer to send up another vet, but Gabe would have none of it. Even though she'd told him she didn't want his horses, that Janis and Joplin belonged to him free and clear, he couldn't afford to believe her. She was a woman, after all.

Unfortunately, he didn't have time to worry over legal ownership. If Janis didn't improve . . . Gabe swallowed hard. He couldn't think about that. Not right now.

"Your mama's bad, Joplin," he said again. "God knows how I'd have managed without those pills." The words hovered in the frost-coated air, and after a moment Gabe self-consciously smacked Joplin's hindquarters one last time, then limped out of her stall.

Strange, but he'd actually found himself thinking more about the existence of a Supreme Being lately than he had in close to thirty years. Maybe he'd been alone too long. Maybe he was going off the deep end. Or maybe the anger and bitterness were finally losing their grip a little, thanks to Janis and Joplin. And, he might as well admit it, Kathleen Winthrop had somehow slipped past his guard, too. She hadn't treated him like dirt. In fact, she'd treated him like he was somebody. She'd left behind a handful of papers and such for him to look over. Carefully listened to his halting plans, even written them down.

Gabe shook his head. Next thing, he'd actually start believing that Kathleen really meant for him to keep Janis and Joplin. The little tickle of confidence grew.

Pressing his arm close to his side, he approached Janis's stall, and the good feelings dribbled away. For several moments he watched her. The mare stood, infected foot dangling, head still down, seemingly indifferent to Gabe's presence. Even worse, she refused to come out of the stall. Gabe had to clean around her, which, with one arm and a bum leg, meant her stall was never as clean as it needed to be.

The leg wasn't improving, and Gabe didn't know what to do. By digging out a hole in an apple, he'd managed to sneak a couple of pills down Janis, but she was still coughing, and even though he'd managed to coat the leg with ointment, he hadn't been able to fasten the bandage in place. Staring at the decrepit animal was a constant fist in his guts. Janis looked so . . . defeated.

Like he himself had felt most of the time till Janis and Joplin. He had to save Janis. He *had* to. If there really was a God up there looking over things, Someone who'd take pity on a helpless animal, then Gabe reckoned it wouldn't hurt to act like he believed. Right now, he'd do whatever he had to—enter the Boston Marathon or a tree-climbing contest—if it would help Janis.

That smooth-talking Winthrop woman better find him a place like she'd promised. Soon.

He spent an hour trying to coax another pill down the indifferent mare's throat, but finally he had to give up. Janis had started trembling again, and if he caused her to panic she could hurt him badly without meaning to. Swallowing the bitter taste of fear, he fumbled the boards back in place across the stall, patted Joplin's nose, then trudged back to the shack.

Didn't look like he could help her, after all. Maybe God didn't plan to, either.

Back in the cabin, he stoked the fire in the woodstove and eased himself down on the sofa. His leg ached, his back ached, his hand was chapped and red, and right now he barely had the energy to twitch. What feeble-minded notion had possessed him to think he could take care of a ranch? He sure as spitting wouldn't be able to do it alone.

He'd have to hire some hands, if he was lucky. But who'd want to work for a cripple with a chip on his shoulder the size of Montana? He might have half a million bucks in the bank piling up interest, but it could have been ten times that amount for all the good it was doing. He used to think that money was power, that all he needed to do to have people look at him with respect was to make a bundle.

Yancey had tried to tell him different. But back then, bursting with the arrogance of youth, he'd told his old Army buddy to take a hike. Staring at the flames, Gabe laughed a bitter, self-mocking laugh. Right now, he'd give every penny of that half-million to anyone who could save a dying reject of a horse. He'd even give her back to Kathleen Winthrop. Who was he fooling? He'd even give Janis to Hunter Buchanan, if either of them knew how to save her life.

If there *was* a God, He was probably splitting a side right now, laughing at Gabriel Wisniewski.

Twenty-Three

Montclair

I want to try riding alone today."

Hunt measured Sabrina in silence. It had been a long week for both of them, each trying to ignore feelings too dangerous to acknowledge. This morning she looked different somehow. Strain still shadowed the rainy-day eyes, but a glimmer of resolution shone there as well. And her posture . . . She stood beside a placid Lady Fair, firmly holding the reins just beneath the bit. Her shoulders were thrown back, no longer hunched. As for her chin, it made a good mood barometer. At its present tilt, determination was flying high.

A stirring of answering excitement sparked inside Hunt. "Sounds like a good plan to me. Want me to give you a leg up?"

"Yes—no. I'll try. . . ."

He did smile then. "I'll stay close, just in case." Looking mulish, she started to speak, but Hunt shook his head. "Take it or leave it. I won't have you thudding into the sand if I can prevent it."

Without a word she turned to Lady, gathered the reins, and swung aboard the mare's back with the natural grace that always took Hunt's breath. He stepped up beside her left leg. "Move out. Keep it to a nice gentle walk . . . Lighten up on the reins, Sabrina. That's better. Good. Good. Now look down at me and smile—just to let me know you're okay."

She didn't budge.

"Sabrina." He laid his hand on her knee. "Come on, now. Unless you want me to vault up there behind you, give me a smile. One of those mysterious, haunting Sabrina smiles." Beneath his hand, her leg jerked.

"I don't smile like that."

He grinned up at her pale face. "Well, I admit that right now I don't see any sign of one, but I keep hoping, Sabrina." His own smile faded, and he held her gaze with the sheer force of his will. "That's what I want you to remember. That I keep hoping, and that I won't give up on you."

He gave Lady a hand signal to which the highly trained horse instantly responded, and they began a slow walk. After an involuntary gasp, Sabrina had gone rigid, but she didn't freeze. And she didn't faint. Hunter paced the horse, keeping his eye on Sabrina's face. A quarter of a circuit, then half. Three quarters of the way around the arena he saw it happen. Like ice breaking up in a frozen river, her body began to relax and move with the horse. The blind desperation that had turned her face to a colorless mask melted first into astonishment, then into budding hope, and finally joy.

"Hunter . . ."

"I know. I know." His throat was tight. "You've done it, Sabrina. Look—in the mirrors along the wall. Can you see?"

Slowly, carefully her head swiveled toward the mirrors. "Oh," she breathed, riveted to the sight. "Hunter, I'm riding."

"Yes . . . yes, you're riding! And you're *beautiful*!"

She pulled on the reins in an involuntary movement that brought Lady to an immediate halt. "I'm riding, but I'm *not* beautiful."

So she had heard him, after all. "At this moment, you're the most beautiful sight I've ever seen," he returned, his voice very gentle.

She shook her head, froze. Then she took a deep, quavering breath. "Will you . . . move to the center of the ring? Please?"

"All right." Every fiber of his being screamed in protest, but Hunt casually stuffed his hands in his pockets and strolled away. "Go ahead. Take Lady around the ring again."

He watched, feeling his heart thudding in his chest, while Sabrina completed two more circuits. The second time, she stopped in front of the mirrors again, gazing intently. "I'm not afraid," she whispered, the announcement floating across the ring, barely audible. "I'm not afraid. I can do this." Abruptly her face crumpled and tears streamed down her cheeks.

Hunt didn't remember moving, but suddenly he was there, hauling her off Lady's back and into his arms. "Yes. You *can*—you already have." He held her close against his chest. "Don't doubt it any longer. Don't be afraid. I'll help. *God* will help, Sabrina. You don't have to doubt Him. He's always there, and so am—" He throttled back the passionate vow. *One jump at a time, Hunt.*

Behind them a door slammed. Sabrina tore herself free, twisting around to hide her face next to Lady's head. Hunter turned, his narrowed gaze honing in on Carla's resolute figure.

"Sorry, Hunt, Sabrina," she called as she approached. "But we have a slight . . . problem. Somehow a reporter made it as far as the boarding stable. Jay and Charlie cornered him, but there's no telling how many photos he's taken—and he's not talking much at the moment. Says he'll speak to you and nobody else."

"I'm on the way, Carla." Fury and frustration throbbed through the words.

"I'll stay with Sabrina, if you like," the trainer offered.

Hunt's hands closed into fists. He forced himself to relax. "Thanks." Turning, he touched Sabrina's shoulder. "Okay? I'll be back as soon as I can."

She nodded and cleared her throat. "That reporter . . . he's probably after me." Her gaze swung from Hunter to Carla and back. "Give me a few minutes, then let me go on and talk—"

"No." Even Carla jumped at the leashed violence simmering in the single word, and with an effort Hunt curbed the anger pounding through him. "This was breaking and entering. No way do I reward a crime with an interview."

"He claims one of the staff gave him permission to wander around, take photos." Carla nodded. "Fella doesn't remember this staff member's name, of course, only that it was a woman with an accent."

"I'm on the way." If the reporter *was* Babcock, then it appeared as though Hunt might have to resort to more extreme measures to teach the fellow some manners. "Sabrina, are you sure—?"

"I'm fine, Hunter. Truly. And I don't mind granting an interview. At least, not as much as I did two weeks ago. It has to be faced sometime, so why not—"

"Not today. And not like this." He forced a fleeting smile, nodded at Carla, then strode back across the ring.

They had locked the pesky intruder inside a little-used storage room full of tools, broken tack, and dust. Hunt could hear the threats and curses all the way down the aisle. He could also see that the ruckus was disturbing the horses, though Jay was doing his best to calm them.

"Mickey's guarding the door," his head groom told Hunt. "And I've sent another hand to telephone the sheriff." He turned back to the restless bay whose stall was only a dozen feet away from the source of the noise. "Do something quick, boss, or I'll no' be responsible for the lads and lasses we're boarding here."

Nor his own Scots temper, Hunt added silently as he approached Mickey. Perhaps that would solve the problem: let Jay Erskine at the hapless reporter. Poor man wouldn't know what hit him. He gestured to Mickey to step aside, then threw open the vibrating door, which seemed to be suffering the brunt of multiple blows. Gil Babcock almost fell into the aisle.

"You sent for me, Mr. Babcock?" Hunter asked.

The infuriated reporter whipped around. "I'll see you in court!" he began, then looked into Hunt's face. A vein jumped in his temple, and he swallowed twice, hard, but his next words were more conciliatory. "There's been a mistake. Your *staff* refused to let me explain."

"Very undiplomatic of them, I'm sure. It's a shame they're so loyal. Law-abiding, too." Hunt swept the still seething Babcock a slow, thorough study. "Maybe a tad naïve, though. They still think that strangers lurking around private property without permission— albeit under the guise of the First Amendment—are engaging in an illegal act of trespass."

An ugly flush mottled the reporter's sallow cheeks. "I got permission," he insisted.

"From my housekeeper?"

"Go ask her yourself."

"Nah. We'll just wait for the sheriff. Got anything you'd like to say before he arrives, now that you've forced my presence as well as my attention? I'll be sending along a bill for my time, of course—" Hunt named an hourly rate that set Babcock to sputtering again— "so unless you're paid *very* well, maybe you'd better keep this short."

"Oh, I'll be paid, all right, and so will you. After you got me fired from my last job, I found an even better one with a newspaper where you and Montclair are nothing but a juicy bone ripe for picking!" The other man took a step forward, then retreated when the hefty Mickey tensed and half lifted his arms.

Hunter shrugged. "All I did was alert your former employer to certain of your spurious tendencies. As for your new employer . . . we'll see, won't we?"

"You used your influence, man. Don't hand me a load of double-talk," Babcock sneered. "And you're supposed to be a *Christian*."

"That I am. That's why I uphold the laws of the land as best I can. Now, if you'd approached through the proper gate, so to speak, this wouldn't have happened."

"Yeah, right. Like a couple of weeks ago? You threw me out."

Hunt was stalling now, thinking fast and furiously. He didn't want trouble, but he knew with the savvy gained through years of living in the limelight that the tabloids only hounded more relentlessly when they were repeatedly thwarted. And their tactics with an avowed Christian tended toward the downright vicious. He couldn't subject Sabrina to—

"Hello. Sorry to intrude, but I need to speak with Mr. Buchanan for a second." Sabrina herself walked down the aisle, looking poised and in command, wearing faded breeches and a sweat shirt, her face scrubbed clean of makeup. She'd twisted her hair up into a sleek bun, however, and two centuries of aristocratic breeding were in her gracious greeting. "We haven't met, have we?" She thrust out her hand. "I'm Sabrina Mayhew."

An explosive moment of silence reverberated in the air. Hunt's mind had gone absolutely blank. Then Babcock elbowed in front of him.

"Well, well, well. Sabrina—okay if I call you by your first name?"

Sabrina shrugged. Her face, Hunt noted, was carefully blank. All vivacity and life snuffed out.

"Like I was trying to tell Hunt here, if you'll give me an exclusive interview, I can promise you'll never have to worry about anyone asking 'Sabrina *who*?' for the next decade."

"Sure." She began scuffling her toe on the floor. "What did you want to know?"

"Sabrina—" Hunter rushed in.

She lifted her blank doll's face and looked at him. "This won't take long, Hunter, since I really don't have anything to discuss with Mr. Babcock."

"Sweetcakes, you're the greatest thing the equestrian world has had going for it since Christopher Reeve." He moved in closer, practically salivating. "How does this grab you? 'Former Darling of the Grand Prix Circuit Leaps to New Life, Thanks to Hunter Buchanan.' "

Hunt's teeth snapped together. Behind him, he heard the sputterings of his staff. Sabrina shrugged again. "Nice. Except I'm not competing. Mr. Buchanan's giving me a few lessons, that's all."

"You're pulling my leg, aren't you?" The reporter glanced from Sabrina to Hunt. "What do you mean, you're not competing?"

"Yeah, Sabrina," Hunt chimed in. "Tell Mr. Babcock what you mean."

"Well . . . I don't know how to be much plainer. I came to Montclair because I hadn't ridden in several years and wanted to . . . ah . . . recover some of my old skills. Nothing newsworthy, Mr. Babcock."

"Gil."

"Hunter agreed to help." Another lightning glance his way before she fixed her gaze on Babcock. "I'll be leaving soon and flying home to Virginia. I have a business to run now, Mr. Babcock. I don't really have time to compete, especially on the grand prix show-jumping circuit." Her voice, her posture, her demeanor could not be more indifferent.

The reporter looked as baffled as Hunt felt. He hadn't seen this particular Sabrina in over a month. "That's not what *I* heard," Babcock began, peering closely at Sabrina. "I heard you were afraid to ride . . . but that Hunt Buchanan has great plans for you."

"I *was* afraid to ride. Now I'm not. As for Mr. Buchanan's plans . . . well, that's *his* concern. *My* plan is to return to Virginia before I lose some clients, Mr. Babcock."

Now the guy was starting to look miffed. Hunter altered his stance, preparing to intervene if things turned ugly.

"But you were one of the best." Babcock wasn't going to give up. "You can't turn your back on something that big. What about the Olympics? According to my sources, you've got what it takes, if you—"

"I might have, once," Sabrina interrupted quietly. "But that was another life, another time." She held Babcock's gaze. "Another story.

I'm sorry if this one hasn't turned out the way you expected."

"You got that right, sweetcakes."

"I think you've about outstayed your welcome." Hunt tilted his head. "What do you think, Babcock?"

Eyes blinking like a trapped rat's, the other man stood, gaze darting back and forth. He still smelled a story, Hunt saw, but he was also growing disillusioned with Sabrina Mayhew. On that score, they shared a bond.

Hunt clasped his hands behind his back. The bitter taste in his mouth was a pretty accurate picture of what was going on inside. He found himself praying for peace. For self-control . . . patience . . .

"Might as well shove off," Babcock grumbled. His bony shoulders hunched. "Say . . . I left my car and hiked in. Can one of your staff—"

Not in this lifetime, Hunt wanted to say. The words crowded all the way to the tip of his tongue, but somehow he managed to swallow them. "No problem," he replied pleasantly, turning to scan the aisle. "Jay?"

"Boss?" Jay's voice was incredulous.

"See who's available, will you? It's the least we can do for Mr. Babcock, considering he came all this way for nothing."

Hunt gestured to the lanky young stable hand who had answered the summons. "Thanks, Matt. Mr. Babcock here needs a lift to his car. Use one of the Center's jeeps—tell Charlie I said it was all right."

Babcock gave Sabrina one last thoroughly disgusted perusal, then strolled out of the barn without another word, Matt tagging along behind him. Hunt waited until they were out of earshot before he turned to Sabrina. "Now," he said in a soft, friendly tone, "you and I are going to have a little talk."

Sabrina wasn't fooled. "Not right now. I'm talked out."

"That's what *you* think, Ms. Mayhew. . . ."

Twenty-Four

Bald Mountain

Gabe Wisniewski, ranch owner.

Had a nice ring to it, Gabe decided, though he was so busy he didn't waste time basking in his new status. He still couldn't believe how fast it had all happened: One minute he's out in the paddock, working Joplin on a lead rope. The next, Kathleen Winthrop comes bouncing up the track in her Caddy, waving her arm through the window.

"I've found it!" she'd called. "Gabe, I think I've found your ranch."

"Rolling Rock Ranch" had once been a small family-run resort that featured trail rides. The former owners had decamped to Florida years earlier, abandoning the ill-fated spot to the ravages of time and weather.

But it was salvageable—like Janis and Joplin—and the price was right. Kathleen had insisted on driving him to see it, talking ninety miles an hour the whole way. "It looks pretty sad on first impression," she'd warned. "But it has everything you're looking for. A hundred acres, with mountains, woods—a creek, even. Buildings are run down, fences sagging some. But since money's not an issue here . . ." She'd flashed him one of those toothy smiles of hers. "I want you to look at it for what it's *going* to be instead of what it is now."

Gabe had never heard anyone talk like that. And blamed if she hadn't been *right*. He'd taken one look at the Rolling Rock and turned to Kathleen. "Do whatever you got to, to push the sale through. I want to move Janis and Joplin soon as I can."

"You ready to sell me Bald Mountain yet?"

She asked every time she saw him, but for some reason Gabe was reluctant to part with the place where he'd found Janis and Joplin. "I'm still thinkin' on it," he always replied. So far she'd been smart enough not to challenge him.

"You're a hard man, Gabe Wisniewski. But I won't give up. Now . . . let's talk about your new home. You'll need to start repairs on the barn first. I can make some contacts for you, if you like."

"I can take care of my own business," he'd retorted, irritated when Kathleen laughed at him. But she hadn't argued. Dadgum, if he wasn't beginning to *like* the woman!

Over the next days he worked twenty out of twenty-four hours, making preparations to move before the next snowstorm. In November, one could hit anytime. First priority, as Kathleen said, had been the barn. It boasted twenty stalls, and Gabe hired a man and his son to do the necessary repairs. Gabe divided his time between the Double R and Bald Mountain, burning up the road in his truck.

On a freezing day, with snow clouds hanging heavy over the tallest western peaks, Gabe purchased a two-horse trailer, then drove it up to Bald Mountain. He planned to move Janis and Joplin the next morning.

But when he went to check her, Janis was lying down in the straw and refused to rise.

Gabe had faced down fear many times; even after thirty years he could still smell the stench of cordite and blood in a steamy jungle. He'd sneered at death then and had no truck with talk of a hereafter. Now he knelt in the straw beside Janis, overcome by a helplessness more agonizing than the day a barrage of mortar fire left him only half a man.

He stroked Janis's sweat-soaked neck with a shaking hand, then swiped at his wet eyes. "I'll get help," he promised hoarsely. "I'm not going to let you die, gal."

Janis didn't even seem to know he was there—or care. "I'll get help . . . don't give up," he begged, blinking hard. "Don't give up on me, gal. Not now."

He covered her with a blanket. "I'm leaving, but I'll be back . . . and I'll bring someone with me who'll know what to do."

Montclair

An early snowfall dumped six inches of snow, but after half a century of rugged Colorado weather, the orderly routine at the Center did not falter. Because the rings were kept clear of snow and coated periodically with sand, flatwork continued outdoors as long as the chill factor remained above freezing. Both indoor arenas were coordinated to accommodate lessons by the three instructors with free exercise time.

"At least horses are blessed with an extra-heavy coat." Janet Sherbing, a cheerful free-lance writer from Utah, tugged on thermal underwear and bib-overall down ski pants. "Too bad we hairless human beings have to add so many layers."

Sabrina pulled a long-sleeved silk undershirt over her head. "I've wondered why they didn't just move Montclair back East, where the winters aren't so brutal."

"Everyone asks that at least once."

"So I discovered." After three months, she was almost used to her revolving-door suitemates. Most of them were friendly. Unfortunately, most of them liked to gossip as much as Sabrina avoided it.

"It's so romantic, isn't it?" Janet enthused. "The story of Hunt's parents? Can you imagine any man doing something like that these days? Not only did Mr. Buchanan move the Center out here so his dying wife could live out her remaining years in *her* home state, but he actually rebuilt Montclair to match his family's hundred-year-old estate back in Virginia." She laughed. "I know you probably know more about this than I do, being a native Virginian and all—not to mention the fact that you've been here at Montclair for several months now. I've never heard of anyone staying here that long. Is there something going on between you and Hunter, besides your rehabilitation, I mean?" Janet teased, the friendly brown eyes betraying her unabashed curiosity.

"I'll be leaving soon." Janet's gall, based solely on the intimacy of a shared bathroom for two whole days, rankled. It was also unnerving. But then Janet was probably only voicing the silent speculations raging among staff and students alike.

Their well-publicized row over Gil Babcock had set everything off, and time had not dimmed the talk or the interest.

She trudged down the well-worn path to the barn, head down against the bitter wind. For at least an hour, she automatically cleaned stalls, fetched food and water, and groomed thick hides, dreading as always her next confrontation with Hunter.

She fastened a blanket over Nutmeg, a sorrel gelding Hunter was training for a rancher's daughter. "There. You'll do," she told the placid animal, giving him a final pat as she left the stall. Every day she felt old habits, old feelings clicking back into place as easily as the mist drifted down over the mountains. With every swish of the currycomb, every halter latch buckled around a horse's head, she felt the three-year hiatus slipping farther into her subconscious.

Except when she was trying to ride—*which is mostly Hunter's fault.*

Right, Sabrina. Blame your own weakness on someone else.

"Yo, Sabrina!" Mickey called from down the aisle.

She jumped, almost dropping her grooming kit. "Down here—Nutmeg's stall, Mickey."

"Call from the boss up at the big house. He wants you up there, pronto."

"I'm on my way." How like Hunter, she fumed all the way up the path, to summon her like a lackey because he didn't want to confront her himself. Well, if this was his way of settling the Gil Babcock incident, so be it.

Elsa pointed a feather duster toward a door halfway down the hall. "The *jefe* is in the study."

Sabrina didn't knock. She opened the door and firmly closed it behind her. "Are we finally going to talk about this, or are you giving up and sending me home?" Not until she'd said the words did she realize how much she dreaded hearing them. From Hunter.

He heaved a sigh, pinching the bridge of his nose in a gesture Sabrina had seen more often of late. "We're going to have it out," he acknowledged. "Until we do, it's just going to keep interfering."

Relieved, Sabrina fired the first shot. "I still think my tactic worked. Gil Babcock left, didn't he?"

"I like a woman who wades right in." He crossed the room to stand directly in front of her. "Yes, ma'am, Gil Babcock left, all right. But he left knowing that the end justifies the means. He left knowing that rules are made to be broken, that privacy is expendable, because nothing matters as long as you land that all-important scoop."

"I was *boring*. You saw yourself how disappointed he was. I convinced him I was nothing but a has-been who didn't rate more than two lines on the back page, which means he won't bother to come back."

"You know what irritated me the most, Sabrina? It's the realization that you believe you were simply telling the truth. You really do see yourself as a has-been. That's why it was easy to convince a hardnosed reporter that his story was dead in the water. You're absolutely right, we're rid of Gil Babcock . . . but don't expect me to thank you for it, because I'm not thankful at all." His eyes, cold, stone gray, were grinding her into dust.

"I suppose . . . I've disappointed you," Sabrina began, the words halting.

"You should be *more* concerned about disappointing yourself." Abruptly he turned and strode back across the room. "There's something I want you to see."

Warily Sabrina wandered over to a fire burning in the fireplace. With her back to the crackling flames, she waited, disquiet growing. What was Hunter going to do? More to the point, what was *she* going to do? She was definitely making progress, but she certainly didn't consider her rehabilitation complete.

God? What am I going to do?

There was no answer.

Hunter was still messing around at the television, and a moment later she heard the sound of a videotape sliding into the VCR, and a television announcer was off and running. "Our viewers have a special treat in store for them today. Sabrina Mayhew, the young equestrian who has captured hearts as well as ribbons on both coasts, is favored to—

"No!" She stepped forward, hand lifted. "Hunter, don't do this. Please."

"You don't have to watch." He settled into an easy chair and lifted his feet onto the matching ottoman. "This looks like it's going to be the only way left for me to see one of the most gifted riders of the decade, so . . ."

Ice congealing in her veins, Sabrina watched in silence as rider after rider performed—some brilliantly, some like the novices they were. Why was she standing here like a piece of furniture, letting a video—and Hunter Buchanan—inflict wounds more painful than a physical blow? *Walk over there, turn off the video. Tell Hunter he's a selfish, insensitive brute.*

Instead, she perched on the edge of a love seat, eyes glued to the screen.

". . . next contestant up is Sabrina Mayhew, riding Greased Lightning, from Juniper Farms. Owned by Peter Cummings. This one may make history, folks. Sabrina Mayhew has a magic touch with horses, and she's unbelievably young to be competing at this level."

"That's right, Lisa. Sabrina's only nineteen, and her story's as incredible as her skill. Parents killed in a shipboard fire in the Mediterranean when Sabrina was only eight. Her love of horses gave her a reason to keep going, and she—"

"She's off. Look at that, folks! They seem to float over the jumps . . . what do you think, Jim? Is it too soon to speculate on the future? If Sabrina Mayhew continues to—"

The screen went blank.

"Sabrina . . . I'm sorry."

She kept staring, glassy-eyed at the screen, wondering why the picture had disappeared. Then Hunter's firmly muscled body filled her line of vision. He dropped down beside her, balancing easily on the balls of his feet. "I only wanted to show you how wrong your self-perception is—that's all. I've been chewing over this all week, trying to think of the best way to drive home the point. I didn't mean to cause you . . . I never intended—" He surged to his feet. "Dear God in heaven, what am I going to do?"

The heartfelt cry mimicked her own so perfectly, Sabrina felt a chill race up her spine. "You're right, you know." Her hand reached out so that her fingers barely brushed the contorted muscles of his forearm. "I never realized, until just now—" She shook her head. "I really was . . . a good rider."

Hunter sat down beside her on the love seat. "I've never seen a more naturally gifted rider in my life," he said quietly. "As God as my witness, Sabrina, I've *never* seen another soul ride like you. That's why your behavior with Gil Babcock caught me on the raw."

"Hunter?" Her heart had started to pound. She needed to talk with him, needed to ask him—and this might be her only chance.

"Go ahead, Sabrina. Say anything you need to. Rip a strip off me if it'll help. I behaved badly, I know. If it helps, you should know I've spent several miserable nights being lectured by my conscience."

Do it, Sabrina. There will never be a better time. Even if she didn't like the answer, even if Hunter again looked at her with the same disillusionment he had that day with the reporter, she wanted to *know*. "Is . . . is God . . . punishing me because I can't love Him enough to overcome this fear? Is that why I feel so empty? As though there's nothing of—of *me* inside anymore?"

Hunter's eyes widened. He waited until her outburst ended, but just as he opened his mouth, frantic knocks pounded on the study door.

"What—?" Hunter left her with reluctance and strode rapidly across the room, throwing open the door. "Jody! This better be *more* than important."

"It is to *them*," Sabrina heard her reply.

Hunter went out into the hall, shutting the door behind him. Before Sabrina could make up her mind whether to follow, the door reopened, and Hunter's eyes searched hers. As he stepped into the room, two people followed hard on his heels. One was Kathleen Winthrop. The other was a bearded man with wild eyes and one arm missing.

". . . and I didn't know what else to do," Kathleen was finishing. The blue eyes flashed toward Sabrina. "I don't know any reputable vets, or we never would have butted in like this."

The one-armed man didn't so much as glance at Sabrina. He was staring at Hunt with a trapped-animal ferocity. "You gotta help. She's dying." Beneath the salt-and-pepper beard his throat muscles stretched taut as violin strings. "She's dying. . . ."

Twenty-Five

"Come on in," Hunter invited. "Kathleen, introduce us, why don't you?"

"Gabe Wisniewski—Hunter Buchanan," the realtor responded, and Sabrina wondered if the two men caught the note of irony in her voice. "Hunt's been trying to meet you for months, Gabe. Too bad it had to happen like this."

Hunter ignored Kathleen's baiting. "Have a seat and tell me about your horse." He inclined his head. "Oh, and this is Sabrina Mayhew, by the way. Don't worry—she's a sympathetic listener."

Incredulous, Sabrina scooted over enough so that she could see Hunter's face. His body was coiled, tense. And yet . . . he sounded *peaceful*, easygoing, as if a neighbor had dropped by for a chat, though the concern in his eyes was unmistakable.

The scruffy, one-armed man appeared disconcerted. "Don't have time for chitchat. This is an emergency, man!"

"It's okay, Gabe," Kathleen intervened. "Hunt will help. He's a good man."

"You don't understand. She's *dying*." He looked past Hunter at Sabrina, and for the first time she saw beyond his hostility to the fear. "There's no time! She's lying down in her stall, and I can't get her up."

Kate plainly didn't understand the significance, but Sabrina and Hunter did. They exchanged glances, chilled by the ominous ramifications of a horse too ill to stand. "Hunter?" Sabrina touched his arm. "Shouldn't we call Noah?"

"How long has your horse been down?" Hunter asked.

"I'm not sure." Red-rimmed eyes blinked rapidly as Wisniewski's gaze shifted back and forth between them. "She was up when I left her this morning. When I got back an hour ago with the trailer, she was down." He swallowed hard. "I bought me a ranch." He jerked his chin toward Kathleen. "*She* found it, made the arrangements for me. I was planning on moving 'em today—got their new stalls all fixed—you gotta come," he rasped.

"All right, Gabe. Hang on." Hunt picked up a cordless phone on a table, punched in some numbers, and rattled off some instructions for the vet.

"Why're you doing this?" Gabe growled the instant Hunter disconnected. "What's in it for you?"

Hunt smiled a little. "Your property—or at least the place where you're living at the moment—borders Montclair, doesn't it? That makes us neighbors. Actually, Kate here might have mentioned that I promised over a month ago to get up there, introduce myself."

"Kathleen!"

"Why?" He glared from Hunter to Kathleen. Sabrina was beginning to feel like a photograph hanging, unnoticed, on the wall.

A light seemed to glow in the back of Hunter's eyes, gathering brightness as he stood watching the bristling man. After a minute he stepped forward and gave Gabe a friendly slap on the back. "Let's just say I love my horses as much as you love yours. Besides, there might come a time when I'll need a favor from *you*."

Since Gabe refused to sit, Kathleen joined Sabrina on the sofa, leaving Gabe to Hunter. She gave Sabrina a rueful look. "You must think all I do is barge into homes, uninvited and unannounced."

"This time I think you barged for a good cause," Sabrina returned.

They talked little, mostly listening to Hunter subtly calming Gabe, at the same time learning tidbits of information about him and his two horses. Eight interminable minutes passed before the sound of boots treading rapidly down the hall brought Kathleen and Sabrina to their feet. Noah Dickerson, Montclair's longtime veterinarian, strode into the room, carrying his black bag. He nodded. "Okay, I'm here. Let's get going."

"We'll follow you, Gabe," Hunter added, then glanced over at Kathleen. "Or did you drive him?"

"He called from a convenience store. Dale paged me, and I met him at the gate outside Montclair." She stood, slicking back her hair with long-nailed hands. "I'd tag along if I could, but I have an appointment in—" she glanced at a slim gold watch—"less than forty-five minutes. So, y'all will have to let me know about Janis." Sabrina watched her silent exchange with Hunter—another of those intimate glances that twisted her heart. "The bossy Texas bully won't be cluttering up the landscape." With a last fluttering wave, she disappeared out the door.

"Can we quit the yapping?" Gabe shifted restlessly. "I gotta get back to Janis." His gaze switched to Noah. "I'll be watching every move you make, so don't think you can get away with any tricks."

"There won't be any *tricks*," Noah promised. He paused at the door. "Gabe, I can't promise to save her life until I see her. Understand? I can only promise to do my best."

"You save Janis, you hear? I don't care how much it costs. I'll pay . . . just save my horse."

"Gabe, would you mind if I came along?" Sabrina blurted. "I won't get in the way—I might even be able to help."

Gabe snorted. "Females! Nothing but trouble."

"I might be a female, but I also understand fear. And I know what it means to lose something dear to you," Sabrina shot back.

"Aw . . . come on then!" Gabe growled. "But stay out of my way. I got no use for women, especially women like that pushy Winthrop dame." He swiveled, almost lost his balance, then stomped around them and headed for the door. Sabrina noticed for the first time that he was limping. "I'll be outside in my truck."

Hunter walked over to Sabrina, his expression sober. "This might be ugly," he warned. "Are you sure you want to come?"

Sabrina wasn't at all sure, but she nodded. "He seems . . . so alone," she faltered, fumbling for words. "I know how that feels." Never more so than when she watched Hunter with other riders . . . Stu and Carla . . . the stable hands. Even Gabe had received the unshuttered warmth of Hunt's personality. Only with Sabrina did he wall off a large chunk of himself.

The way she had walled herself off from him—and everyone else.

Hunter was looking down at her that way now—veiled eyes, watchful, reserved. "I know you do," he admitted quietly. A muscle in his jaw twitched. "But there's nothing I can do right now to help.

So let's go where we *can* help—something I should have done weeks ago."

"Hunter, you're not responsible for the whole world."

"Maybe not." He tucked a strand of her hair behind her ear, the tips of his fingers brushing against her skin. "But I *am* responsible for living my faith in my own little corner of it. So . . . one last thing, Sabrina. We didn't have a chance to finish our discussion. There's something I want you to think about on the drive up to Gabe's place." His gaze burned into hers. "God feels Gabe Wisniewski's fear and pain, just as He feels yours. Even when you're hostile. Or hopeless. Even when you're full of fear, Sabrina. He understands how much you hurt. And He wants to help, because His love is far more powerful than your fear—or Gabe's."

Stricken, poised on the edge of a chasm too deep to see the bottom and too wide to jump, Sabrina stared up at him mutely.

Hunter's expression softened. "Someday—soon, I hope—you'll understand. You may *feel* empty inside, but you're not. God's Spirit moved in there, a while back, and His love really is enough to drive all that fear away. Now come on. Let's see what we can do to help teach Gabe that there are still some decent folks left in the world."

On first sight, Gabe Wisniewski's homestead could have been mistaken for an abandoned dump. Hunt wished he'd talked Sabrina into staying behind at Montclair; he had never enjoyed taking a course sight unseen. "Maybe you should wait in the Jeep," he suggested, pulling to a halt next to Gabe's rust-covered pickup in front of a dilapidated two-stall barn with a flimsy paddock attached.

"I'll stay out of the way."

"It's not that." Hunter waited until Noah grabbed his bag and headed after Gabe. "Wisniewski's pretty . . . unstable right now, and there's no telling how he'll react if Noah can't do anything to save that horse."

Sabrina slid across the seat and stepped out of the Jeep. "Don't worry about me." Without another word she followed the vet, and short of tying her inside the vehicle with some of the rope used to piece together Wisniewski's homemade fencing, Hunt didn't have a lot of choice.

"She's afraid of people," Gabe was explaining to Noah. "Some *other* no-count lowlife in the past worked her over real bad—not *me*."

He sounded both defensive and fearful. In fact, he reminded Hunter of Sabrina, which told Hunter more than he wanted to know about his own feelings toward her. Resigned, he tromped across the snow-covered slope.

". . . and then I trained Joplin, her baby. Easy, there, girl, you're squishing my toes." Gabe had unhooked the latch to one of the stalls, and a young filly with surprisingly good conformation eagerly stepped out into the aisle. She nuzzled Gabe, snorting playfully, and without hesitation welcomed Noah's touch as well, butting her head against his chest. "She missed me," Gabe said, rubbing Joplin's forelock. "Don't like it when I'm gone so long."

"She's lovely," Sabrina ventured, though Hunt was pleased to see that she stood back a little, not crowding Gabe.

He ignored the compliment. "Doc . . . you gotta save Janis. But I don't know how she'll act. She's only got used to me this last month."

"I'll be careful," Noah promised. He glanced inside the stall next to Joplin's. Hunt was not encouraged by his vet's expression. "Hello, little lady. Will you let me inside to see if I can help?"

Hunt took Sabrina's arm. "Let's leave them alone for a little while," he murmured in her ear.

They walked back toward the car, boots crunching in the new-fallen snow, breath spiraling upward into the pearl-gray afternoon sky. Sabrina shivered. "I couldn't see Janis, but Joplin's a sweetheart."

"She's got Arabian lines, as well as Thoroughbred. Did you notice?"

Sabrina nodded. "Long legs and a nice deep chest. She'd be a honey of a jumper—" She stopped and pressed her gloved hand over her mouth.

"It's in your blood, just like it's in mine," Hunter said. "You can bury yourself all you want, but it'll never go away, will it?" He gazed around Wisniewski's meager domain, a minimally cleared couple of acres at the top of a smallish mountain, dwarfed by the surrounding peaks. A ramshackle cabin sat forlornly beneath a clump of ponderosa pine some twenty yards beyond the parked vehicles. "I wonder what Gabe's been hiding from?"

"Everybody hides from something, every now and then." Sabrina studied the cabin, then Hunter. "Even you. I wish I . . ."

"You wish what?" Hunter prodded after it became clear she wasn't going to finish the thought.

"Nothing. Can we go see what's happening? I'd like to make friends with Joplin, at least."

"Still hiding, Sabrina?"

"Of course. After all, that *is* what I manage best."

Torn between amusement and frustration, Hunter trailed after her. Halfway across, Noah reappeared, wiping his hands on a towel.

Sabrina ran to meet him. "How is she, Noah? Will she be all right?"

Noah's expression was grave. He waited until Hunter approached, then gave them his prognosis. "She's in pretty bad shape, and I can't promise she'll pull through. She's suffering from a variety of ailments—pneumonia, influenza, an abscessed hoof. . . . I'll have to come back to do an endoscopic exam. Possibly try another antibiotic if the one I brought with me doesn't do any good."

Sabrina had turned pale. Hunt met the vet's gaze. Pneumonia and influenza were bad enough, but a hoof infection could cause permanent lameness. "How did Gabe take it?"

Noah shook his head. "Not too well. He threatened to take a shotgun to me when I broke the news. He's done a good job with her, and I confess I'm frankly amazed, considering the looks of things." He dug inside his parka for his gloves. "I think he managed to get just enough of the pills the last vet left down her to give her a fighting chance. As for the hoof—" He shrugged. "Gabe's care and the good Lord's help might make the difference. I've seen what people who love their horses are willing to go through, but that man carries it to new heights." He hesitated, then added dryly, "Hunt, we'd best watch him as closely as the mare. If she doesn't make it, I'm afraid he might really use that shotgun on me."

Hunt's mouth thinned. While Noah headed for the Jeep, he and Sabrina approached the little shed that housed the two horses. The raw lumber and unskilled workmanship could not disguise the effort it had taken for a man with only one hand to achieve.

They halted just inside. Gabe was weeping, tears thickening the gravely voice as he pleaded with Janis to get well. Without thinking, Hunt's arm wrapped around Sabrina's shoulders. He felt her quiver and realized she was fighting tears herself.

God help us all, he prayed, wishing he could find the words, suddenly feeling hopelessly inadequate.

They peered into the stall. Fortunately, Gabe's back was to the aisle, and he gave no indication that he was aware of their presence. The mare's head lay cradled in his lap, her breathing noisy, labored. She looked pathetically malnourished. Hunt thought of the rows of sleekly groomed, well-fed animals bristling with health back at Montclair, and he was overcome by a wave of shame so forceful it almost knocked him to his knees.

The drive back to Montclair was accomplished in gloomy silence.

Twenty-Six

$\mathcal{E}$very Thanksgiving Day, Montclair opened its doors to a stream of people from all walks of life, Sabrina learned—from local families who enjoyed the chance to rub elbows with Hunter Buchanan, to homeless winos transported from outlying towns to Montclair in the Center's van. Hunter, Jody warned her in fond exasperation, never turned anyone away.

"Do they ever run out of food?"

Jody twirled one of her corn row braids between two fingers, looking puzzled. "You know, it's really weird. Even when as many as a hundred people show up, we've never run out of food in the six years I've worked here. In fact, there's usually a lot left over, and Hunt has the kitchen staff fix up baskets for people to take home."

Sabrina typed in some information on-screen and saved it, marveling at the complexities of Hunter Buchanan's personality. For Sabrina, holidays meant either dinner for two with Uncle Sebastian, or a noisy meal with Renee and Evan's brood. Even in competition, she had never enjoyed crowds, though her background and training enabled her to hide her discomfort. This Thanksgiving promised to be . . . interesting, since Hunter had insisted she stay at Montclair.

"You've got to help me convince Gabe to show up," he'd joked. Then, with a teasing shudder, "You've also got to shield me from Kate."

Sabrina didn't mind helping convince Gabe, but Kathleen Winthrop was way out of her league on every level except financial. Still,

Hunter had told Sabrina he wanted her to stay, and weakling that she was, she agreed.

Naturally, Uncle Sebastian had been delighted. "I'll have all my grand nieces and nephews crawling over me, so don't you worry about me, Little Bit. . . ."

Sabrina glanced across at Jody. "When I asked Hunter why he goes to all this trouble, instead of just enjoying a quiet family celebration, he told me these people *are* family."

"Except for some distant cousins somewhere down South, he doesn't have any blood relatives left, you know. Not since his father died. I think he started throwing these shindigs a couple of years after that."

"How come you chose to stay here instead of flying home to be with *your* family, Jody? Didn't you tell me you were from Chicago?"

Jody stared at her, then lifted one shoulder indifferently. "I thought you knew. I ran away from 'home'—such as it was—when I was twelve. Couldn't take any more of my stepdad's abuse. My mom was killed in crossfire shooting between rival gangs when I was ten, and I tried to put up with my stepdad because of my kid sister and two brothers." Her face closed up.

"I'm so sorry. I . . . didn't know."

"Yeah—it's okay. Anyway, Hunt caught me shoplifting when he was up in Chicago once. Instead of turning me in, he found a shelter where I could . . . well, clean up my act. Then he talked me into taking night classes to finish high school, and by that time I would have eaten nails for him. He promised me a job if I kept up my grades, and . . . here I am." Suddenly she smiled. "He's all right—for a horseman."

Sabrina nodded, her throat tight. She wondered if she would ever fully understand the man. "He's overly fond of getting his own way, if you ask me," she eventually retorted to lighten the atmosphere.

For several moments they continued to work, but Sabrina's mind was only half on her assorted tasks. She couldn't help but wonder how much of Hunter's behavior toward *her* was due to his oversized conscience. Wasn't she just another hard-luck case in need of patching up, like Jody?

Even though she was in love with him, it was love without a future. She should have flown home for Thanksgiving. The dorms were closed for cleaning, and there were no students left in residence—

except for Sabrina, who had been moved into a guest room up at the big house. So much for pride.

"Do you have the total number expected for the fancy bash?" Jody called over her shoulder.

The "fancy bash" was Montclair's famous Open House, given the Saturday after Thanksgiving, in which guests from the horse set streamed in and out of the estate from four until nine. Caterers from Denver were hired, and a string quartet played classical music. The contrast between the Open House and Thanksgiving Day defied imagination, everyone informed her, though Hunter only grinned and shrugged over the incongruity.

"The Open House helps keep Montclair economically afloat, in spite of the expense. It's great PR. And I suppose I enjoy it. These parties have been part of Montclair's history for half a century now." Incredibly, he'd looked embarrassed. "But Thanksgiving Day means more to me personally. *That's* what the holiday is about. I . . . well, I guess I need them both."

Sabrina wasn't wild about eating with strangers on Thanksgiving Day, but she didn't know how she would endure five hours of socializing among people she had known in her past life on the show circuit. All of whom would want to know why she was apparently *living* at Montclair. . . .

She glanced down at the list of names in front of her. "Eight more last-minute acceptances, three regrets." Panic surged, then was ruthlessly subdued—not without difficulty. It had been a really *bad* idea, giving in to Hunter on this.

She should have flown home. She should *not* be staying here, even if she rarely saw Hunter outside of her lessons, which he insisted on maintaining for the sake of appearances . . . and Sabrina's welfare, he had assured her.

Jody returned from the room across the hall, her arms full of office supplies. "How many usually show up for the Open House?" Sabrina asked.

"Upwards of three hundred, though thankfully not all at the same time, of course. The drive looks like that scene from *Field Of Dreams*. This year there will probably be even more." Jody's chocolate brown eyes swept a resigned look over Sabrina. "*You're* here."

"I tried to talk Hunter into letting me fly home. You saw how much headway I made." Sabrina kept her face averted, pretending to examine something on the computer monitor.

Jody was unimpressed. "Only because you didn't really want to go. We both know the boss can charm mountains into moving, but if you'd dug in your heels, he would have driven you to the airport himself."

Wisely, Sabrina dropped the subject. "I've got everything under control here, I think. I'm going to run down to the barn a minute and see if Noah's returned from Gabe's place yet."

"That's right. Leave me alone to be buried alive in paper work. Those two kids Hunt hired to help with this infernal Open House are a joke. I don't know why—"

Sabrina fled, knowing by now that Jody's constant carping was more habit than genuine complaint. She hurried down the hall and up the back stairs, which Hunter had teasingly told her would have been the servants' stairs a century ago at the original estate back in Virginia. "But everyone out here's liberated, western-style," he told her. "In fact, Elsa derives great pleasure in sailing up and down that monstrous set of stairs in the main hallway, even if these are more convenient."

Hunter. . . .

Sabrina was grateful for the relentless beehive of activity the past weeks, for it had provided her needed breathing room. She continued to ride—alone now—twice a day, gentle warm-ups in the arena. She never allowed Lady Fair beyond a trot—as per Hunter's explicit instructions. Now that she was riding again, his behavior toward her bounced between obsession, solicitude—and indifference. Sabrina could handle the first two, but his offhand, casual treatment *during* her lessons the past month had become a creeping hurt she could not contain. He wouldn't even shout at her, as she had suggested, to see if she could handle his normal teaching style.

"What for?" he told her. "You're not going to compete, so why toughen your hide?"

She really detested it when he used that bland, reasonable tone of voice with her.

"But I gave my word," he went on, "that I'd have you back to form before you left—just as you gave your word to do as I asked." Then he'd leaned forward and brushed a fleeting kiss against her tightly pressed lips, completely shredding her concentration. Not to mention her aggravation. "Now let's try a posting trot, from letter

B. Relax your hands and your back. . . . Go, Sabrina."

I ought to go, Sabrina thought now as she climbed the stairs. *All the way back to Virginia.*

Elsa was hurrying down the upstairs hall, arms laden with linens. "Señorita, you are finished in the office?"

"Well, let's just say I've temporarily escaped. I want to see if Noah's back so I can find out how Gabe's mare is doing."

"The boss . . . he is not pleased that your attention is divided." The housekeeper towered over her. Even with an armful of towels, Elsa Menendez manifested a calm authority.

Sabrina bristled. "I know, but I don't see that there's a lot I can do about it."

"Hmph." The penetrating black eyes searched her face. "You can spend less time in the office—more in the barn. Also you can quit running off to Bald Mountain. *Ay de mi*, it's like waving the flag at el toro every time you leave the Center."

"Hunter visits Gabe almost as much as I do." Hands on her hips, Sabrina returned the housekeeper's penetrating glare. "Elsa, did Hunter put you up to this lecture, by any chance?"

The housekeeper swelled to her full height and looked down her nose at Sabrina. "You disappoint me even to mention it." She shifted the towels, her expression set. "Señorita, you must know something. For over thirty years I work here at Montclair. I watch the boss grow from boy to man. I watch the señorita he ask to marry him spit and claw and try to make him love her like he love Montclair. Señor Buchanan always kind. Always . . . gentle with her. But in the end, he did not marry her. Now—"

Elsa paused, shaking her head and mumbling in Spanish. Then, "He is . . . uneasy in his heart." She looked straight at Sabrina. "Do not hurt this man, señorita. He is a good man . . . a godly man. But, of course, it is none of my affair." Still muttering under her breath, she bustled off to attend to her duties, leaving Sabrina in stunned silence.

Hurt him? What in the world was the woman talking about? How could *Sabrina* hurt Hunter Buchanan? A disturbing possibility dawned. Had he picked up the signals that she'd fallen in love with him and felt uncomfortable dealing with that?

Oh, brother! she thought, hurriedly bundling up for the trek to the barn. She'd been so selfishly consumed with her own problems that she'd failed to consider *Hunter's*.

Yet *why* did he take advantage of every opportunity to *kiss* her? It didn't make sense. Hunter was neither a flirt nor a womanizer. He never lost control—or almost never. To be honest, Sabrina *enjoyed* those brief interludes—probably invited them. She couldn't help it. His every touch, his every look filled her with a dizzying warmth, a painful yearning. In spite of the chasm between them and all her uncertainties about the future, when she was with Hunter, she forgot about the fear, forgot about her lost faith . . . even forgot that she was living a fantasy.

Noah was just climbing out of one of Montclair's utility vehicles when she reached the barn. "Janis was on her feet when I left her," he greeted Sabrina, quiet satisfaction in the words. "And she's been eating the mash I recommended to Gabe. Hoof still doesn't look as well as I'd like, but I think we're about to kick the flu and pneumonia."

"I'm glad," Sabrina returned, almost adding, "Thank God!" But the words stuck in her throat. "How's Gabe?"

"Cantankerous as ever, except with his two babies." Noah squinted in the afternoon sun, shaking his head. "He still doesn't plan to attend the Thanksgiving dinner here, by the way. He's antsy to move. Ms. Winthrop told me the other day Gabe's wearing himself to the bone fixing up Rolling Rock in between nursing those two horses. He pesters the life out of me every time I check Janis, wanting to know how much longer before he can move them."

"He just wants them to have a better life," Sabrina murmured. "He's really kind of sweet, and Hunter tells me he's some kind of Vietnam war hero."

"Yeah. Saved his platoon commander's life. That's when he lost his arm and took a hit in his leg. The commander's father was so grateful that he set up a perpetual annuity for Gabe. That's the good part." Noah shifted his gaze to the distant peaks. "The sad thing is that when he was shipped home, his young wife couldn't handle his injuries. Divorced him before he ever left the hospital."

"No wonder he's so bitter toward women." Sabrina let out a long breath. "But he's wonderful with horses. Joplin follows him around like an overgrown lap dog." In spite of herself, a wistful note crept into her voice.

"Hunt told me how you raised your horse from a colt. Vesuvius, wasn't it? Must be tough to watch Gabe with those two animals of his."

She could feel Noah's eyes studying her as she gazed at the vivid orange sunset splashing the western sky and spilling over the snow-capped peaks. "It's getting better. That's one reason I go up there so often. I've seen how Gabe shuts people out, focuses all his love and attention on Janis and Joplin." She tried to smile. "In a crazy sort of way, it's helped me see that I'm not the only one who's lost something or someone they loved." She shrugged, suddenly feeling awkward. "But I'm keeping you from your work. You'll be here tomorrow, won't you?"

"As long as there are no emergencies." He patted her on the back. "You'll do fine, Sabrina Mayhew. You're all right."

So she was—worlds better than she'd been six months earlier. But when she finally *did* leave Montclair, she wondered how long it would take her heart to stop yearning for the man she would leave behind.

⁊⁊⁊⁊⁊

Thanksgiving Day passed in a flurry of snapshot impressions, all of them bittersweet, because they only bound Sabrina's heart more thoroughly to Hunter Buchanan. He had dressed casually for the day in corduroy slacks and a soft rust-colored cashmere sweater, and Sabrina's eye found him even in the crowd.

Hunter . . . moving among the tables set up at the dorm cafeteria, serving his guests, chatting easily, his heart-stopping smile embracing everyone.

Hunter . . . blessing the food, his voice deep and sincere as he offered a simple prayer of thanks that brought a lump to Sabrina's throat. When he opened his eyes, he looked around at the sea of faces. "This is a day when we celebrate all the blessings God has given us." His expression sobered. "But there may be some here today who feel they have little for which to be thankful. In fact, the last thing some of you may feel like doing is thanking the Almighty for a mountain-load of trouble."

Hunter searched out Sabrina's face, and it was as if he could read what was written in her heart. "We aren't expected to thank God *for* the mountain, but we can be thankful that He's always there, ready to help us *climb* it. All we have to do is trust enough to ask. . . . Now, everyone enjoy your meal."

How could she *not* love this man?

How *dare* she love him, when he was utterly devoted to God, and her own spiritual life was such a hopeless snarl?

By the time Sabrina fell into bed late that night, she had decided to borrow one of the Center's vehicles and escape to Denver. She'd never make it through the Open House on Saturday. No way. *I can't do it. I'll have an attack . . . I can't*—

The Open House reminded her of the parties she and Renee used to attend with Uncle Sebastian, growing up in Virginia's horse country. Only Montclair, like the West itself, did everything on a far grander scale. Laughter and talk echoed through the huge estate, lit up from top to bottom and decorated in fall colors. "Christmas decorations have to wait until the first of December," Hunter's mother had always insisted, he'd told Sabrina, so he dutifully carried on the family tradition.

Wearing a royal blue sleeveless gown with a flowing skirt that swirled about her ankles, Sabrina spent the first torturous hour greeting guests and answering their painful questions, a smile pasted across her face. Then Hunter had appeared at her side, smoothly drawing her out of the crowd and into a deserted room. In the background, muffled strains of Vivaldi filtered down the hall. "You look breathtaking," he told her. "And you're a lifesaver. Thanks for staying and helping out—both Jody and Elsa assure me they wouldn't have made it without you." Then he cupped her face in his hands, kissed her, and disappeared from the room.

Sabrina's uncertainty shattered like exploding crystal. A fluttering joy blossomed, softening her smile, buoying her spirits so that somehow it didn't seem to matter any longer that she was in the spotlight, her miraculous return to the equestrian world the favorite topic of conversation. She deflected pointed questions with serene good humor and somehow played the part of hostess with, if not enthusiasm, at least enough of Renee's panache to survive the endless evening with her poise intact.

Not an attack in sight. And all because of Hunter . . . and a few breathless moments alone with him.

Sabrina, you really are a limp-willed noodle.

Twenty-Seven

*E*ight inches of snow blanketed Montclair the second week of December. Hunt shook a mental fist at the weather, then pitched in to help complete the never-ending tasks necessary to keep the Center on an even keel throughout the winter months. Several paths and one arena were kept cleared and sanded to guarantee the horses a dose of fresh air and freedom. Lessons, however, remained indoors. The newly paved driveway was plowed almost weekly for the safety of arriving and departing horse trailers.

A frosty blue sky belied the previous day's snowstorm. Morning sunbeams cast prisms of light through the icicles spilling in frozen splendor from the roof of the barn. Hunt grinned and shivered inside the bulky layers of clothing. It was a beautiful day, even if the mercury in the thermometer wasn't expected to rise above twenty degrees. Sadly, few of the eleven students at Montclair this week would agree.

Riders born and bred in warmer climates, especially from back East, tended to complain the most. One of these years, he ought to hire someone to write a paper on the psychological advantages of testing yourself outside a familiar environment. Horses born and bred out here in the Rockies, to Hunt's way of thinking, were some of the strongest in the country—possibly the world. Their lungs were stronger because of the altitude; their legs stronger because of the terrain. Surely people could adapt as well.

Inevitably, his thoughts returned to Sabrina. Since Thanksgiving, improvements in her lessons had leveled out to the point that Hunt had made the decision the previous evening to move her to the next step. Still, he dreaded the possible consequences even though he'd called Dr. Rowan to discuss it.

"Is there a chance this will cause her to regress?" he'd asked the psychologist.

"Possibly. But I don't think either of you will be content if you don't give it a try. This is a process, remember. People overcome a fear of snakes, for example, by finally arriving at the point where they can actually handle them. What you're doing with Sabrina is preparing to hand her a live snake instead of a rubber one. Let me know how it goes."

Hunt only hoped it wouldn't be Sabrina doing the going—away from Montclair.

The past weeks had been difficult for Hunt. He had watched her advance with each lesson. Something inside his chest ached every time he watched her riding Lady Fair with newfound confidence—a confidence not limited to horses. Hunt remembered her miraculous rebirth the night of the Open House, when he had forced her to jump yet another barrier she'd raised against her past. When she descended the staircase that afternoon, she had taken his breath away, looking as elegant and poised as a queen in her designer gown. Even the imperturbable Elsa had approved.

Of course, Sabrina had reverted to her mannequin pose, hiding, Hunt knew, all her anxiety and discomfort. Arriving guests stymied his efforts to do anything about it then. Hunt had only been able to take her arm, introduce her, and leave her to fend for herself. At the time he'd felt as though he were tossing a helpless kid to a pack of hungry wolves.

That was the only reason, he'd been telling himself ever since, for his behavior later in the evening. He knew he shouldn't have risked Sabrina's reputation by dragging her off and kissing her. Yet the reward had been more than worth the risk. Afterward she had practically glowed. People would be talking about her return for months, which was precisely the effect Hunt had anticipated.

Keep telling yourself that, old man. By all means, refuse to examine the real *reason the woman had melted like snow in summer.*

It was much easier, and far safer, to nourish his frustration over Sabrina's insane notion about competing. Much easier to rail at her because her obstinancy threatened all his carefully laid plans. Infuriating filly!

But though Sabrina made him irritable and uneasy, all she had to do was turn that solemn face and those vulnerable eyes in his direction, and he was a goner. That's when he wanted—God help him—to take her in his arms and kiss away the shadows. For the first time in his life, Hunt was at a loss for answers, and for some reason the Lord wasn't choosing to supply any.

Sabrina would be satisfied to be free enough of her fear to ride a hack just for pleasure, when the mood struck. As a pleasant break after a hard day's work sitting at her *computer*.

But what she needed was to *compete* again. He knew that she would never be the person she used to be unless she went into the ring as a competitor.

Hunt stalked into the barn. He didn't have all the answers, but he was through waiting. And whether she knew it or not, Sabrina was through stalling.

⁘

"Mornin', boss. Nice day."

"Morning, Jay. You always *did* have a gift for understatement." Hunt shed his down parka, ski cap, and gloves and grabbed a crash helmet. "Is Tiny Tim ready?"

"He's ready. But I'm not so sure about Sabrina." The wiry groom scratched his chin and leveled a thoughtful gaze on Hunt. "You didn't warn her, did you? She's down in Lady Fair's stall, don't you know, readying the mare for her lesson."

"With Sabrina, warning only breeds anxiety. I want her warming up on Lady Fair. She'll be more relaxed that way."

"You've done a nice job with her, boss. When I remember what she was like that first week . . ."

"Thanks, though I'm not sure how much credit *I* deserve." Hunt took a deep breath. "You might say a prayer or two for me, if you will, so that you don't have to take back the kind words."

She was walking Lady Fair when, leading an impatient Tiny Tim, Hunt entered the ring. He patted the stallion's muscled neck, calming the spirited animal. When Sabrina caught sight of them, he watched a bucketful of expressions spill across her face.

"This is Tiny Tim," he casually announced. "I've been training him for the past several months and decided this might be a good day to accomplish a couple of things at the same time." He tightened the cinch while he spoke, then vaulted into the saddle. Tiny Tim snorted and instantly tried to move out. Hunt grinned. "Feisty fellow, as you can see."

"Yes." The wary look had faded, and Sabrina smiled. "Must be the cold weather. The snow's great, isn't it? I don't know why everyone complains."

"Spoken like a native Coloradan." He guided Tiny Tim into place beside Lady Fair. "Let's try walking tandem. I need to train him to be more tractable around other horses. When we reach letter H, move ahead of me and into a slow trot. All right?"

For twenty minutes they worked in companionable accord. When Tiny Tim had settled down and Sabrina had lost the last trace of unease, Hunt signaled a halt in the middle of the ring. "Looking good. Now let's trade so I can watch. He's still having trouble picking up the signal for a left-leading canter. Maybe if I watch what he does when someone else is in the saddle—"

"Hunter? I'd . . . I'd rather not." She bit her lip, looking down at Lady's neck.

"I know." He slid off Tiny Tim and held the reins close behind the bit. "But it's time, Sabrina." He waited until she met his gaze. "Trust me?"

For the first time in recent weeks, panic darkened the nutmeg brown eyes, and the rosy glow in her cheeks faded. "I—" she glanced at Tiny Tim—"I don't know. . . ."

"He's a bit like Vesuvius, isn't he? Impatient, strong-willed, needing that firm leg and light hand? You'd be good for him, Sabrina." He reached up and his hand closed over hers. "Look at it this way. If you fall, the sand is softer than the ground, and he's well-trained enough to stop instantly." Hunt had spent the last four months insuring that particular habit. "Come on. You can do it."

He watched her, a confident, relaxed smile firmly in place. What he *wanted* to do was haul her off Lady Fair and toss her on Tiny Tim— after kissing her thoroughly. She'd be so flustered she probably wouldn't have the wit to be afraid, until it didn't matter.

Hmm. Not a bad idea, Hunt.

His smile broadened to a reckless grin, and without further warning, he whipped his arm around her waist and tugged her out of the saddle, never releasing his hold on Tiny Tim. Lady Fair shifted but didn't move.

"Hunter, what are you—"

He silenced her with a kiss, holding her close. She stiffened, her hands pushing against his chest. For a fraction of a second Hunt himself almost panicked. Then Sabrina thawed and kissed him back with a passion that matched his own. Her arms crept around his neck and . . . their crash helmets bumped together, ending the moment in a spontaneous burst of laughter.

At the disturbance, Tiny Tim snorted and half reared, almost jerking the reins from Hunt's grasp. He released Sabrina, setting her down gently, then turned to quiet the stallion. "I think Tiny Tim's jealous," he murmured.

Then, because Sabrina was standing there, looking as stunned as Hunter felt, he summoned a smile. "I won't apologize . . . you looked too irresistible." His fingers caressed her shoulder, then slid down to close around her wrist. "Now it's your turn. Come along. I'll give you a leg up."

In an instant she was in the saddle, looking down at him with that wrenching blend of bewilderment and doubt. Hunt handed her the reins. "He's not Lady. You'll have to control him. But you can do it, Sabrina. Trust me—trust yourself. Okay?"

She swallowed hard and blinked twice. Then she took a deep breath, gathered the reins, and nodded. "I can do it." A wavering smile flickered and grew. "I can do this," she repeated more strongly.

And so she did . . . until Tiny Tim decided he was tired of a slow trot, leaping without warning or instruction into a frustrated canter. Sabrina panicked, the stallion erupted into a runaway gallop, and she crashed onto the arena floor to lie in a motionless heap.

꩜

At the sound of an engine, Gabe glanced up, a furious scowl darkening his face when he caught sight of the driver. Blamed interfering females! They were crawling out of the woodwork these days. What in tarnation was so fascinating about his crummy two-bit spread that kept bringing Sabrina Mayhew back, anyway? He'd tried for weeks to keep her away, but even downright rudeness didn't work. He hunched inside his leather bomber jacket, pulled the brim of his Stetson lower, and turned to Joplin.

"You're no help," he growled when Joplin nickered a greeting. "Soft-headed mule. Just because she brings you treats—"

"Hi, Gabe."

He grunted and pretended to be checking Joplin's hooves for packed snow and stones.

"I . . . just wanted to see how Janis and Joplin were getting along."

Gabe straightened. There was a pleading note in her voice today he hadn't heard before. "They're fine. If that's all you came for, you can crank up that Jeep and get off my mountain."

Her face went frozen and blank as a snowbank. She searched his face, then switched her gaze to the shed. For some reason, Gabe felt lower than a snake's belly. "Aw, go on and have a look, if you got to. Won't hurt, I expect. Just don't try to pat her."

"I won't." She trudged through the snow, head down, shoulders slumped.

In spite of everything, he was curious. And when Joplin trotted along the fence after Sabrina, Gabe gave in, stomping after her and swearing every step. He wanted to tell the prissy female to cut the act and stay away. Janis and Joplin were *his*, and he had no intention of sharing them. Once he made the move to the Rolling Rock, he'd be rid of her *and* that sneaky realtor.

While Sabrina was standing there looking at Janis, her hands clasped behind her back so she wouldn't risk spooking the mare, he got a good look at her face. "What happened?"

"I . . . fell." She turned so Gabe could no longer see the swollen, blue-tinged scrape along her cheekbone. "Janis is looking really good. Noah said he was pleased." She hesitated, then added tentatively, as though she expected him to bite her head off, "He said you deserve all the credit."

A flush burned up Gabe's neck. "I . . . she let me lead her out of the stall yesterday. It's the first time," he blurted out, busting with the news, with the need to tell someone, even if it was a nosy, interfering woman.

She turned back then, and her smile made his flush deepen. "That's wonderful. What about her foot? Noah did say he was still a little worried."

He was instantly on guard. "I been bathing it in ice water, just like I was told, and turnin' her round the stall. What's the matter? Think a cripple can't do the job right?"

"Not at all," Sabrina returned. She sounded distant again, and the light had gone out of her face. "I'm sorry you took it that way. I came up here because I wanted to see Janis and Joplin, not to bother you." She walked out of the shed, ducked through the fence, and headed toward her car.

She said something else, but Gabe didn't catch the words. "What did you say?" he demanded, trailing after her. "Hang it all—quit your pouting. I didn't mean nothing." He wiped the back of his hand over his mouth, fiddled with the brim of his hat, then gruffly added, "Sorry, then."

"It's all right. I was invading your privacy. Trust me, I know how it feels when someone forces you out—" She bit her lip. "When are you moving to your new ranch?"

"Doc says Janis can travel in another week. If the weather cooperates, I'll have 'em settled by the end of December."

"That's great. Hunter's told me about your plan to take in old and unwanted horses. He's going to help, I know, but he told me it was your idea." She looked wistful and weepy-eyed all of a sudden. "It must make you feel really good, knowing that you'll be helping. . . ." At that moment Joplin thrust her head over the fence and nudged Sabrina. She smiled and dug around in her jacket pocket, tugging out a carrot. "Here. You really are a spoiled brat, aren't you?"

Gabe's hand came up defensively to rub Joplin's jaw. "She just needs someone to care about her is all."

"She reminds me of my horse," Sabrina whispered.

In the brutal white light of the midday December sunlight, the red scrape on her cheekbone against her pale skin made her look curiously defenseless. Gabe had never known a woman like this one. For some reason, his softness toward her made him angry. "I guess your horse is like all the others at your fancy-pants place, all sleek and pampered. Does he have hot and cold running water in his stall? Do you feed him out of a solid brass bucket?"

"No." After a painful moment of silence, she lifted one hand, then dropped it. "He's dead, Gabe. He was killed four years ago during a show. I . . . I was riding him. It was in the middle of a jump. A little boy in the stands popped a balloon. It startled Ves and he . . . he caught his legs in the jump. He broke his neck." She finished speaking in a voice as desolate as the naked mountaintop.

Gabe shifted awkwardly. In all his misbegotten life, he'd never felt the urge to offer comfort to another human being. To his way of thinking, none of them deserved it. But this one here—she was different. She was rich, healthy, and whole—had everything a body could hope for—yet she was hurting inside. Just like him. "What about you?" he asked. "What happened to you when your horse fell?"

"I was pretty banged up." She shrugged. "I healed on the outside. But I came here to Montclair because I needed to heal *inside*." She looked at Gabe, and after a moment he had to turn his head away. "I'm afraid, Gabe. Always afraid. Afraid to ride, afraid of new places, new circumstances. Afraid of living—" She stopped, her voice catching. "Most of all, I'm afraid because I can't control the fear, and that makes me wonder if I've lost my faith in God."

Gabe snorted.

Sabrina sighed. "I suppose you wouldn't understand." She put her hand lightly on his arm.

Gabe jerked away. He couldn't remember the last time a woman had voluntarily touched him. But when she spoke, her words cut into him like the blade of a dull axe.

"You might feel like you're only half a person, with one arm and a limp, Gabe. But I'd gladly give you my arm and two sound legs if I could stop being afraid. I want to *feel* God's presence in my life again. I'd give everything I owned to have a purpose in life like you do so that I could understand why God has spared *me* when he allowed the death of my parents . . . and my horse." She shook her head, a look of raw pain on her face. "It's *not* so I can compete again, no matter what Hunter says! There has to be more to life than—" She backed away. "I'm sorry. I—" With a muffled gasp, she whirled and high-tailed it back to the Jeep.

Gabe watched her leave, his mood vile. He removed Joplin's halter and shooed her off to frolic in the paddock a few minutes. *Blast* all women! Spitting out words like bullets, hitting below the belt . . . serve her right if she drove off the side of the mountain. She had no call to tell him what she had. No call at all.

And yet . . .

Later that night he sat on his couch, staring into the fire, thinking. How could that infernal woman set more store by all this God-stuff than to having a sound body? She wanted to "feel" some weird supernatural Presence? Wanted it more than an *arm*?

There was a catch. There *had* to be a catch . . . it was a trick. Both Sabrina and Buchanan were trying to sell him a bill of goods. Montclair's big man had a reputation for being real religious, but so far, Gabe had to admit that he was an okay kind of guy. He sure didn't shove his religion down Gabe's throat . . . or threaten him with hellfire. In fact, Buchanan had promised to help round up some names of people to contact about his idea for the ranch.

If the God these people insisted on believing in acted like Hunt Buchanan, Gabe could almost understand why Sabrina might be willing to give up an arm and two good legs. Almost. It was a shame about her fear. Blasted shame. Gabe stared into the leaping flames, his thoughts tumbling back into the distant past. Oh yeah, he knew all about fear, how it could cripple a man . . . or a woman.

"If there really is a God," he mumbled, half asleep, "He'd need to be powerful enough to pull a body free of all that fear. Sure would be a relief . . . not being scared."

Twenty-Eight

Stu was talking to one of his students at the entrance to the barn when Sabrina slipped through the door, poise barely intact. She had fought off a panic attack after leaving Gabe, but the triumph was bittersweet: inside she *felt* defeated. Worthless. As though the last confidence-building months had vanished in a puff of smoke. Sure, she'd managed to avoid the attack, but by now she shouldn't be having symptoms at all.

Why? For the first time in her life, Sabrina had wanted to scream at God. Demand answers. She was trying so hard, had accomplished so much. And for what?

From the startled look on Stu's face, her feeble effort to at least *appear* normal hadn't worked.

Sabrina nodded shortly as she hurried past them and turned down the aisle; she was not surprised when Stu caught up halfway to Nutmeg's stall.

"You still upset about this morning?" he asked without preamble. "Sabrina . . ." He ran his hand through his wiry blond hair. "What a can of worms."

"I'm okay."

"Sure you are." Stu glanced up and down the aisle, momentarily deserted. "Look, Hunt's been searching for you, in between lessons, ever since you went tearing out of the arena this morning. Give the guy a break, all right?"

A painful flush crept over her skin. "What do you mean? He knows

I wasn't badly hurt. I remounted and rode Tiny Tim for another fifteen minutes, didn't I?''

"From what Hunt *didn't* say, your lesson was still not a roaring success, especially when—his words—you ran for the hills to avoid discussing it.''

"There was nothing to say. I disappointed him. We both know it. I wasn't up to a postmortem then.'' She stared stonily at a coiled lead line hanging on a peg. "And I'm not now.'' She turned away.

"Sabrina.''

The warning in his voice halted her in her tracks. "What?''

"Go easy on the guy. He's crazy about you, and if you'd open your eyes, you'd see it as plainly as the rest of us do.''

"I'm just another one of Hunter's mercy projects—like Jody . . . and Gabe.'' Sabrina glanced over her shoulder, giving Stu a tight smile. "Someone who needs help. That's all, Stu. Don't read anything more into Hunter's actions.''

"Sure, Sabrina.'' He leaned against the wall, crossing his arms over his chest. "You want to crawl farther out on that limb and try convincing me that you're not in love with him, either? That you're only using him as a means to an end?''

The hectic color receded. So. Her secret—if there had ever been one—was out. She had been pretty naïve to believe she could hide her feelings for long. "What do you hope to accomplish, dragging it out in the open?'' she asked finally. "Did . . . did Hunter—?''

"Hunt would nail my carcass to the barn door for talking to you this way,'' Stu admitted, stepping forward to take Sabrina's shoulders in a light grip. "But he's my friend, as well as the moving force behind Montclair. I care about him. I've known the guy since we battled each other on the grand prix circuit fifteen years ago, and I've never seen him like this. Not even after he broke off his engagement. Women have thrown themselves at his feet in droves, so to speak, but none of them ever got past the starting gate. Until you.''

He studied her silently, a curious half smile curving his mouth. "You know what I think? Over the past couple of months I've watched you change from a half-dead robot to a warm, witty, very attractive woman. Frankly, I think you have a lot to offer my good friend Hunt Buchanan.''

"He doesn't want what I have to offer,'' Sabrina retorted. "It doesn't come with an agreement to go back on the grand prix circuit."

"Hey, Sabrina!" Mickey called from the end of the aisle. "Did you know the boss is tearing the place apart looking for you?"

"Where is he?" Stu called back.

"Went to the house, I think." Mickey ambled up alongside, a frown replacing his good-natured smile as he glanced from her to Stu. "Muttering about Sabrina hiding out in the office or something—say . . . you okay?"

She widened her eyes innocently. "Sure. I'm fine."

Stu turned her around and gave her a push. "Go on. Settle things. Tell Hunt I'll take his next student. I think it's George Salvadori, so it shouldn't be a problem. He's mainly here to train his new horse anyway." He paused. "Scram, Sabrina."

Sabrina scrammed.

∽◠◠◠◡∾

Hunt met her halfway up the path to the house. "It's about time! I've been looking everywhere—Sabrina?" His tone sharpened. "What's happened to you? I know you drove up to see Gabe, but you've been back over an hour—I checked with Charlie." His gaze narrowed. "Did something happen up there? Is it one of the horses? Gabe say something to you?"

"What is this—an interrogation?" She lifted her chin. Humiliation churned inside. *Everyone knew.* She might as well have hired a plane to fly over Montclair and spell out the news in skywriting. "I've been at the barn"—where she'd been put through the ringer and hung out to dry instead of doing her chores—"but I decided to see if . . . ah . . . if Jody needed any help." *Good, Sabrina. You can't even tell a lie, much less a* believable *lie.* "Actually, I've just realized I'm tired. I think I'll go rest in my room—"

"I think you'll come with me." He wrapped his arm around her shoulders and herded her down the path toward the garage.

Tension rolled from him in thunderclaps; Sabrina had never seen him look so stone-faced. And yet he wasn't angry. His eyes were more blue than gray—a dead giveaway. "Where are we going?" she asked, striving to be sane and reasonable, because she had a feeling if she dug in her heels, Hunter would simply hoist her over his shoulder and keep walking.

"Away from here."

"What about your next lesson?"

He stopped, and an indefinable expression of exasperation and incredulity washed over the grim cast of his face. "I forgot," he said blankly. "I don't believe this! I forgot." He glared down at Sabrina. "This is all your fault."

"You sound like my ten-year-old nephew." Squirming, she tried without success to break free. *Just get it over with.* Steeling herself, Sabrina took a deep breath and stared straight up into his face. "Stu told me to tell you that he'll take George Salvadori for you."

In the thickening silence Sabrina could almost hear her heart trying to climb out of her chest. Hunter had gone still, head cocked to one side, gray eyes boring into hers.

"Why would Stu do that?" he eventually asked.

She closed her eyes, but the fluttering panic only intensified. "He wanted me to talk to you."

"About—? This morning? Gabe?" Then, impatiently, "Never mind. We'll discuss it later. Come on."

Those were the last words he uttered for the next twenty minutes. They marched down to the garage, where he all but tossed her into the passenger seat of the Jeep. They were halfway down the drive before Sabrina managed to fasten her seat belt. A quarter of a mile later they rounded a curve in the road, then, to Sabrina's astonishment, turned onto a snow-covered lane. It wound around a small foothill and disappeared. Several teeth-rattling moments later, a small stone cottage appeared.

"This used to belong to the grounds keeper a million years ago," Hunter said when he finally broke the silence. He steered the Jeep to a halt directly in front of the door. "I have a key."

Sabrina looked from his set face to the cottage. The steeply-pitched roof was almost free of snow, but drifts from the storm had gathered beneath the frost-coated windows and entrance. It looked cold, dark—deserted. And private. "Are you planning to strangle me or something and hide the body?" she joked. Because she was nervous, even more confused, the feeble attempt at humor fell between them with a dull thud.

"Very funny." He drummed his fingers on the steering wheel.

"You don't really think I'd do anything to hurt you, do you?"

"Not physically, no."

"I . . . see." He stared through the windshield. "If I can start a fire, will you come inside with me so we can talk? In private . . . without a thousand interruptions?"

Sabrina nodded because she didn't trust her voice.

"Then let's go inside."

Ten minutes later Hunter joined Sabrina at the window, where she had been gazing out at the snow-shrouded landscape. "Come over by the fire," he invited. "It's not very warm yet, but it's better than freezing to death."

"I'd rather have privacy than comfort," Sabrina promised, giving him a fleeting smile. She tugged off her gloves and held her hands in front of the crackling, popping flames. Shyness flooded her all of a sudden. Should she just blurt it out—offer to leave Montclair? The least Stu could have done while he was loading her down with advice would have been to include a few pointers on precisely *how* she was supposed to "go easy on" Hunter.

He came and stood beside her. "Does your cheek hurt?"

She shook her head.

"Are you still upset that you panicked?"

"Disappointed. Frustrated . . ." She lifted her shoulders helplessly. "Depressed, I suppose. At least I managed to get back on Tiny Tim, even if I looked like a bundle of sticks." She wondered what he'd say if she told him about the barely suppressed panic attack.

"Style isn't important at the moment. I was proud of you—I wish you'd let me tell you so."

She darted a quick astonished glance at him. "I thought you were . . . disappointed and frustrated, too. You certainly looked like it."

"Well, I was—but *for* you. Not *with* you, Sabrina." He heaved a sigh. "And you scared ten years off my life when you went slamming onto the ground."

"You . . . yelled at me." All the hurt and pain and bewilderment boiled up, spilled over. She whirled and glared up into his face. "I was terrified. Then you picked me up and held me, and I felt . . . I felt— *why did you yell at me?*" She wrapped her arms around herself. "I didn't fall on purpose. I was trying as hard as I could. I shouldn't have panicked. I know that. I—" She gasped as Hunter abruptly hauled her into his arms.

"You didn't do anything wrong, Sabrina." He pressed her head against his heart, the other arm wrapped so tightly about her waist she could scarcely breathe. "I shouldn't have yelled, not when you were afraid and confused." Beneath her ear his heart pounded in deep, frantic thuds. "I just—I was angry at *myself* for forcing you to ride Tiny Tim. And—" Suddenly his hand moved to tilt her chin. In the shadowy room the firelight danced across the taut planes of his face. "I was afraid you were hurt."

His hands cupped her face then, holding it in a tender cage. "Sabrina . . . Sabrina . . . I never thought I'd ever feel this way. I'd given up, until I saw—"he dragged air into his lungs—"your photograph." His mouth descended and covered hers in a slow kiss full of passion. "Now I realize," he whispered, "I fell in love with the woman in that picture."

"What?" Sabrina felt the same sensation of dizziness and disorientation she had that morning when she'd hit the sand. "Hunter?" She wormed her hand between them to touch his jaw.

He grabbed the fingers and pressed a kiss to them. "I think I've been waiting for you for years. I know I've never felt like this about another woman—even the woman I was going to marry. Something was always missing. But with you—it's as though we've had a *connection*, somehow, ever since we met at that charity show. Then, when you came here that first time, you were so excited I thought I'd have to weigh you down with sandbags. And when you were riding, you soared. And I wanted . . . I wanted—"

Beneath her fingers, Sabrina felt heat steal into his face. "I'm mangling this." He closed his eyes and took another deep, shuddering breath. "I love you, Sabrina Mayhew. I never thought I'd say that to a woman again, but as God as my witness, I do love you."

His arms tightened, and Sabrina knew he felt her trembling. She laid her head on his chest and struggled to comprehend. Hunter . . . *loved* her?

"Sabrina"—his voice was agonized—"say something. . . ."

"I didn't know," she choked, unable to look at him. "It never occurred to me that you . . . you're *Hunter Buchanan*. . . . When Stu said . . . I thought he meant—"

Gently he forced her chin up, then pressed his fingers over her lips to still the incoherent flow. "What did Stu say?"

"He told me to—at least I think he was telling me to tell you"—

a tear seeped from the corner of her eye and trickled down her cheek—"that I'm in love with you." A second tear followed the first. "I think everyone else already knew. I've tried to hide it. I didn't want to embarrass you or make you feel awkward."

"Blind as a bat," Hunt whispered tenderly. "Both of us." A grin spread across his face. "I figured it was just hero worship. . . ." Suddenly he lifted her completely off her feet, swung her around, laughing. "You love me! It's a miracle!"

Heart bursting, Sabrina clutched him, feeling as though a thousand sparklers had ignited in her stomach and were shooting sparks in every direction. "*You* love *me!*" she managed to gasp back. "That's even *more* of a miracle!" When Hunter lowered her feet to the ground, her eyes were swimming. "I don't understand . . . are you sure?"

His hand burrowed beneath her hair and closed over the nape of her neck. "I'm as sure of my love for you as I'm sure that God loves me and brought us together. All my life I've waited to find a woman I could love like my father loved my mother. A woman a man would willingly sacrifice everything for—his heritage, his job. That's why none of my other relationships worked. Those women—they weren't *you*."

"You'd give up Montclair for me?"

He stared down at her with eyes as blue as the heart of a flame. "You know . . . I think I actually would. Scary thought, huh? But I doubt you'd hold me to it. I think you love Montclair as much as I do." He kissed her then, a loving kiss full of joy and promise.

She didn't want the sudden shadow of doubt to intrude. Not now—not when God had finally handed her a slice of heaven, showed her a happiness so profound she was almost . . . afraid. *No. Please, God.* "Hunter . . ." she murmured when the kiss ended.

"What is it, sweetheart?"

"What if I can't live up to your dream? I'm really not like your mother at all; I've never enjoyed entertaining . . . or crowds. I—" She fumbled for words, fighting the curdling uneasiness. "And the riding. What if I never fully recover? You'd be disappointed, I know you would."

"Hush." He brushed her cheek with his knuckles. "I love you. You love me. That's enough for now. Trust me. Someday soon you'll understand how much I love you, and you'll be soaring over jumps again."

The tiny spur of doubt sharpened. "Hunter . . . I still don't want to compete."

He held her close and kissed her temple. "Sabrina . . . will you at least agree to wait and see how you feel, say, by spring? Give *me* a chance to work with you, prove that your fears about competing are groundless. Will you . . . for me?"

When he looked at her like that, the love showing nakedly in his eyes, Sabrina couldn't refuse. "I'll try," she whispered. "For you, Hunter, I'll try."

The niggling doubt still pricked her heart. But Sabrina, drowning in the first tremulous joy she'd felt in four years, closed her mind along with her eyes and allowed herself to be swept away on the flood tide. *Hunter loves me.* Surely he was right, and his love would be sufficient to drive the last of her fear away.

Twenty-Nine

Gabe had softened up some since Christmas. He could tell it himself. Maybe it was being in his new home, or maybe it was Kathleen's Christmas gift to him. Gabe didn't like to think overmuch about such matters. He couldn't quite bring himself to trust the woman, but between her and Sabrina, he was beginning to realize that there were a few decent women left.

It was the Christmas gift that did him in, though. Kathleen had handed him two official-looking documents. "I figure this is the only hope I have of ever getting you to sell me Bald Mountain," she'd drawled in the sultry tone that made the back of his neck feel hot. "As you see, Janis and Joplin now belong to you, and you alone. Officially. Legally. Nobody—including me—can take them away. Gabe! You're not going to cry on me, are you?"

"'Course not, blast it! I just got cinders in my eye from the fire. . . ."

Ever since, he'd grudgingly admitted to himself that she wasn't too bad, for a female. She still stopped in once a week or so, in between all her running around trying to buy and sell. Gabe knew by now she wanted to build a fancy resort. He hadn't told her he agreed with Hunt Buchanan and that there was no way under the sun he'd sell Bald Mountain to her. It gave him a chuckle to keep her guessing.

In January, Kathleen Winthrop stopped by the Rolling Rock to bring Janis and Joplin a horsewarming present. "I knew you'd pull the shotgun on me if I brought *you* anything for the house," she informed Gabe without batting an eye.

He looked at her, feeling the back of his neck start to prickle again. It was snowing, and she was all bundled up like an Eskimo and wearing a fur-lined hat. "Your hair's growing out. Looks better."

He was surprised when her face actually turned red. "Why, Gabe Wisniewski! That's the nicest thing you've ever said to me," she teased, smiling. She removed the hat and fluffed the black hair into shape. "Quit stalling. Open the horses' present. Go on—you know you're dying of curiosity."

"Always did say you were a bossy bit of goods." He stared at the huge box she'd dumped on the kitchen counter. Mumbling, he fumbled the lid off, then stared.

"They're monogrammed," Kathleen said. She lifted out the two horse blankets and opened them up. "See? 'Janis' on this red one, and 'Joplin' on the plaid." She looked uncomfortable all of a sudden. "I've always thought Joplin would look good in plaid."

"They're right . . . nice." His throat muscles felt tight, and a ticklish sensation inside his nose made it burn. He started to swipe it with his arm, caught himself, and limped over to the sink to snag a paper towel. Panic was crawling in his belly like worms in hot ashes. He was afraid he was going to break down.

"Gabe? I hoped you wouldn't mind. . . ." She sounded almost timid, like a shy little girl. "I know how you feel about Janis and Joplin, but I . . . well, I'm rather fond of them myself."

He wanted to yell at her to take her stupid present and leave. He wanted to throw the ridiculously expensive blankets out in the snow. The feelings this woman was forcing on him were far more terrifying than even the black hole Trina had kicked him into when she walked out on him all those years ago. He'd vowed never to trust another woman—ever. And yet . . .

"Janis and Joplin . . . they like you, too," he heard himself say gruffly. "And the blankets are nice. Real nice." He walked back over to stroke the soft fabric with his rough fingers. "Thanks."

He cleared his throat, started to mutter an obscenity, and checked himself. "You want to come on down to the barn with me? You can help put 'em on the girls, I suppose."

"I was hoping you'd ask. . . ."

Over the next weeks Kathleen dropped by often, timing it, Gabe eventually noticed, when he was either working Joplin on the lead line or walking Janis up and down the length of the barn. The barriers tumbled a little more each time her bright blue eyes and that thousand-watt smile turned on him, and he found himself letting her help with the horses. She wasn't near as skilled as Hunt and Sabrina, but he could read the pleasure in her face.

Strange . . . how he was coming to enjoy having folks around.

One evening, near the end of February, he found himself inviting her to come back to the house with him to warm up a spell before she left. When she accepted, he was sorry he'd made the offer. But after she made the best hot cocoa he'd ever tasted, he changed his mind. . . .

⊙⊙⊙⊙

Montclair

A spring chinook blew through the valley early in March, melting much of the snow. At Montclair, horses and riders alike battled an endless sea of mud, wet snow, and occasional gale-force winds whipping down the mountains. Warmth was deceptive. Within hours, a blizzard could easily sweep down from Canada and bury them under a foot of snow. Hunt had spent a lifetime learning to respect—and mistrust—Colorado weather.

A little past sunset one Friday afternoon, he drove through the gates, returning at last after a two-week horse-hunting trip to the West Coast. Never had it been so hard to leave Montclair. Never had the urge to return called to him so compellingly.

Would Sabrina be waiting for him?

Since Christmas, the months had passed in a golden haze. For the first time in his life, Hunt was head-over-heels in love—an all-consuming, glorious sensation not unlike the thrill of soaring over a cross-country course on a world-class jumper. Even the bitter black-and-white Colorado winter could not dim the vibrant colors that had exploded into his life when Sabrina had confessed she loved him. They had flown back to Virginia for the Christmas holidays, where a smug Sebastian had shaken Hunt's hand, announcing that he'd known for months how things would turn out.

"Sabrina had a poster of you hanging in her bedroom when she was a teenager." He'd chuckled at his niece's heightened color. "More than once I'd catch her standing there, gazing up at it with the same look on her face she has right now."

"Uncle Seb, don't you think you're stretching the truth just a little?" Sabrina had retorted, giving his beard a playful tug.

She'd never been so relaxed. So . . . natural, Hunt thought, smiling at the memory. As for Sabrina's sister Renee . . . the stunning blonde with cat green eyes had swept Hunter into an enthusiastic embrace, kissed him with a loud smack, and warned him that if he hurt her little sister, Renee would ship all three of her kids to Montclair for revenge.

Sabrina. A family. He felt as though God had answered so many prayers at once that his bucket was not merely full, it was spilling over. Hunt had never been busier or more contented. He had permanently moved Sabrina up to the main house, laughingly reminding her that with Elsa around, they were well chaperoned. He continued to work with Sabrina every day, though both Stu and Carla pitched in whenever Hunt had to be out of town. She was riding now—really riding— and before he left, she'd promised him that she would try jumping again as soon as he returned.

He maneuvered the car around a slush-filled pothole just before the turn-off to the stone cottage. When the trees budded, he'd have to bring Sabrina back there—*would she be waiting?* The previous night, he'd phoned from his hotel to let everyone know what time to expect him, but he hadn't talked to Sabrina. That was a unusual, and Hunt admitted to himself that he was a little concerned.

He loved her; she loved him.

And yet even after all these months, Sabrina still kept a lot of herself under wraps. Though Hunt made an effort to respect her privacy, he didn't like the jabs of uncertainty nudging his subconscious. It wasn't anything he could take out and examine—more like a feathering sensation at the back of his neck every now and then. A fleeting expression on Sabrina's face. A chance encounter when he'd find her standing perfectly still. Too still. . . .

Her persistence in denying that she was still troubled by occasional panic attacks.

As far as Hunt knew, she hadn't had one since the first of the year.

The only reason he knew about that one was because Carla had happened to stumble over her, hiding in the back of the tack room. ". . . and her eyes, Hunt," Carla had told him, sounding distressed. "It was her eyes that gave her away. She looked so . . . desperate."

Impatiently, Hunt thrust aside the uneasiness.

A blood-red sun disappeared behind the imposing bulk of the mountain, splattering the sky in a bold vermillion stain. He rounded the last curve in the drive, impatient as a lovelorn teenager, and pulled up in front of the house. He jumped out, taking steps to the front door three at a time.

"Anyone home?" he called, grinning when his voice resounded through the cavernous foyer. As a boy, he'd driven his mother crazy, yodeling like a Swiss shepherd from the top of the stairs.

Elsa appeared in the doorway leading down the hall to the library. "Welcome home." She studied him, her black eyes gleaming. "She is not here, Señor Hunt. She drive over to that ranch this morning and has not returned."

Deflated, Hunt gave Elsa a sheepish smile. "Well, at least my favorite housekeeper is here to welcome me."

She harumphed, shaking her head. "She say she wanted to be here when you return. But now you show up early, ay de mi."

"I caught an earlier flight—didn't Jody tell you?" He waved his hand. "Never mind. I'll take the car down to the garage and check in at the barn." Did she have to go visit Gabe today, of all days? Now that Wisniewski had moved, it was a thirty-five-minute drive each way. The Rolling Rock Ranch seemed to consume more and more of Sabrina's time lately, especially with Gabe expecting his first load of horses from a bankrupt dude ranch within a couple of weeks. But Hunt had only himself to thank for it—he'd set the whole thing up.

It had been a while since he'd heard from Kathleen Winthrop, too. Sabrina had mentioned that Kate was visiting Gabe quite often. He and Sabrina had shared a smile, imagining the polished, cosmopolitan Kathleen and the rough-as-a-cob veteran together.

"But's Gabe's changed, Hunter," Sabrina had told him just before he'd left on this last trip. "He's . . . softer, somehow. It's almost a miracle in itself. I don't know whether it's Kathleen or the horses or the Rolling Rock—or all of the above. But he's almost like a new man."

All the way to the barn Hunter fought a losing battle with jealousy.

It was an ugly emotion, and he was ashamed of himself—but knowledge didn't always result in control.

An hour later he pulled a jittery gelding to a halt for a brief rest. He'd put the green jumper through an easy course of low jumps, but the animal was still uncertain, a little nervous. He was patting the sweat-soaked neck when a flash of blue caught his eye.

"Sabrina!" He trotted the horse over, vaulted from the saddle, and swept her into a hard one-armed embrace. "I missed you . . . you weren't here. . . ." He covered her face with kisses.

"Hunter . . . at least wait until I call a groom for your horse!" Laughing, she twisted free and dashed out. Seconds later she returned, a giggling teenaged girl in tow; one of the local rancher's daughters, Hunt saw. Sabrina whispered in her ear, and the grinning groom took Hunt's mount and led the horse out without a word.

When Sabrina turned back, Hunt caught his breath at the glowing welcome that lit her face. She threw herself into his arms. "I missed you, too!" She hugged him tight. "Hunter, I have so much to tell you. It's incredible! I've been over at Gabe's—Elsa told you, didn't she? We had a 'discussion,' Gabe and I, that is—only it was more of a shouting match. Gabe shouting, I mean, and—"

"Whoa!" Hunt covered her mouth with his hand. "Slow down, sweetheart." He held her at arms' length, his gaze moving over her in a swift, comprehensive survey. "Are you *sure* you're Sabrina Mayhew? What happened to the reserved young woman I left a couple of weeks ago? The one who looked at me with such wistfulness shining out of her eyes I almost canceled my trip?" He kissed each eye, then cupped her face. "I love you."

Tears sparkled, and her mouth began to tremble. "I love you, too," she whispered with a heartbreaking catch in her voice.

Hunt's insides clenched. "Sweetheart? What is it? What's going on?"

She closed her eyes and took a deep breath. "Hunter . . . I finally know what I want to do with my life."

"What do you mean?" His heart began to pound. "Sabrina? What are you talking about?" Her life was going to be spent with *him*, wasn't it? They'd only talked about marriage once before, but Hunt had easily read the panic just below the surface. Over the Christmas holidays, he and Sebastian had talked at great length, the lawyer warning him that Sabrina might have difficulty accepting the commitment required for a permanent relationship.

"She's lost so much," the older man had told him. "She loves you, son. Trouble is, she's afraid of loving *too much*. She'll approach marriage, I imagine, with even greater caution than she showed when she went out to Montclair." He'd removed his bifocals and stuffed them absently in his shirt pocket. "So good luck. I have a feeling her rehabilitation with horses is going to seem easy compared to the fight you'll be facing to convince her to marry you."

Hunt watched her now, hands crammed inside his pockets as he fought to keep the anxiety from showing on his face.

"I've been watching the old videos of the shows—the ones where I competed—this past week, trying to . . . to remember what it's like to jump," Sabrina was telling him. Her face was shining with excitement. She took another breath and began talking even more rapidly. "I still plan to try. You don't need to worry about that. But Hunter, there was a clip during the middle of one of the videos. One of those human interest stories. The commentator was interviewing an owner/operator of a school that teaches handicapped children to ride."

She clasped her hands together, her gaze glued to Hunt's, as if willing him to understand. "It was incredible! The horse's move-ments, the position of the mounted rider, are not only beneficial *physical* therapy, but *emotional* therapy as well. The bond between horse and rider? Hunter, don't you see the possibilities? With my own ex-perience, combined with Gabe's handicap, we could turn the Rolling Rock into a school like that. Only *our* school would go one step be-yond; we'd be helping handicapped *horses* as well as people! And today I finally got Gabe's promise to think about it. In fact, he admitted that Kathleen has been pestering him some, as he put it, because *she* wants to be involved in Gabe's project, too. Hunter?" She searched his face, her eyes beseeching. "I . . . I haven't felt this much excite-ment since my fall. It feels . . . *right* . . . as though God has finally given me a purpose. A *reason* why I'm here."

She felt "right." *He* felt numb. Sabrina expected a response, needed his unqualified endorsement. His support. And he couldn't give it. *God? I can't give her what she needs.* "What about your train-ing?" The words came out almost like an accusation, and he winced, but once begun, he couldn't stop. "What about competing, Sabrina? You need to start a pretty rigorous regimen now, to prepare even for schooling shows this summer. . . . What about your promise to me? To *us*? How does that fit in with your grand purpose in life?''

For several moments a thick silence spread like a poisonous cloud between them. A rafter creaked overhead, and somewhere in the background a door slammed.

Sabrina stood stiffly, her face frozen into an expressionless mask. "I had a feeling you'd take it this way, but I had to try." She backed a step, moving carefully, as though Hunt might suddenly attack her. "Hunter . . . I'll try to compete, but you may as well know, the thought terrifies me. I've tried for months—" her voice cracked, and she backed another step—"but it isn't getting any better. I can ride, but I feel you *willing* me to do more, want more. I think about jumping, and inside I freeze up. It's the same . . . when I think about marriage. . . .''

"Sabrina . . .'' He barely recognized his own voice.

"You want me to be something I can't be anymore. I don't understand why—I love you with all my heart, but it isn't enough.'' The words struck like acid pellets, burning holes in his heart. "I've tried to be what you needed, Hunter. . . .''

"But you don't want to compete.'' He clenched his hands, still inside his pockets, to keep from grabbing her. He couldn't address the marriage issue right now or even think about it. He knew he'd hurl out words he'd regret for the rest of his life. But the riding . . . "You have no desire to regain what you once were—you'll throw away your incredible gift.'' She winced, but Hunt, hurting more than he'd ever hurt in his life, barely noticed. "This idea of yours is a good one. I'll admit that. But *anyone* can do it, Sabrina. If Kathleen's sticking her nose in it, let *her* have a go at it—along with Gabe's idea for rescuing horses.''

He pinched the bridge of his nose. A headache threatened to split his skull. "But you—why can't you understand?'' He searched her face and saw only despair and hopelessness. He didn't know whether to pray or pound his fists against the wall. "The way you ride—what you offer the sport—that can't be learned. I've trained some of the best in the world.'' He ran his hand through his hair. "Blast it all, Sabrina! *I've* won enough cups and ribbons myself to know I'm good. But you could be *better*. I know this. Why can't you see it?''

All expression left her face. "Probably because I don't want it badly enough anymore." She turned and walked away, moving as though she were an old woman. At the door, she turned back around. "There's more to life than being good at a sport, Hunter. Why can't *you* see *that?*"

Thirty

*T*he jumps were higher than she remembered—great blocks of solid granite. Protruding, jagged-edged posts, waiting to gut the horse like a fillet. Heart racing, she tried to gather the reins, but they kept slipping out of her fingers. Ves reared, dancing sideways. He brushed against a dense thicket of needle-sharp briars. The thorns gouged her leg, shredding her riding boots.

She tried to calm Vesuvius, but he was wild, uncontrollable. Gathered around the fence, completely surrounding the ring, a sea of faces watched, black holes for eyes, mouths stretched in macabre smiles of anticipation.

Hunter stood in the middle of the ring. He held a whip in his hand, and he was yelling at her. Screaming. Egging her on. Jump!

"No . . . no, he can't do it! He'll fall. . . ." She tried to shout the words, but nothing escaped. "He can't do it—I can't do it! Hunter . . . I can't do it—"

"Sabrina! Wake up, Sabrina! It's just a dream. It's all right."

Sabrina came awake in a scalding rush. Hunter's face loomed over her, but she shrank back, still reeling from the vividness of the nightmare.

"Easy. It's all right, sweetheart." His voice was strained, unnatural.

"Ay de mi! Such screams. *Pobrecita*. Never have I heard the like." Elsa Menendez appeared behind Hunter, her large frame wrapped in a thick robe, a heavy black braid spilling across one shoulder. "Shall I make some cocoa, boss?"

"Yes, please. And explain to any other staff who might have heard her."

The housekeeper nodded and left.

Sabrina blinked, shuddering, "Sorry. I'm so sorry."

"Don't, sweetheart. God forgive me, but you had cause." He pulled a chair up beside the bed, sat down, and took her hand. In the dim light of the bedside lamp, his gaze was shadowed, unreadable. "Can you tell me about your dream?"

"It was . . . just a dream," Sabrina murmured, moving restlessly against the pillow. "I . . . I don't remember much."

"You don't lie well, my love," Hunter murmured back. Abruptly he sat up, burying his face in his hands. "Your nightmare—it was my fault, wasn't it?"

Sabrina longed to lift her hand to calm the tense, stubbled jaw. Instead, she kept her hands fisted at her sides. "Hunter, what's going to happen to us?"

He inhaled sharply. "What do you mean?" His hand shot out to grasp her chin when Sabrina tried to turn her head aside. "What do you mean by that, Sabrina? Don't even think of leaving me. I won't let you." He paused. "You think my love for you depends on—"

"Doesn't it?" Sabrina interrupted, jerking her head back. She felt battered. "You said it yourself. You fell in love with me—with my photograph—years ago. But *that* Sabrina is dead, Hunter. She doesn't exist anymore."

"Here is the chocolate." It was Elsa, lumbering back into the room. "I'll fetch Sabrina's robe, shall I, and she can meet you downstairs?"

"Five minutes," Hunter snapped. He exchanged a level look with his housekeeper, then leaned down and pressed a hard, possessive kiss against Sabrina's mouth. "In my heart, you are already my wife," he growled and stalked from the room, leaving an electric silence in his wake.

"Oh, my," Sabrina managed after a while, lifting her hand to touch her lips.

"Ay de mi," Elsa agreed. She set the mug of steaming cocoa on the bedside table. "Whatever is this disagreement between the two of you, I wish you will not doubt the boss." She slanted Sabrina an indefinable look.

"What makes you think *I'm* the only one with doubts?" Sabrina muttered, sitting up and swinging her legs to the floor.

Elsa sniffed. "When Señor Hunt give a woman his heart, it is not done lightly. You did not know his parents. Never have I seen a man love a woman like Señor Buchanan love his wife"—she handed Sabrina her robe—"until these past months, when I watch the way the boss look at you. If you throw so great a love aside . . . you are less of a woman than I thought."

And she sailed out of the room, leaving behind an even more deafening silence.

〇◍◍〇

Sabrina entered the study several moments later, carrying lukewarm cocoa that she'd refused to allow Elsa to reheat. A fire had been started in the fireplace. Hunter stood in front of it, head bent, hands clasped behind his back. He'd thrown on jeans and a sweat shirt, but his hair was a mess. A quivering uncertainty snaked up Sabrina's spine and coiled into a choking lump in her throat, though she fought not to show it. He looked so alone. "I'm here."

His shoulders stiffened, then he slowly turned. "Come over by the fire." He pulled a chair closer to the flames, then backed up, as though he were afraid to come too close to Sabrina.

She walked across the room, and Hunter waited until she sat down on the edge of the chair. "I've been thinking," he began, staring into the fire. "You've forced me to realize a few things about myself, and . . . well, they aren't very attractive."

"Hunter—"

"Shh. You can have your turn after I'm through." He paused, adding almost roughly, "I'm praying, you see, that what I have to confess might change what *you* were going to say."

Drowning in the swamp of her own doubt and guilt, Sabrina could only nod. Her own prayer consisted of a single word, repeated in a pitiful litany. *Please.*

"It was two things, actually." In the firelight, his shadowed face was almost gaunt. "First, I'd never realized that I might have demanded more of you than I had a right to. Expecting you to want to recapture those magical years . . ."

Sabrina shifted uncomfortably. She didn't want to remember those years, didn't want to confess to Hunter that, in the deepest part

• 223 •

of her, she still remembered them. Because she would also have to admit that once she *did* feel . . . magical . . . when she rode a horse.

When she jumped a horse.

Hunter shifted. "I also had to face the fact that—" he stopped and swallowed hard—"there *is* more to life than riding. I've always known that, of course, but lately . . . with you . . . I guess I forgot." His voice deepened, rough with urgency. "Sabrina, I just wanted to help you. Will you believe that, at least? I never meant to force you to compete with an idealized image of yourself." His hands fisted, and he slanted her a brief, indecipherable look. "I just wanted to give you back the gift. But—it isn't mine to give."

Sabrina bit her lip. "I . . . I need to ask you something, Hunter, but I don't know quite how." She toyed with the sash on her robe.

In a swift graceful move, he knelt in front of her chair. "What is it you're afraid to tell me? I can take whatever you throw my way, sweetheart—except two things." He waited until Sabrina met his gaze. "Don't tell me you're going to leave . . . and don't try to tell me you don't love me."

"It's *your* love I need to ask about." Cornered, defensive, Sabrina threw caution to the wind. "You loved the person I used to be. What about what—and who—I am now? I'm riding, Hunter, but I'll never be an Olympic-caliber equestrian again. And my faith still isn't what it used to be, either." She lost her nerve then and turned to watch the twisting tongues of flame.

"Look at me," he ordered, very softly. Sabrina reluctantly obeyed, relieved that much of the aloofness had dissipated from his face. "If I had to guess, I'd say that the heart of this whole problem lies more in your loss of faith—in yourself . . . in God—than your insecurity over my love for you." He paused, then added more gently, "Am I right?"

"I never blamed God for any of it," Sabrina mused. "Not the fall or Vesuvius. Not even my parents. Bad things happen . . . nothing in life's a sure thing. I've always understood that. But . . ."

"But. . . ?" Hunter prompted.

The wall of silence finally crumbled, destroyed by her compelling need to *understand*. To test Hunter, if she were honest. "I think God has removed His presence from my life because I haven't been able to overcome the fear. If I loved Him like I'm supposed to—if I loved *you* like you deserved—I wouldn't be afraid, would I?" She stared him straight in the eye. "Don't bother to deny it. I can see it in your face—have seen it every time we talk about my riding. It's no good. *I'm* no good. I don't deserve—"

"Enough!" Hunter's arms shot out, and he hauled her up against his chest, lifting her to her feet until their eyes were level. "I don't *ever* want to hear you talk such utter garbage again, do you hear? Ever." He plunked her down but didn't release her.

"Let *go*! You're hurting me!" Sabrina snapped, almost as angry as she was astonished. She had never seen Hunter lose his temper before.

"I'm sorry!" Hunter released her instantly. He looked and sounded anything *but* apologetic. "What do you think it does to *me* to hear you talk like this? I love you—*God* loves you. Today, here and now, the way you are. Full of fear. Full of doubts. Full of . . . full of—"

"Manure?" Sabrina supplied, lifting her chin and crossing her arms.

The anger vanished from his eyes, and the uncompromising line of his jaw relaxed. His mouth twitched. "That, too," he agreed and snatched Sabrina back into a bear hug.

Sighing, he dropped a kiss on the crown of her head, then held her close, rocking her. "You've told me that you don't blame God for *causing* the bad things that have happened," he murmured after a minute. "I'm glad you've learned that much. That's what I think life is, you see—a series of lessons. I'm a teacher, after all."

"The best . . ." she whispered, earning a quick smile.

"Well, I think all those 'lessons of life' are designed to teach us how to be more like God's greatest role model, Jesus. The trouble is, sometimes people learn the wrong lessons. Or they apply them—wrongly—to their circumstances."

Sabrina tensed, but before she so much as took a backward step, Hunter's hand burrowed beneath the back of her neck, gently imprisoning, calming her with his touch.

"You've had your share of life's tragedies, *especially* the death of your parents at such a young age . . . But the Sabrina Mayhew who took the grand prix circuit by storm and electrified the world didn't let that loss defeat her. Unfortunately, though, there was the second tragedy."

A log fell in the fireplace with a muffled thud and a shower of sparks. Startled, Sabrina jumped. "I . . . it's late," she stammered. "I'd just as soon not talk about—"

"The teacher hasn't given you permission to leave the room."

"The student is considering leaving _without_ the teacher's permission," she grumbled, shoving her hands against his chest. She didn't want to talk about Vesuvius—never should have brought up the matter of her faith. And yet . . . if Hunter could help her to at least understand . . .

He waited until she quit resisting and stood quietly, though inside, her stomach was churning. _Please_, she found herself pleading inwardly, but she wasn't sure whether her supplication was meant for God's ear . . . or Hunter's.

"I think," Hunter told her then, "you learned the _wrong_ lesson from your fall and the death of your horse. This time you learned to fear life's cruelties more than you trusted God to see you through them. And for some reason, you're convinced God is going to punish you for the rest of your life."

"Not _punish_ me, exactly," Sabrina objected weakly. "Just not"— her hand began to pleat the thick fleece of his sweat shirt—"_bless_ me, like He used to." Spoken aloud, the words sounded petty. She tried to pull free again, then gave in and let him hold her. She needed to be held . . . needed to feel _something_.

Then Hunter's hands were cupping her face. "Sweetheart"—his voice was tender—"cut yourself some slack, all right? _Nothing_ can separate you from God's love, Sabrina. Not your fear. Not my bone-headed arrogance. Not your feelings of inadequacy or guilt. You can still make a choice here. Only this time, choose to trust that God's arms are wrapped around you just as firmly as mine were when I was sitting behind you on Lady Fair."

"But I can't _feel_ Him! Hunter, I can't feel God's presence like I can feel yours." She swallowed, blinking moisture from her eyes. "If I could just feel Him, maybe I could—" She stopped, for the first time in years finally hearing the meaning behind the words. "I'm asking for proof, aren't I? Like Thomas did after the Resurrection."

"We'd all like that kind of proof." Once again Hunter's matter-of-fact acknowledgment calmed her. For the first time, she felt faint stirrings of hope. "Look at it this way. You _do_ feel fear, right? You see the results—you're afraid to ride, to jump. You've suffered tangible consequences—isolation, a lifestyle change. . . . Are you pleased with the results of what you can feel and see?"

Subdued, Sabrina stood for a long moment, searching her mind.

"You must know I'm not," she finally admitted in a low voice.

"Then what have you got to lose by trusting God? That is, except the fear and guilt? You still might not *feel* any differently for a long time. But if you act on what you *know* instead of how you *feel* . . . well, I have a *feeling* you might be surprised."

The tenuous feeling of hope spread, unfurling fragile streamers of light deep inside the dark holes of her spirit. Sabrina felt confused and cherished, all at the same time.

Come to think of it, it was as good a description as any, of faith.

Thirty-One

$\mathcal{E}$arly one morning near the end of March, Gabe plodded stiffly out to the kitchen. His hip was on fire—not a good sign. For the last five years, it had proved to be a more accurate weather barometer than the weatherman's fancy calculations. Groaning, he filled the coffeepot and turned on the gas burner of his handy-dandy new stove, then perched gloomily on one of the kitchen stools while he waited for the water to boil. Dollars to doughnuts, a nasty storm was brewing.

At least Janis and Joplin were snugly wrapped in their blankets, safe inside their new barn. He wouldn't have to ride out the bad weather, fearing that the roof would leak or that they'd freeze to death in the flimsy shelter. But confound it, the first delivery of more horses was scheduled for the end of the week, and this storm better not delay their arrival. He'd waited too long, invested too much time and energy.

The Double R was turning out to be a crackerjack place. He glanced around the kitchen. Even the house—at least the kitchen— looked downright *homey*. The plant Kathleen had brought over the previous week helped. A corner of Gabe's mouth tilted. That woman! She'd sashayed into the room with a gleam in her eye and thrust the basket of greenery under his nose.

"You need some plants to dress up this place a little," she'd announced. "This is a philodendron. You can't kill it, and I'll be along often enough to make sure it's watered."

With typical "Kathleen efficiency," she screwed a fancy metal hook in the ceiling over the sink, and now the glossy leaves spilled halfway down. Gabe liked to gripe about the thing interfering with his view, but to tell the truth, he sort of liked the looks of it.

Kathleen was that way. Once she got hold of an idea, a man might as well let her run with it. Of course, they'd had some wildcat fights over her involvement with the Double R, until she forced him to admit that her business savvy and her "networking," as she called it, could provide him even more horses and exposure than Hunt Buchanan.

"He's got Montclair. All I have is time . . . and interest." The blue eyes had lit up then. "I've come up with an idea myself, actually. I'm still doing research, so I don't plan to mention this to Hunt yet, but I don't mind telling you, Gabe," she said a little sheepishly. "Grumpy old bear that you are, you still *listen* to what I have to say."

"Not much else I can do, the way your mouth runs on." But he could tell that she knew he was pleased.

"Anyway, I've changed my plans for the resort. I still want to build it, just not *here*. Hunt's probably right, much as I hate to admit it. Colorado has enough ski resorts eating up the mountains. So"— she'd given him that sassy grin, then—"I'm going to investigate land *east* of the Rockies. What do you think of this—a *golf* resort somewhere in eastern Colorado. An option to Las Vegas and Lake Tahoe. . . ."

"Long as you're not cluttering up the mountains with more people, you can build another Disneyland, for all I care," Gabe had retorted.

Kathleen had stuck her nose in the air. "I just might," she'd drawled. "But that's not what I wanted to tell you about." She scooted closer, all but wriggling in her excitement. "I want to be part of the Double R rehabilitation program. If you'll make me a partner, we can even expand it—use some of that land I've bought up. What would you think of turning some of it into homes for the wild mustangs? I have a friend who's pretty high up in the Bureau of Land Management. . . ."

The coffee finished perking, and Gabe filled himself a mug. Between Kathleen and Sabrina, his head was downright spinning—them and all their plans for the Double R. Lately he wondered if they'd decided between them that he existed solely as a target for their shenanigans. But the smile on his face grew, in spite of the pain in his hip and the weather. Why not admit it? Those two women made him feel like a real man. Someone who could still get things done.

Even Sabrina's latest harebrained scheme couldn't dim Gabe's bone-deep glow of satisfaction. Of contentment. He collapsed on his new couch to sip coffee and plan the day, though he kept thinking of Sabrina. In her own quiet way, she was every bit as muleheaded as Kathleen. And . . . he might as well admit something else. Her idea was worth chewing on.

It was nice having . . . friends. People who acted like they respected him instead of treating him like dirt. His thoughts turned now to Hunt. Like Kathleen had pointed out, Montclair's head honcho had more irons in the fire than a burro had burrs, and Hunt's visits to the Double R of late had been short and scanty. But it had been Hunt who'd helped make Gabe's dream come true, Hunt who had delivered a truckload of books on horse care, farm maintenance, training manuals; Gabe had been up to his eyeballs in reading material since Christmas.

Hunt had also given him another book. Gabe hadn't opened this one—a butter-soft leather Bible, very old. He kept it by the side of his bed because Hunt had told him this particular Bible had belonged to Ellen Buchanan, his mother. It made Gabe feel uncomfortable . . . yet somehow *connected*. Hunt wouldn't have given such a prized possession to a man he didn't give a lick about. One of these days, Gabe would get around to looking at it, too, seeing as how it was so special to Hunt. But for right now Gabe was content merely to touch the leather cover from time to time.

If Montclair's head man wasn't able to stop by as much anymore, Sabrina kept turning up at the ranch like a homesick pup. She'd follow Gabe around, taking care to stay out of the way. Unlike Kathleen, Sabrina never had much to say, but those big solemn eyes got to him. Yep, the little gal even made him laugh with her brand of humor that was dry as desert dust. So why not let her help out with Janis and Joplin?

"Dadblamed female," he muttered now out of habit. He drained the last of the coffee and heaved himself to his feet. "Nothing but trouble." Then he chuckled out loud.

He wondered if Sabrina would show up today. For the past few weeks they'd been working with Joplin, breaking her to the bridle; the previous week Sabrina had even been riding the filly bareback since Gabe hadn't gotten around to buying a saddle yet. He pawed his hand through his beard, marveling at the woman's grit. Hunter had told him her story. "Wonder what's going to happen when we show him what we've been doing?" he mused as he limped across the room. Sabrina had wanted to surprise Hunt, but Gabe wasn't too sure. He had a gut instinct the boss would go ballistic.

She'd talked him into keeping the secret anyway, just like she'd talked him into mulling over her idea to turn the Double R into some sort of school for handicapped people.

"We'll have to think of a different description, of course," she'd told him with that wry humor of hers. " 'Handicapped' is considered politically incorrect back in Virginia."

"Call it what you please," Gabe had snorted. "Having one arm and a bum leg is a handicap. Why dress it up?"

He whistled as he bounced down the lane to the barn in his new pickup. The place was looking good, if he did say so himself, especially with the newly completed paddock he'd had constructed behind the barn. Yep, it sure felt good being alive. For the first time in his life, he could hold his head high and spit in anyone's eye who tried to call him a worthless bum.

". . . and your new roommates ought to be here in a couple of days. So what do you think?" he asked Janis an hour later, rubbing his hand along her flank. "You'll have some company other than your pesky kid, two women, and an old man. Maybe you can swap stories or something. . . ."

Janis's tail swished idly in response and her ears swiveled to listen to his voice while he spoke. She'd lost most of her fear of people, but she would never be as tame as Joplin. Gabe carefully folded her blanket, then fetched a halter, absently noting that Sabrina had hung the bridle next to it instead of on the peg on the opposite wall. Grumbling as he slipped the halter on the mare, he reminded himself to put the bridle where it belonged after he let the horses out for some fresh air. This was *his* barn, and if Sabrina wanted to help out, she'd better learn to put everything back where it belonged.

Janis had healed up nicely, had even put on some weight, and Noah's visits had ceased a month ago. But Gabe knew he'd probably always fret over her. "You've had a raw deal," he told her, loving the even sound of her hooves clattering along the aisle. Not even a limp. "Funny, though, how things work out. Who'd have thought your first owner would turn up on the doorstep? Good thing I don't know where that piece of pond scum is she fired."

He scratched Janis's chin—the spot that always made her half close her eyes in enjoyment. "Guess you'll always be a little gun-shy of me, just like I'll always be a mite worrisome toward *you* . . . aw, don't go getting your water hot!" he called to Joplin, who was stomping her feet, straining her head as far over the stall door as she could reach. "I'll fetch you in a moment."

Half an hour later, Gabe was leaning on the fence, watching his two horses enjoy the freedom of the paddock. To the west, towering cauliflower clouds peeped ominously over the mountains. He scowled, lifting a finger to test the wind. The scowl deepened when his suspicions were confirmed; the wind was blowing from the south.

Instead of a thunderstorm, they might be in for a late blizzard.

Grumbling, he debated whether or not to run a couple of errands he'd been postponing all week, then decided he'd better go on and get it over with. He should be back in an hour. If this turned into a snowstorm, at least he'd have his supplies. He'd hate for Kathleen to stop by one evening, and him be out of the dark chocolate she'd taught him to buy so she could make them her famous hot chocolate.

He started to whistle for Joplin and Janis, then caught himself. They looked so peaceful and relaxed, nosing contentedly at the damp, half-thawed ground, occasionally sniffing the wind.

Gabe glanced at the sky again, debating. Storm was a good two hours away, possibly more. If he left immediately, he'd be back in plenty of time.

⚬⚭⚬

By the time he roared back down the track to the barn, almost an hour and a half later, the clouds had spilled over the entire sky, turning the deep blue to a dirty gray. He hurried through the barn to the paddock, planning to fetch Janis and Joplin back inside before he unloaded the supplies. No sense in taking unnecessary risks, especially with Janis.

But the paddock was empty. Both horses were gone!

Fifteen nightmarish minutes later, Gabe discovered the splintered top board in the fence, at the far back corner of the paddock. Churned-up earth and panicked hoofprints marked the ground in front of the spot where they'd jumped. Cold terror choked off Gabe's breath. He couldn't swallow, couldn't breathe. Unnoticed, the first snowflakes drifted down. Mouth twisted, he scrambled through the fence to look for their trail.

After falling twice, he knew it was no good. *He* was no good, with his hip on fire and a loose sleeve flapping in the wind. The taste of defeat churned in his stomach as he retraced his steps to the paddock.

"Why?" he ranted toward heaven, his fist pounding uselessly on the fence post. "Why now?"

He had to act fast. Had to find them before it was too late. He cursed the storm, swiveling on his heel to lurch drunkenly back across the field to the empty barn. But it was sure as shootin' he couldn't find them alone.

There was only one place to call for help.

⁂

"Why do you think they bolted?"

Hunt manhandled the Jeep around a turn in the road, relieved when the tires held on the snow-slick pavement. "I don't know, sweetheart. Could be any number of reasons."

"Elsa said Gabe was babbling over the phone, and she almost hung up on him before she realized what was going on." Hunt heard her take a hiccuping breath and knew she was fighting tears. "Hunter, if we can't find them—"

"Let's not think the worst right now." They skidded around another curve. Mouth tight, Hunt forced himself to slow down. They wouldn't do Gabe *or* the horses any good if he crashed the vehicle. "You're wearing plenty of layers, aren't you?"

"For the tenth time, yes! And for the *last* time—before you ask again—no, I will not wait in Gabe's house. I won't even wait in the barn. Janis and Joplin trust me almost as much as they do Gabe. Besides, we need all the eyes available in this county."

"We need *radios*!" His hands flexed on the wheel. "I shouldn't have loaned them out, regardless of circumstances." The thought of tracking two near-wild horses through snow, accompanied only by a one-armed man and a woman with no wilderness experience, made him break out in a sweat.

"Hunter, you had no way of knowing we'd need them," Sabrina

reminded him. Again. They'd been debating back and forth ever since Gabe's frantic call.

She was right, but Hunt didn't have to like it. Several foolhardy hikers had been caught in the blizzard as well, and when the county sheriff had phoned to ask if he could borrow Montclair's emergency radios for the search team—to supplement the ones they had—he'd handed Montclair's over willingly.

"We've brought enough supplies to outfit a dozen people," Sabrina reassured him. "Besides, you've told me these spring blizzards usually blow over within hours."

"I don't like the way I feel about this whole situation." He flashed her a quick look. "What we're doing is just as foolish as what those hikers did. If we get lost, we have no way to contact anyone for help."

For the next few minutes they drove in strained silence. When the road leading to the Rolling Rock appeared, Hunt expelled his breath in a sigh. Out of the corner of his eye, he saw Sabrina's hands ball into fists. "At least it's quit snowing," he commented as they roared down the lane and he pulled to a screeching halt in front of the barn.

Wild and disheveled, Gabe paced back and forth like a frustrated animal.

"Sabrina." Hunt halted her with a hand on her arm. "Promise me you'll show some common sense. You're in good shape, but this is no mountain walk."

"Hunter—"

"Promise me," he insisted, ignoring Gabe's frenzied approach. "If you can't promise to take care of yourself, I'll drive you back to Montclair—now." She turned on him then, her eyes spitting mad until she met his gaze. He wasn't sure what she saw in his expression, but at least she kept her mouth shut. He touched her cheek with a gloved finger. "I can't concentrate on the search if I'm worrying about you."

"Don't worry about me then. I—"

Gabe yanked open Hunt's door. "Hurry up!" he exploded, thrusting his head inside. "What are you doing, yammering and wastin' time! It'll be dark in less than four hours."

"Settle down. We'll catch up," Hunt told the terrified man. He'd maintained a small hope that he could talk both Gabe and Sabrina into waiting until they could scrape up more help and some radios. One look at Gabe told him the hope had been futile. "Did you track them at all?"

"They headed toward those hills." Gabe pointed to some steep snow-covered hills, where a long sloping meadow disappeared into a thick stretch of trees. Beyond that, endless waves of foothills and canyons.

Hunt ground his teeth. "Can we drive in?"

"Maybe a mile." Gabe wiped a trembling hand over his mouth. "It was a cougar. I found the tracks after I called. We gotta hurry. . . ."

"We will, but we're going to do this right." Hunt speared the older man a telling look. "I've brought along backpacks with emergency supplies for each of us. Get yourself some head gear and gloves. A scarf as well. You've lived here long enough to know not to set out in the mountains ill-prepared. Now, where did they jump the fence?" Gabe told him. "Fine. We'll meet you there in five minutes. Make sure you bring along halters and lead ropes for the horses."

After Gabe stomped off, Hunt turned back to Sabrina. "Well? I haven't heard that promise."

"You really can be a bully at times." She shook her head. "All right. I promise. I'll be careful. Can we go now?"

Hunt started the engine. He couldn't explain the trickle of dread that swept through him. Grimly he scanned the empty paddock, then the leaden sky.

"What is it? Do you see something?" Sabrina asked, craning her neck to peer through the windshield.

"No. I just—" He shook his head. "I just have this feeling. . . ."

"Concentrate on what you *know*, remember?" She reached up to brush his cheek. "I won't do anything stupid, Hunter. I promise."

He gave her a fleeting smile. "It's not that. I can't really explain it." They reached the far side of the paddock. The ghostlike chill had dissipated. He sent a silent prayer heavenward as they scrambled out of the Jeep.

Ten minutes later Gabe's truck bounced across the paddock and pulled to a rocking halt beside them. Hunt lifted Sabrina into the cab, then followed her in. Gabe drove in tight-lipped silence for three-quarters of a mile before the rocky terrain and thick undergrowth ended the truck's usefulness.

"Okay," Hunt ordered calmly. "Let's go. I've been thinking, and here's what I think we should do."

⟨⟨⟨⟨∞⟩⟩⟩⟩

Two hours later Hunt scrambled up a steep, rocky slope. At the top, breathing hard, he scanned the valley below while he rested a moment and caught his second wind. Thankfully, the sun had broken through the clouds, clearing the last of the swift-moving storm. Blinding sunbeams transformed the snow to a glistening white, so bright it was difficult to see. Shivering in the icy wind, Hunt shaded his eyes, straining to glimpse any movement in the vast snow-covered wilderness. He was silently debating the safest way to descend into the valley when his ears caught the faint sound of a human voice.

It seemed to have generated from the western side of the slope. Scrambling like a stag, Hunt vaulted over scrubby bushes and crevices the width of a man's hand, knee deep in powdery snow as he made his way along the crest. "Sabrina!" he called moments later. "Gabe! Can you hear me?"

"Down here!" came Gabe's faint response.

Hunt picked his way over a pile of snow-covered boulders to find himself on the precipice of a small cliff. Several hundred feet below, he spied Sabrina's bold turquoise and yellow ski parka. She waved her arms. Relief flooded through him at the sight of her, and he waved back, then cupped his hands over his mouth and yelled down, "Any luck?"

"We found them! They're in that stand of pine!" Sabrina yelled back, pointing. "Can you climb down that slope?"

Hunt didn't waste time answering. Already the sunlight had lost its mid-afternoon brilliance. Below him, the jumbled rocks leveled out into a steep, treacherously smooth slope, which ended some twenty feet above Sabrina. Though the descent was covered with two-foot drifts, Hunt managed to maneuver his way down, falling only once. When he finally reached the lip of the ledge, he grinned down at Sabrina. "See? No problem at all for a born-and-bred mountain man."

"You still need to climb down off the ledge." She glanced toward the trees, where Gabe stood huddled between Janis and Joplin. "Try to hurry. The horses are fine, but I think Gabe's leg is hurting pretty bad."

"It's also going to be dark in less than two hours," Hunt pointed out. He started to say something else, but a strange sensation, almost like vertigo, overwhelmed him without warning. Suddenly he felt the earth shift beneath him in an ominous slide of settling snow.

"What is it—*Hunter*!" Sabrina screamed, horror filling her face, her voice. "Behind you! Hunter—*jump*!"

Hunt swiveled and met head-on a monstrous cloud of deadly white, descending with appalling silence and the speed of a runaway freight train. Sabrina's terrified scream reverberated through his ears. It was the last sound he heard. There was an eerie sensation of falling through mid-air, and then he was swallowed beneath a crushing tidal wave of snow.

Thirty-Two

*T*he small but powerful avalanche missed Sabrina by a scant six yards, though the force of the wind still blew her backward, showering her in stinging shards of snow, ice, and rock. Sabrina didn't even notice. "Hunter!" she screamed again, clambering to her feet.

Behind her, Gabe was yelling like a madman. Sabrina ignored him. She threw herself into the deadly mound of snow, pawing at the frozen mass, unable to think, unable to grasp any reality beyond Hunter—lying there. Buried somewhere underneath the snow and rocks, trapped, helpless.

Gabe joined her, spitting curses, his eyes red-rimmed, wild with shock and disbelief. Time ceased to matter. The world tunneled into a blur of muddy white. All thought, feeling—even breathing was suspended as they focused every effort on finding Hunter's body.

"Here!" Gabe gasped out. "I got him. I got him!" He flung a football-sized rock over his shoulder. "Help me dig!"

Sabrina choked back a sob, frantically scooping up more handfuls of snow and dirt. "Dear God . . . his head is covered with blood!" *Hunter. Hunter. . . .*

"Just keep diggin'," Gabe snarled, his hand churning.

Moments later they had uncovered Hunter's head, chest, and arms. Limp, unmoving, face deathly pale except for the blood oozing sluggishly from the gash on his forehead, he looked . . . lifeless.

"No!" Sabrina yanked off her mittens and fumbled with useless fingers, trying to unwind the soaked, frozen scarf from Hunter's neck.

Feeling for a pulse in his neck, his temple. The zipper on his ski jacket was frozen, embedded with snow.

Pushing back the panic, Sabrina blindly persisted. She ran her hands over Hunter's neck and head, checking for injuries. There was a lump on the back of his head, and her fingers turned red with blood—Hunter's blood—from the gash on his forehead. Sabrina grabbed the wet scarf and clumsily pressed it to the gash.

The blood still flowed. . . . That meant Hunter was alive!

"God . . . please." She whipped off her ski cap and leaned over, turning her head so that her ear hovered just above his blue-tinged lips.

Though faint, the whisper of breath tickled her ear, and relief made Sabrina light-headed. "He's alive. Gabe . . . *he's alive!*"

"He's also trapped." Gabe had continued to dig, but now he straightened and swore under his breath.

Sabrina's head jerked around. The lethal avalanche had been full of hundreds of stones and small boulders. Hunter had miraculously escaped being crushed, but his lower body, from the waist down, was wedged awkwardly beneath several large rocks, one a boulder the size of a large washtub. Sabrina and Gabe stared at each other, stricken into silence.

"His legs . . ." she finally croaked, feebly shoving at the boulder.

"Not to mention his ribs, his pelvis—" Gabe broke off, and his muddied gloved hand clenched into a fist. "We can't get him out—not by ourselves."

Sabrina stared at him in horror. "Merciful Father . . . and we don't have the radios." She remembered the look on Hunter's face when he'd reluctantly agreed to help Gabe with the search. Remembered as well the forebodings he'd tried to hide. She closed her eyes, then opened them and lifted her chin. "How far to the Double R? Do you know?"

Gabe twisted around, scanning their surroundings. After a moment his lips tightened, and he shook his head. "It's a good hour at least, even walking fast." His voice went flat, bitter. "And there ain't no way I can make it any faster, lady." The bitter gaze raked over Sabrina. "You neither."

Sabrina shook her head. "I'm not going to let him die, Gabe, do you hear? I'm *not* going to give up and just sit here!" She turned back to Hunter, struggling against a despair as deadly as the avalanche. He was so still. So lifeless.

"It'll be dark in less than two hours."

The defeat in Gabe's voice shattered something inside Sabrina. She whirled back to the man and jabbed her finger in his chest. "Then we'd better move fast!" she snapped, though her voice shook. "Stay here. Take off your glove and start rubbing his face and hands to get the circulation moving. I'll get the backpacks we left with the horses."

"I don't see—"

"He isn't going to die!" She shot to her feet, reached out, and grabbed Gabe's hand, tugging at his glove. "He—is—not—going—to—die."

"All right, all *right!*" Gabe jerked his hand free, then glared at the glove dangling from Sabrina's fingers.

They changed places, and Sabrina staggered across the field, lurching like a drunk with a hangover. Moments later she returned, dragging both hers and Gabe's packs. Hunter's backpack, like his cap and goggles, was buried somewhere in the rubble and snow. "Here," Sabrina said breathlessly. "There's still coffee and some food. A survival blanket and another hat. You'll need to keep his head protected; you lose more heat through a bare head—"

"I know what to do." Gabe glowered at her. "Blamed waste of time. You can't walk three miles in this terrain."

"I can . . . and I will." Her heart pounded so heavily every breath hurt. The fear for Hunter was alive, wrapping her in choking coils that tightened with every passing second. Kneeling, she leaned over Hunter and pressed one brief trembling kiss against the cold, unresponsive lips. "I love you," she whispered. "God . . . take care of him. Please."

"God would have done a sight better caring if He'd kept the avalanche away in the first place."

Sabrina stumbled to her feet. "Well, He didn't. But He's still God, and He still cares. . . ." Hunter had said so. She took a deep breath, scanning the unfriendly wilderness. Off to the right, in the stand of trees, Joplin whinnied nervously. She sensed that something was wrong with the same sixth sense that enabled Sabrina to recognize the animal's uneasiness.

Like a thunderclap, the thought resounded through her skull. She stared across at Joplin, then whirled around, her eyes meeting Gabe's.

"I don't have to walk," she announced. "I can ride Joplin." She spoke automatically, her thoughts, her spirit so focused on Hunter's well-being that nothing else mattered.

"You're crazy, lady!" Gabe burst out. "Joplin might know how to flit around these mountains like a goat, but she's not broke good yet. Besides . . . you're afraid to ride a horse unless you're strolling around a ring."

A flutter of panic stirred but was ruthlessly squelched. "We've both been working with Joplin. I've ridden her enough, and she trusts me almost as much as she does you. I've also been working with a high-strung stallion—at a canter at times—for the past two months."

"You got no bridle, no saddle. You'll break your neck and I'll have *two* dadblamed corpses!" Gabe yelled. His cold-reddened cheeks flushed with more angry color.

Sabrina spared one last agonized look at Hunter. "It's his only chance," she stated, and the bald truth resounded in the arctic silence. "I have to try."

"Let *me* go. You stay here with Buchanan."

Sabrina began searching Gabe's backpack, looking for a spare lead line to use as a bridle. "No . . . I can ride. A lot better than you." She stared blindly at Gabe, then resumed her search. "Hunter will tell you. I can ride better than just about anyone. He's told me so, countless times." Her frozen fingers tugged out what she thought was a lead line. She was wrong. Amazement, gratitude, and hope flooded her as Sabrina held Joplin's bridle up to show Gabe.

"What the—" Gabe stared, and then a smile spread across his cracked lips. "You put it back, the other day—in the wrong place, with the halters. I planned on movin' it this afternoon. . . ." He shook his head in wonder. "I just grabbed a handful of tack earlier . . . anything to help Janis and Joplin."

"I'll be back," Sabrina promised. "I'll be back *soon*, Gabe. You just take care of Hunter. Take care of yourself, too." And she tore off across the meadow.

༄

You'll have to help me, God.

I already have, Sabrina. Trust Me, the quiet Voice whispered in the wind.

Janis and Joplin watched her approach, Joplin with a welcoming nicker. Willing herself to calm, Sabrina patted both horses, talking to them in low tones. Then casually, easily she slipped the bridle over Joplin's head, fastening it in place. Her heart was racing, the pulse roaring in her ears. "You'll have to help me, too, Joplin." She stroked the filly's neck, scratched her forelock. "It's been a while, riding cross-country, for me."

Relax your hands. Still the trembling. *Concentrate . . . breathe deeply. You can do this, Sabrina.*

"Hunter's hurt. We're going for help, girl. . . . That's it, come over here, by this boulder, so I can mount. I'm a little clumsy right now. You'll be good for me, won't you?"

Joplin happily followed her, standing next to the boulder, watching Sabrina with quizzical brown eyes alight with trust.

There was no time for fear.

Sabrina scrambled on top of the boulder, then coaxed Joplin closer. "Easy now. Remember the other day, when you wanted to fly like the wind? I wouldn't let you because I—" The words died in her throat.

You can do this, Sabrina. I'll be with you . . . don't be afraid.

She eased herself onto Joplin's back and gathered the reins. The filly snorted, dancing a little sideways, but Sabrina controlled her easily. "Thank You for the bit and bridle. Thank You!"

Now . . . trust Me.

All her reflexes sprang instantly into place as the patient months of working with Hunter merged with the past, so completely it was as though the last five years had melted away.

She turned Joplin's head toward the ranch. "Come on, girl. We have to help Hunter. It's up to us, Joplin."

And, Lord? *All* of it is really up to You.

The sensation of oneness spilled into her veins, pouring in a cataract throughout her body and spirit. *Hunter, can you see me?* She called to him in her heart as Joplin walked eagerly across the meadow, unimpeded by four inches of fresh snow. Daintily she picked her way up a slope. *Hold on*, she begged, even as joy splintered through her. *Hold on, Hunter . . . because you have to see that . . . I'm not afraid anymore!* Even in the midst of her terror for the life of the man she loved with all her heart she was free! Freed by her love for him. . . .

And *God's* love for them both. *You were right all along, Hunter. You were right about the love. . . .*

Joplin stumbled, pitching Sabrina forward. She clamped her legs to the horse's flanks and steadied Joplin with the reins. Her body relaxed, shifted, bent to the motion of the animal as though their muscles were intertwined. They skidded and slipped down the other side of a steep hill, but Joplin didn't falter.

Neither did Sabrina. Nothing mattered except saving Hunter.

Forty minutes later both horse and rider were soaked with sweat, spattered with mud and wet snow, but Sabrina didn't notice. Joy bubbled in her heart, mingling with the fearful urgency over Hunter.

Joplin scrabbled across a brush-choked ravine, with Sabrina clinging like a burr. They trotted and cantered down a gully, then burst into the meadow that stretched in front of the Rolling Rock Ranch. A hundred yards in front of them, a frozen creek sliced the meadow in half.

"Okay, girl." Sabrina leaned forward, urging Joplin onward. "This one's for Hunter."

They took it in a soaring leap, and the strong-legged filly landed on the opposite side with the smooth grace of a veteran steeplechaser. Then they were galloping across the meadow, Joplin's ears pricked eagerly forward as though she realized they were close to home.

Sabrina slowed her to a trot as they neared the paddock. She could sense the filly's rising uneasiness, and with her voice and hands and legs, tried to reassure her. "The cougar's gone, girl. It's okay . . . it's okay. Trust me." She patted the sweat-slickened neck. "You don't have to be afraid."

Neither did Sabrina. Not about riding a horse—nor about Hunter.

God was in control, as He always had been. As He always would be. Because He loved. Because He would always love.

It's about time you accepted that, Sabrina.

She ran on wobbly legs for the barn phone to call the county rescue squad. After she hung up she stood for a long moment, breathing hard, ears ringing. Then she shook her head and made two other calls. The first was to Montclair. The second call—to a number neatly penned by a feminine hand, directly into the wood—was to Kathleen Winthrop.

Thirty-Three

$J$is head hurt. Not the normal tension headache. Not the normal dull pain between the eyes. Hunt tried to lift his hand to pinch the bridge of his nose.

A muffled exclamation sounded from somewhere nearby. He tried to turn toward the sound, but his body refused to move. In fact, he felt as though he'd been plunged into a barrel of ice cubes. When he shivered convulsively, the movement brought a fire-hot stab of pain streaking from his ankle all the way up his left leg. "What—?"

"Take it easy, pal. You're hurt."

"Gabe?" Hunt forced heavy eyelids to open, but the world was a kaleidoscope of whirling colors; the sensation, nauseating. What was wrong with him? Had he fallen off the horse? And what was Gabe doing here?

He felt the other man tucking something around him with surprising efficiency. "You almost turned into a popsicle," the gravelly voice rumbled in a confusing mixture of relief and fear.

Memory returned in a rush. "Avalanche . . ." Hunt whispered. "I was caught in an avalanche. How long?" It was hard to talk, hard to think in coherent patterns, but he instinctively fought for consciousness, driven by a desperate need. "Sabrina?" he muttered, his throat tight. "Where's Sabrina?"

"Easy. Quit thrashing around, man. Sabrina's . . . gone for help." Gabe planted his hand in the center of Hunt's chest, keeping him still. "You're trapped from the waist down, Buchanan, and unless you have a hankering to end up a useless bum like me, put a lid on it and keep still.''

"You're not a useless bum." He winced and tried again to focus on Gabe. "I think I have a concussion."

"Not surprised. Got yourself a gash on your forehead that bled all over the place, and a lump the size of a grapefruit on the back of your head. At least you're conscious now. I was gettin' worried." The other man sat back, and Hunt heard him rummaging around. "Here. Coffee." Carefully Gabe propped Hunt's head up a little, using the folded-up backpack as a pillow so he could hold the cup to Hunt's lips.

The warm liquid revitalized him, but it also awakened his nerve endings to a host of unpleasant sensations. "Glad to be alive, thank God." He managed a weak grin at Gabe's blurred face. "Even though you have two heads at the moment. You say Sabrina's gone for help? She's really okay?"

"She's fine," Gabe said, his voice strangely short. "And you're one lucky guy. You should be dead, man."

"God isn't finished with me yet," Hunt feebly quipped. He turned his head slightly, biting back a moan. Pain battered him in waves. "How long?" he managed to ask again after a moment.

"Oh, 'bout an hour now." There was a pause. "And we got about that long before sunset."

Hunt thought for a while, but he kept drifting off somewhere without realizing it, until cold or pain or his battered senses jerked him back to awareness. "You okay, Gabe?"

"Don't worry none about me. Here—drink some more of this coffee, then you can try a candy bar if your belly's behaving."

"Gabe?"

"What now?"

"The horses. Are the horses all right?"

There was another one of those strange silences, and a shiver that had little to do with the temperature spiked down Hunter's back. He stirred and managed to turn his head very slowly toward Gabe. "You may as well tell me what you're holding back. It's worse *not* knowing. . . ."

"Janis is all right. She's over there in a stand of trees. I've got her tethered and fed her some of the grain. As for Joplin . . . well, I reckon she's probably back at the barn by now, enjoying all the comforts of home." Gabe cleared his throat and gulped several swallows of the coffee. Finally he muttered something beneath his breath and looked down at Hunt. "Sabrina *rode* her out of here, Hunt. Rode Joplin like I never seen a body ride before—like she was one of those centaur creatures." He shook his head, and the deep voice was bemused. "Never saw anything like it. Sabrina sat on that horse like she was part of her, and Joplin . . . well, she acted like she'd been carrying a rider all her life."

Hunt couldn't take it in. "She . . . rode? She wasn't afraid?"

"She lit into me with hobnail boots for wanting to give up on you," Gabe answered frankly. "Told me she'd do whatever it took to save your sorry hide. She was aiming to ride that green broke filly with just a dadblamed halter, but—"

"What?" Hunt jerked, oblivious to the thudding pain as he flung out his hand and grabbed the hem of Gabe's down parka. "And you let her go?"

"I didn't have a whole lot of choice!" Gabe barked, peeling Hunt's fingers loose. "Or would you prefer to be a dead man?" He leaned over, his face close to Hunt's. "You need help, ya blamed ox, and you needed it faster than *I* could fetch it. As for Sabrina, riding Joplin . . ." His voice mellowed, and that bemused look softened the harsh, bearded countenance. "I wish you could have seen her."

"Without a saddle—no bridle . . . she's probably lying in a gully somewhere. . . ."

"I don't think so." Abruptly Gabe laughed, a rusty sound that startled Hunt into silence. "She didn't need a saddle, and Joplin's bridle was in the backpack. I grabbed it along with a bunch of halters . . . by mistake. Whatcha think of *that*, Buchanan?"

Hunt closed his eyes, too overcome to speak. When he finally re-opened them, they were wet. "I think," he whispered, "that God is . . . God."

"That's about what Sabrina said," Gabe put in. "The two of you are the strangest pair I ever met. What you got to thank God *for*? You're trapped, with a concussion and who knows what else, and nothing but half a man standing between you and a coffin."

"Well, I'm alive. We're *all* alive." He managed a weak grin. "And . . . you *are* here."

"Well, *God* had nothing to do with it, so don't go thanking Him for me."

There was a hushed silence before Hunt spoke again. "Underneath that thick hide is a good man, Gabe Wisniewski. Thanks . . . for saving my life."

"Didn't have anything else to do this afternoon."

Hunt laughed, then grimaced in pain. "Tell me again about how Sabrina looked."

Gabe shifted him a little, trying to arrange him more comfortably as he began to talk. Hunt tried to concentrate on the words, but they started to blur together—like Gabe's face.

"Gabe?"

"Yeah?"

"You got anything else I could drink or eat? I keep blacking out, and I don't think that's such a hot idea."

"No problem. I reckon between the two of us, we packed enough to feed an army platoon. . . ."

Time passed in a bizarre hopscotch. Seconds crept along, while minutes leaped with dizzying speed. Gabe, with little help from Hunt, managed to wrestle him inside a spare ski jacket, and exchanged the blood-soaked scarf for Sabrina's spare. He bandaged the gash with supplies from the first-aid kit, trying with less success not to jar Hunt's throbbing head.

"You're a handy man to have around, Gabe," he ventured, feeling marginally better in spite of the relentless pain. "Thanks again."

"I hope you don't plan to try and pay me for saving your skin."

"The thought never crossed my mind." Eyes closed, Hunt reached out until his hand brushed against Gabe's knee. "Gabe?"

The man heaved an exasperated sigh, pulling his hand free. "*Now* what?"

"When you saved that boy's life, back in Vietnam, and his father paid you all that money? Wasn't pity. . . ."

"You're outta your gourd, Buchanan. Quit trying to think, and be quiet, will ya?"

"The father . . . was just grateful. Wanted to *do* something for you." Hunt grimaced, feeling drops of sweat popping out on his brow in spite of the cold. "I . . . know how that father felt," he managed. "I'm grateful, too. But I'd never offer you money, Gabe."

"I'd cram it down your throat if you tried."

Their eyes met, and after a moment, the older man's bristling hostility drained away. Hunt's cracked lips spread in a smile. "It's okay for other people to depend on you, to need you, you know. You're a good man, with a lot to offer."

Gabe grunted and busied himself, straightening supplies. More time passed.

"Gabe?" Hunter mumbled at some point, his words beginning to slur. "You here?"

"Yeah. I'm here."

"Can we talk some more? Keep dozing off . . ."

Gabe busied himself checking the makeshift bandage on Hunt's head. "Don't have much to say. You talk. I'll listen."

Hunt tried to think through the haze of pain and Gabe's astounding revelation earlier about Sabrina. He needed to see her, and his desperation was almost more painful than his injuries. He needed to know she was safe. Needed to know . . . how she *felt*, now that she'd ridden—according to Gabe—like the old Sabrina. "God," he whispered, "take care of her."

Not until Gabe spoke, in a strangely hesitant voice, did Hunt realize he'd spoken the agonized prayer aloud.

"I tried . . . uh . . . talking to God a while back. Didn't feel any different. You . . . ah . . . you talk to God like that a lot?"

"All the time." He shifted again, and a white-hot bolt of pain seared his body, jarring him to alertness. "God isn't a *feeling*, Gabe. More . . . a matter of *knowing*, even when you can't feel." He could almost see Sabrina, hear her quiet voice asking almost the same thing. "Gabe?"

"Yeah?"

"You ever read my mother's Bible?"

There was a long pause. "Naw. Didn't know where to start. But I keep it by my bed. Funny—"he tugged off his glove with his teeth so he could scratch his beard—"I sort of like knowing it's there." His bloodshot gaze glanced off Hunt's. "I mean, you giving me something of your mama's and all . . . you're an okay guy, Buchanan."

"So are you."

Gabe snorted. Then, "You sure you wouldn't mind if I try reading your mama's Bible? Maybe you could even point out some parts of it or something. If you're sure you'd trust me with it."

"I'd trust you . . . with anything I own. Trust you with my life, Gabe." His hand fumbled around, and this time he felt Gabe's hand close around his gloved fingers and squeeze. "Trust . . . God." A tingling warmth was enfolding him, surrounding him, bathing him in a rich, golden tide of love.

"Hunt! Talk to me, man!" Gabe's voice sounded panicked for some reason. "Don't leave me—you gotta stay awake. Hey, Hunt! You gotta . . . you gotta tell me more about God, all right? Sabrina too. I want to know how she could ride, and why the two of you—*Hunt!*"

"Iss okay, Gabe." Hunt's speech was staring to slur. "Don't be afraid. You can read about it . . . show you later. Perfect love . . . drives fear away."

Relaxing completely, Hunt allowed the golden tide to sweep him into the darkness.

⌁

He regained consciousness briefly when the rescue team pried the boulder from his leg. He roused, sweating and disoriented from pain, to reassuring hands patting his shoulder, holding him still. Calm voices promised that everything would be all right . . . he just needed to hold on. But Hunt needed to hear a particular voice. "Sabrina?"

"I'm here, Hunter. It's all right. I'm here."

A tear splashed down onto his cheek, and he felt her trembling lips against his own, felt her fingers brushing the tear from his face. "You . . . rode Joplin?"

"Like an Olympic hopeful. Hunter . . . I love you."

"Love you, too."

"Now behave and get some rest. You'll need to recover really fast, you know." Her voice broke. "You have to help me get ready for the Gold Cup. We've only got a couple of months, but I'm not worried. I've got the best coach in the business."

His head felt as if it were being trampled by stampeding horses, but he didn't care. "Best . . . equestrian . . . in the world. But, Sabrina, what about . . . your school. You and Gabe wanted—"

"Shh. Don't worry. Everything's under control." There was a thread of laughter lacing the watery sound of her tears. "Gabe can be a partner—and God, of course. Hunter, we just have to trust Him, remember? Don't be afraid. It's going to be a *blast!*"

The joyful confidence ringing through her words followed Hunter as he sank back into oblivion, a smile of utter peace filling his face.

Epilogue

*I*t's been a great week here at the annual Stock Show at the Denver
Coliseum. The highlight has been the phenomenal comeback of
Sabrina Mayhew. As we mentioned earlier, she is now married to
Hunter Buchanan, one of the world's foremost equestrian trainers.
It's a heartwarming story, isn't it, Lisa?"

"It sure is, Jay. If you're just joining us and didn't know, folks,
four years ago Sabrina was the rising star of the grand prix show-jumping circuit, until she suffered one of the most brutal tragedies of the
sport. Her mount was killed in a fall, and as a result of her extensive
injuries, Sabrina was subsequently afraid to ride."

"You'd never know it now, would you? Her horse, Tiny Tim from
Montclair, took the jumps like a champion. It's been a long time since
we've seen that kind of poetry between rider and horse. They certainly thrilled the crowd here today, didn't they?"

"You bet. We had a brief interview with Hunter Buchanan right
before today's show. No one could miss his pride in his new wife. Remember that TV clip on the two of them this past March? Hunt had
been trapped in an avalanche. Broke an ankle, suffered a concussion—
and Sabrina rode a green horse through three miles of wilderness for
help."

"Makes a wonderful story, doesn't it? Hunt's still not letting on
whether or not Sabrina plans to make a bid for the 2000 Olympics in
Sydney."

"Well, they're pretty busy with the therapeutic riding school

Sabrina's been instrumental in establishing southwest of here at Rolling Rock Ranch. It's generated a tremendous response statewide. Kathleen Winthrop, a prominent real estate developer, has helped sponsor some of the R-&-R's programs. We'll share an interview with her right after we watch the demonstration of a couple of riders from the ranch. Proceeds from the show today, by the way, are being donated to this worthy cause."

"As you can see, entering the ring now is Gabriel Wisniewski, leading one of the children who has benefited from the programs offered at the R-&-R. Gabe is Sabrina's partner at the ranch, which is also used as a shelter for mustangs, as well as other unwanted or abused horses. I don't know about you, Jay, but watching him here today with these kids and his salvaged horses is every bit as thrilling, in its own way, as watching Sabrina Buchanan jump."

"Yes, they've all beat the odds and come out winners. Like we said, folks, it's a heartwarming story. A true testimony to the power of love."

"For I know the plans I have for you," declares the Lord, "plans to prosper you and not to harm you, plans to give you hope and a future."

Jeremiah 29:11 (NIV)

From the Author

Dear Readers,

In some ways, *Montclair* was a difficult book for me to write. As with all my books, this is a *love* story. But Sabrina, the main character, suffers from an anxiety disorder. For many people, emotional or mental "conditions" are far more difficult to accept than physical ones. Friends and relatives, employers and fellow employees generally make more allowances for a person undergoing chemotherapy for cancer, or hobbling around on crutches while a broken leg heals.

It is far more taxing to sympathize with someone suffering from a cancer of the spirit, or a heart broken by fear . . . or anxiety. Or panic. A crippling phobia. Christians, after all, are supposed to be full of peace and patience, hope and confidence. They aren't supposed to be afraid or anxious—all the time.

Several years ago, God allowed a car accident to change my perspective about faith and fear. I learned how it felt when—without any warning at all—fear swoops down like a vulture to feed on my shaken faith. The doubts and self-torture Sabrina suffered? I've been there, dear readers. And there's a difference between the person who chooses to remain a victim, and the person who wants to be victorious but who doesn't know how to fight the battle.

This book was written for the one person whose heart is hurting so deeply you no longer feel God's love in your life. It's written for the person living a life of emptiness and defeat, because shame over your condition has robbed you of confidence in yourself and God. This book was written for the one person who feels utterly alone, who feels even God has turned His back.

If *Montclair* helps just one hurting heart, then His purpose—and mine—will have been accomplished.

With Love,

Sara Mitchell

BOOKS BY SARA MITCHELL

Available From Bethany House Publishers

Montclair

SHADOWCATCHERS
Trial of the Innocent
In the Midst of Lions